IDEWIPED

Crime, thriller, mystery story.

By

M.L. Weatherington

ISBN 10: 1-942622-08-2
ISBN 13: 978-1-942622-08-6

This book edition is published by:
Pynhavyn Press
First Edition: April 2017
http://www.pynhavyn.com

ACKNOWLEDGEMENTS

You've heard that it takes a village to raise a child; it's true. Sideswiped is my second creation and along the way, I found many helpful hands. Those people were eager to see me succeed in my new career. Listing them becomes a problem for me, first because I don't want to forget anyone, and second because each one should be the first mentioned as they are all equally important to me and the project.

Lessie Bond, Yvonne Tansley, Sherri Oneto, Suzanne Bruns my friends who supported my many needs. Mike and Marie Jewett, Gerry and Linda Taylor and Gayle Prentice. Jan Ellis for the introduction to Betty Yoder. Aubrey Lane for insight and information and those cream cheese bagels. Dear friends that were always there when I needed their help. To Thelma Welsbacher, for the rolling cart that made moving all my author's stuff from place to place so much easier. To Irma Westbrook, who took up the reins of my needs and introduced me to Judy Petersen, who promoted me with my first book signing at her store, Pret. All these people and so much more encouraged me to complete Sideswiped. To Amanda Burton, my daughter, and Zak Schulps for the easel it made painting the cover for this book a breeze.

Thank anyone that has helped me, and I have not listed them here, I apologize.

The task of editing fell to four brave souls. Thanks to Betty Yoder, Nick Adams, Eleanor Ackerman and Sheryl Raumann, they've earned a long restful vacation.

To my final and critical editor, Rene Averett, sideswiped could not be without you. To Rochelle McGrath, Shamrock Designs, for my fantastic cover.

To everyone, thank you, Mary

Reviews

Betty Yoder, reviewer of books.

Here ya go.

SIDESWIPED is another Arthur Franklin mystery! And who doesn't love small town mysteries? Set in Lodi CA, this country town who-dun-it starts out first page with a murder no one saw right in front of the high school at Grape and Oak. Featuring lovable, soft hearted, Lt. Art Franklin in the police department in Sacramento Valley's wine country. Caught up in the intrigue immediately it's easy to settle into page turning to see how Franklin and his police pals take you on this local journey. Throw in a nice little romance, a couple of scary moments and you are hooked. I couldn't wait to share this book with my teenage grandchildren!

Eleanor Ackerman, avid reader.

In SIDESWIPED M.L. Weatherington's detective Art Franklin is in love and is feeling his way in the new relationship, while in his regular life he's being faced with one challenge after another. He is on leave because of a wound to his shoulder he received while on the job and has to find ways to stay involved with the latest local murder investigation. His relationship with his teen-aged daughter is strained to add to his problems. All in all I found this a fast-moving narrative that kept me looking for what comes next. An entertaining read.

*In all your trials, arm
yourself with faith,
confidence in God,
and deep humility
of heart.*

Fear Nothing.

St. Paul of the Cross

Chapter One

3:35 P.M. Thursday, August 31, 1995

A husky male voice answered, "Nine-one-one, what is your emergency?" He listened as a voice broke, grabbed air and rushed forth.

"She's just in the crosswalk, lying there. She's not moving. I can't see her face. It's covered with hair, lots of hair, and blood. There's blood everywhere. You've got to come." The woman stopped talking; dispatch heard what sounded like her hand moving over her phone, then breathlessly, "I think she's dead!"

Dispatch asked, "Ma'am? What's your location?"

Her voice shook with each word, "I'm on Oak and Grape Ave, across from the high school."

"Stay there please, I'm sending an officer now."

"Yes, okay."

1

3:35 P.M. At the same time, several blocks away.

Sweating over steaks is one thing, sweating over seeing a psychiatrist another. My palms are wet. How can I clasp hands and feel confident? Arthur Franklin asked.

Walk out of here. That's the best next move. Art's leg muscles tensed to lift him just as the door opened and Amanda Burtoni sailed through and into his heart. He was a lost pup as they strolled into her inner office.

"The knife wound," she said as she put her cell phone on the table, "how is it coming along?"

Art rubbed the back of his hand and looked the room over. It seemed the same. He remembered every detail from that day they came here for the Nelson case. The white tulips with their long, lime-green stems sat in the tall, clear, aqua-tinted vase on the coffee table. Art eased into one of the side chairs next to the couch, his knee close to hers. He rubbed his hand slowly over the texture of the beige fabric. Maybe this will dry my palm. It felt velvety soft. The walls were peach. The room fit Amanda, business-like and yet feminine.

She sat on the couch almost across from him and crossed her ankles. He admired her expensive leather pumps. Today she wore gray; her blouse, a shiny silk, had a bow under her chin and a string of pearls cascading midway down her chest. She had those teeth, beaver teeth, but perfect and her makeup was flawless. She was a beautiful woman.

Art brought his hand up to the place where the knife had cut his upper left arm. He rubbed the area. "They tell me with time and therapy I will get most of the movement back. Until then it's pretty useless," he said, adjusting the arm sling.

"Are you back at work?" she asked.

SIDESWIPED

He studied her. She sat with a pleasant smile on her face and brought her blue eyes up to meet his. Her blonde hair shone from the overhead light. She set her elbow on the chair arm and the movement wafted a pleasant floral scent his direction.

Art caught the deep fragrance of lovely petals and the heavy undertones he couldn't quite identify and he thought her perfume fit so her well. He fought to bring his attention back to her question. "I'm on disability, can't go into the office right now." He sighed and shrugged his shoulders. "Walt brings me files to look over. I'm Walt's handyman these days." He frowned and said, "It's a far cry from being a homicide lieutenant." He shifted his focus down at the floor. "At least I keep up on what's going down."

He couldn't help enjoying the perfume. It drew him to her. Art felt desperate to find the right words to say to ask her to go out with him for a night on the town. Fear kept him, a grown man of forty-five and father of one teenage daughter, hostage. Art smiled as he thought what woman would want a gimp, a loser? You're not a loser his inner self screamed. He brought his head up his attention toward her.

She gazed into his eyes. "You've lost a few pounds since July." Her eyes made her statement a fact. "I like you in civvies, a blue checked shirt and tan Dockers. Very nice, goes well with your green arm sling." She beamed, a caring softness flooding her eyes. "I was surprised when you called for this private, off-the- record meeting."

"Amanda, I'm sorry for taking up your time. I guess I shouldn't have called you," Art said as he shifted restlessly. He remembered sitting at his home office desk this morning and thinking how he was a waste of space these days. Both he and Melissa were suffering the after effect of one Raymond Michael McNamare. Something happened this morning. He'd drifted out of depression for

3

just a little while, and during that time he'd called Amanda and made this appointment.

She turned more toward him, uncrossed her ankles. "Why don't you start where you were prompted to call me today? What made you do that?" she asked.

His good hand rubbed his weak one while he studied the floor. "I don't know. I was thinking how stuck I felt, and I thought of you and what you do. I thought you might get me, um ..., unstuck."

"Got a pry bar with you?" An astute smile crossed her face.

"You need to be somewhere?" Art asked noticing her glance at the French table clock. Its heavy brass base sat on the side table. Art admired the convex glass lens that magnified the dial. Although the six inch high body of the clock was demure in size that dial seemed to jump out at him. It was easy to read and he liked it very much.

She smiled. "Just wondering when you are going to get to it, whatever 'it' is."

"Oh, Amanda, I think..." he said and sighed. He turned his attention off to the side of the window then brought his eyes back to her knees. He studied the shine of her hose. His eyes came up when her hand pulled at the hem of her skirt. He knew he was making her uncomfortable.

"Amanda. I need some help, your kind of help. I feel frustrated. I want to break things. I feel that way a lot and I know it's not good. For Melissa or me." Art slowly brought his eyes from the glow of her pearls up to the gentleness of her eyes as he said that, checking to see if she heard what he was really saying, then turned away.

She nodded, her gaze drifted to the floor as she said, "For all the wrong reasons, I had hoped you were here to ask me out." Her eyes came up and stayed on his.

He sat forward. "I want to. Not sure how. Amanda, I'm not sure of anything lately." A sheepish smile covered his face and reddened his cheeks darkening the freckles.

4

"Things have shifted, changed for me. You sure you want to hitch up with me?"

She smiled. "We could make it something non-threatening. We could meet somewhere, spend some time together then go our separate ways. No stress, no expectations. Just see how things go."

"I wanted to ask you if you were busy this Saturday evening. I thought we might go wine tasting. That is if you don't have anything to do," he said. "You do like wine?"

"Art, I'd love to. I can take off this weekend."

They had a date before he knew it, and both of them sat there looking a bit surprised yet pleased. That settled, they both rose, standing and facing each other.

"So, it's this Saturday evening." He grinned at her. "For wine tasting, you and me?"

"Oh, Art." She fished in her pocket and brought out a card. "I have a friend who would be perfect for you to see concerning being stuck. I am glad you decided to come in to talk to me. You understand, I can't see you professionally and socially. It's unethical," she said with a warm smile and sparkling laugh as she extended the card. He took it barely looked at it as he slid it into his pocket. Art headed for the door and as he did his pager went off. It startled him as his thoughts were completely on Amanda. Pleased to be with her and talking to her. He reached for his pager.

"That's timing for you," she said.

He glanced at the pager's screen. The message read; "Homicide." He slid the pager back in place and fought to contain the emotions he sensed from the date he had with her for this weekend and now there was a job to do. He slipped the card into his pocket and smiled, thrilled that Walt needed him.

"A homicide?"

Art didn't answer her. His brows furrowed over his eyes, the lips tightened as his mind sank into deep thought. He'd slid into cop mode.

Chapter Two

4 P.M. Thursday, August 31, 1995

Art stepped outside and dialed Walt, then listened while moving to his car. Walt gave him directions and he drove to the intersections of Grape Avenue and Oak Street near the high school. The place was filled with police cars, yellow crime scene tape, interested bystanders, and the body. He parked back from the other cars and made his way forward. One of the officers pulled the tape barricade up for Art to walk under, allowing him into the inner circle of activity. His right hand guarded his injured arm as he ducked down, then up to thank Officer Murphy.

Murphy let go of the tape and inquired, "How are you?"

"Hangin' in there," Art said as he grabbed the young man's strong hand. He let go as hunched over and slow moving Walt meandered to a stop. Foreheads inches apart the detective spoke in hushed tones. "Art, the body was found in the crosswalk. There were no witnesses. No one heard anything, no gunshots. Two shots took the victim out. We have her purse, and she's identified as Adele Blandford, aged forty-four. She lived just down Pacific Ave. We've got officers knocking on doors. We're looking for anything and everything at the scene. So far, we've got nothing. Walt raised his hand so slightly that

Art barely caught the movement. He swept his eyes in that direction. "That driver standing by the Toyota parked at the curb made the discovery and called it in. She's pretty shaken up." Art's eyes moved to the open window of the passenger's side of the car. There, a small brown dog pushed its nose out into the air. Art chewed on his mustache and stared at her. "I doubt she's going to be much help. What time did she call it in?"

Walt paged through his note pad. "Around 3:55 p.m. As soon as I got here I called you."

Art nodded and let his eyes drift to the men and women officers moving in a formed line, scouring the street surface and the lawns, sidewalks and driveways, some with metal detectors. They were searching for clues, shell casings, anything that would lead the department in the investigation.

Walt had said all he had to say. Art nodded more to himself and straightened up. He walked over and peered at the body, draped now and waiting for transportation from the scene. That couldn't happen until the coroner arrived. He studied the ground. The paint stripes defining the pathway were clear and easy to see. Nothing else other than street dust appeared to be in the crosswalk. His attention swung to the covered body of a middle-aged woman. Her right shoe exposed a red sole peeking out. Art moved his eyes as he mentally recorded everything. What's her story? How did she come to be here at this moment and so very dead? What is her connection with the shooter?

Art stood two feet from the crosswalk line that edged Grape Ave. He turned and looked at the school. Could the shooter have been standing there? Well, they weren't going to know that until the line of trajectory was known. If the shooter did use the school ground, where would he or she have been standing at the time of discharge?

He pursed his lips together and swung his gaze to the open areas before him. A sidewalk, some lawn, and more cement walkways, a crème colored round building with a dark red peaked rooftop. He looked at the few trees that grew in the lawn area, their trunks too narrow to hide behind. He peered down open breezeways leading to classrooms. Someone could draw a bead from any number of places on campus. Could the killer have been on the roof? His eyes rose and checked the roof line.

He studied the areas to the right and the left of where he stood. Too many opportunities and each one will have to be checked out. His gut told him this was a sniper hit. Art wondered how far from the victim was the shooter when he fired? Was this personal?

That left the homes on Oak Street. He turned toward them and for a long moment he soaked up the appearance the community made. He guessed they'd been built in the 1970's, homey places.

Art felt it in his being, something was off. He just couldn't put his finger on just what. Too many questions presented themselves, rushing at him. He needed to sort them out. It would be best to make a study list and he'd do that as soon as he got the report. One question gnawed at him; did a student from the high school shoot this woman? He wanted it to be far-fetched. With so many other school tragedies on the books, he couldn't let the idea go so easily. He gave this some intense consideration about the time a metal detector went off. His thrill of excitement at the find faded as the officer announced he'd found a coin.

Art let the cover remain over the woman, even though it would help him to look at the body for clues. There were too many citizens watching this show, and he knew the newspaper would have coverage, and he didn't want to help them out in any way. He'd have to wait for the photos to hit his desk. That would be tomorrow at the earliest.

Besides, he couldn't lean down and get his arm aggravated. He didn't want to start the waves of pain out here in front of everyone. Even the department people didn't know how much that pain took him down. Annoyed, he bit his lip, disgusted at being on the back burner. This was Walt's case, not his. He was here out of courtesy. Although glad to be included, he felt on the outer edge of everything. For now, his job was to stay alerted and abreast of what evidence the department waded though, and to help Walt anyway he could.

He squinted to the west noting that the sun would be going down in a couple of hours. The warmth from that direction rested on his face as he stood there wishing he could dive in and get going on this investigation. Not that there was anything different he would be doing. Art let the sounds around him in and he listened to the hum of activity. The neighbors and other bystanders mumbled as his people worked. These were his people and he knew they would leave no stone unturned. Someone found something and the scraping sounds of a plastic markers being placed were like music to Art. He loved the hunt. He'd make his own story board in his office and run down to the department from time to time to see if they had anything he didn't.

This team will have to work through the night hunting for clues. He wouldn't stay; there was nothing for him to do at this point. His expertise would be called in when the clues were made available.

He spotted Walt in the mix of people and strolled over to him. When he could he spoke. "Melissa's got dinner ready. How much longer are you going to stay?

Walt glanced up at him. "Hum. Not sure. This is going to be a mess by the looks of it, and it could be a cold case if we don't get it right." He surveyed Art. "The kid's cooking?"

"Yeah, and you're invited, tonight."

Walt appeared skeptical, "What's for dinner?"

"Spaghetti, and I've got a good bottle of wine."

"Sounds good. I'll get things wrapped up here and be there in about an hour or so, okay? I'm going to be on call you know so if they need me I've got to come back."

Art nodded and smiled, fished in his pocket for his car keys and backed away. He ducked under the tape Murphy lifted for him and bid him goodbye.

Art didn't like it when homicide happened but he couldn't dismiss that fact that at this moment he could say this has been a good day and he felt happy, needed, and useful. He had a date with life.

Chapter Three

9 P.M. Thursday, August 31, 1995

Mouthwatering spices and herbs simmering filled the kitchen with cooking odors as Art held the door for Walt to enter. Melissa wore an apron folded over at the middle and tied in back as she stirred a big pot. Her hair hung loose and sailed out as she crossed the room, wooden spoon in hand stained with red sauce, and hugged Walt.

"How ya been?" he asked.

She wrinkled her nose before saying, "Hangin' I've got dinner ready. Can I interest you in Italian, Franklin style?" she asked, her face beamed and her eyes sparkled as she put her hands up and out indicating 'what do you think, good idea or bad?'

Walt's mess of hair went uncombed, his rumpled shirt needed ironing, his shoes begged to be brushed. It all fit so perfectly with the gruff voice, as he said, "I am so hungry I could eat..." He caught himself, blinked his owl-like eyes and finished, "That sounds good to me."

Art moved off the stool. "I'll get some wine. And Melissa," he turned to her and pointed, "you can have a glass tonight if you'd like."

Melissa giggled and gushed, "Yes, I'd like that." She spun toward the stove; her hair sailed out and spread in the air coming to land on her back, smooth as silk. She

12

lifted the lid to the container, bent and smelled the contents and stirred the spaghetti, tapping the spoon on the side of the saucepan.

She was happy, Art could tell. The back door stood open, and the crickets were in full orchestration, their strumming filling the room with homey sounds. Art had a fleeting sense of normalcy. He stopped and listened for a moment, savored the peace, took a deep breath as he stepped from the room to get the wine. "Here we are," he said as he came back and handed the bottle to Walt to open.

Art took the opened bottle and announced, "Just what the doctor ordered," as he poured Walt a glass, then one for himself and one for Melissa. Twisting the bottle and lifting it at the last pour he thought of telling them that he had a date with the Doctor Amanda Burtoni. Excitement and embarrassment heated his cheeks, and he dropped his head to hide his face. He would not tell them now.

Melissa hummed with the music as she brought the heavy bowl of spaghetti to the table and set it in place with pride, she walked to the refrigerator, opened the door and slid a salad out and positioned it by the large bowl.

They moved from the bar stools to the kitchen table and took seats. "One good thing about spaghetti is that it seasons with time. Wish I could say the same about me," Art said, then laughed as he pushed the bowl of spaghetti toward Walt. "I suppose we should say grace. Melissa, would you do the honors?"

The soft lashes over her hazel eyes dropped as she reached across the table and caught her dad's fingers. She slid her other hand palm up to Walt. "Uncle?"

Walt set the bowl down.

She felt the heat of his grip as his chubby fingers circled about her hand. These two men had been her family for as far back as she could remember. She cleared her throat. "Thank you, Lord, for the gifts you give, and the friends you bring, and the food we eat. Amen."

Walt slowly rolled a ball of spaghetti on his fork and pushed the wad into his mouth. "This is the best I've ever tasted."

"It's Nicole's recipe, she's teaching me how to cook."

Art ate as if he'd just discovered something rare. "This is really good, Honey. It is stupendous. I could eat this every night," he said finishing his wine. "What did you think of the wine?"

She wrinkled her nose, "I like Coke better." she said passing him her half-filled glass. "Too bitter for me."

Art took the glass and upended it, draining it in one swallow as he dropped his eyes on Walt. "Anything turn up after I left?"

"As a matter of fact," Walt nodded and sliced his eyes toward Melissa. She busied herself rinsing the plates and placing them in the dishwasher.

"It's okay, what happened?"

"Well," Walt paused. "The real Adele Blandford is possibly alive and well and living just down the street from where the body turned up."

Art's mouth hung open in amazement as he said, "What?"

"Yeah." Walt nodded, "Well, I am glad she's alive, but I've just got to wonder who the victim is. And," Walt paused and turned from Art to Melissa, "how'd she come to be dead at that place and at that time?"

The room quieted

Melissa wiped her hands, turned to the table, dropped the damp tea towel, put both hands flat on the surface and said, "Well, Dad, you said you would tell me what happened when you got back. I don't know what you two are talking about, so give."

14

Art nodded his head. "Well, it seems we have a female dead from two shots to the chest area. The body was in the crosswalk on Oak and Grape Avenue right across from Lodi High School. We had identification until the real Adele Blandford showed up. Now I'm wondering, how did Adele's purse get to be at the side of the dead woman?" Art began working his mustache with his bottom lip.

Art and Walt were feeding off each other now like two old dogs with their noses to the ground. Their nostrils flared and their eyes wide and sparkling with electrical flashes. They were locked together as they leaned toward each other to make that contact even closer. Their ideas came fast and furious, silly and stupid as they slung it out to see what would stick.

Art said, "I didn't uncover the body. Sure would have liked getting a firsthand view. I'll just have to go off the pictures." Art poured more wine in Walt's glass and then his own as Melissa approached the table.

"I can't wait to tell Nicole how you liked the spaghetti." They had finished so she picked up the plates and cleared the table, filling the dishwasher, and putting it on start cycle. "See you two later, I'm going up now," she said kissing Walt on the forehead and her dad on the cheek.

"Night Mel."

Art called after her, "Good night Melissa."

"Night Dad. Night Walt."

"Well, I guess we've just about covered everything about this case for the time being. That was one great meal. The kid is growing up Art." They scraped the chairs on the floor as they stood.

He walked Walt to the curb and bid him a good night and thanked him for coming over. "I think you helped us be more normal."

15

Walt nodded. "Good." He studied the ground a long time before finishing his thought. "You and the kid need help, Art."

Art gritted his jaws, shuffled his feet and took in a deep breath. He hated to admit it to others, even Walt. It was true. Melissa was getting help and he didn't know how that was going. He would be seeking help soon. He just needed to make the appointment. Where was that card Amanda gave him today? Oh, yeah, my shirts pocket. Art placed his hand on Walt's car's hood and caught the old detective's eyes on him. "I know."

Chapter Four

10 A.M. Friday, September 1, 1995

The Mokelumne River ran quietly and lazily now, and although controlled by a fast undertow, seemed at a standstill. Melissa's hand caressed the surface of the deep green, cooling, wonderfulness of the waterway. She dipped her hand, wiggling her fingers under the surface. A dappling of sunlight played along her arm. She relaxed completely over the inflated inner tube, her knees just out of the water, her head held in place by the rubber. Breathing deeply, allowing the wilderness roar to fill her ears, she floated in the middle of the river not wanting to break the moment.

Shades of green from light lime to deep sage and all hues of olive-green filled this part of the river. Moss ran up the sides of the trees against the far bank, a sharp contrast to the rough texture of the dark umber oak bark carrying the canopy hovering above. Sunlight fought through the jungle-thick covering and targeted the water below, splashing it with dazzle too bright to focus on for long. Echos filled her ears with a steady sound of leaves moving with the breeze and the constant thunderous reverberation of the river's flow. The fragrance of leaves, water, and wildlife floated around her. All of this shut out her real world, and she welcomed every bit of freedom from that pain.

It seemed peaceful, an ideal morning, a perfect place to exist. She didn't want it to stop. Every muscle in her body relaxed while the inner tube carried her a million miles away from the life that now bugged her to the bone. Dinner last night went great, but that seemed the only thing around the house that worked right. Everything's strained her conversations with her dad especially. He's so uptight all the time. Just can't talk to him. He wants to hit something. I'd like to break something. Things are just messed up. I don't know if they will ever get back to normal.

She pushed the thoughts away, Melissa didn't want to think about anything. She slit her eyes open and gazed at the green, a world that had caught her up, making her oblivious at the moment to the frantic pace of the real world. That other life waited a thousand yards to her left, where, at this instant, Lodi baked in 104 degrees. She didn't want to think about that existence, she wanted to push it away and savor this one forever.

"Hey?" Sandy said.

"Um?" Melissa answered. Her eyes closed. A slight smile pulled her rosy, freckled cheeks into mounds. She listened to the tinkling sound of the water as she moved her hand, and the droplets glistened as they rejoined the river.

"Want a Coke?" Sandy asked while draped over an inner tube tied to Melissa's. She lay listlessly, her bright orange and red colored bikini, covering her tanned body, a contrast to the deep greens of the river. Sandy's blonde hair braided and wound around her head and held in place with two orange clips, made her bronzed face glow.

"Not yet." Melissa relaxed her neck back over the inner tube, her olive-green walking shorts and top blended in with the scenery as she bobbed with the flow. At this place and time that was her secret desire, to be invisible.

Something about being closed up inside the house panicked Melissa. She had to have the lights turned on at

18

home. This river's the only place I can close my eyes and feel safe. She didn't understand, but felt no compunction to question why. Her shrink wanted her to question why but she didn't want to go there.

The heat grew over her knees, she opened her eyes and realized they had floated into direct sunlight. They were coming back to their boat ramp area where the trees grew sparsely and ended their ten-mile inner-tube voyage. She kicked her feet and splashed water over both her and Sandy's legs.

"That feels so good," Sandy said. She rose up and pulled on the cord connected to a submerged six-pack of Coke trailing them. "Melissa, you're sunburned," she said.

"It won't last. I burn and peel off. I just stay the same all the time," she said. Melissa opened her eyes and asked, "Do we still have the Cokes?" She gazed at the river; it seemed about forty feet wide at this place. She could just see large roots ready to snag anything that passed their way as she stared down deep into the water.

"I just checked, and they're there, nice and cold," Sandy said.

Melissa lay back, closed her eyes again, and thought about going back home this afternoon. Her dad would be there trying to work on some project in the garage or other. He liked to think he was a repair person, but he wasn't. She loved the heck out of him, but she didn't know how to love him back to being her dad, the one she remembered before Ray McNamare. That dad wasn't perfect, but she knew and mostly understood that person. Last night with Walt and the dinner he seemed more like himself.

"Are you still going on that endurance ride?" Sandy asked.

Melissa didn't answer right away. She dropped her hand back into the water and enjoyed the soft feeling. Gently she allowed her hand to rest on the surface of the water. "Yeah, I don't know," she answered.

M.L. WEATHERINGTON

Somehow, she had a relationship with the Mokelumne River now; she loved this river. In her mind it became her savior, and she felt protected and loved by this body of water.

She wanted to come by herself to the river. That was not allowed. Her Dad has insisted she not come alone. He acts as if he expects me to die at any moment.

It was driving her crazy and him crazy, whatever it was. She didn't understand what was happening. She didn't understand why she had to have lights on all the time and her window shades open to the night as well as the day. Her heart beat fast each time she used her bathroom. Small confined spaces scared her the minute she entered them. She acted on her first impulse and stepped back seeking safety.

What had happened to make her feel this way? Could she ever trust anyone again? Just to be safe, she had decided that no one would ever get close to her like Ray had, ever again, ever! What a fool she'd been. How could she have believed in him? What a loser. She'd never marry. God, it made her feel hollow inside. A sick swirl tickled her stomach; it would flip in the next few moments. Maybe she should ask Sandy for one of those sodas. She took some deep breaths.

She hadn't told Sandy her fears. They embarrassed her, and she felt ashamed. "We're almost home," she said with certain sadness.

"Yeah, I've got to get home. Mom's on me about my room. She seems to think if my room is perfectly clean I'd be a better person or something," Sandy floated a moment. "I am so relaxed now all I want to do is take a nap."

"Is she home?"

"No, she had a hot client in Sacramento. She won't be home until late tonight. Want to come over?" Sandy asked.

Melissa thought about it and said, "I suppose we'll have to fix chicken again. She's on a chicken kick lately."

"You noticed. I'm sick of chicken. Just once Mom could ask us what we want," Sandy said. "My legs are burned where they were out of the water. How can we be sunburned in the shade?"

Melissa smiled and said, "I have often wondered that too. I guess I'd better stay home. Dad's got a new case the departments working, and I need to make dinner." She managed to sit up a bit and take her bearings before paddling with her hands toward their red and white boat tied up at the wooden dock. The water made her lazy and relaxed, sleepy, that's what she felt like now. The sound of the river a lovely melody to her put her in a special place. One she didn't want disturbed by anyone or anything. The river was the only place she felt this way lately and it saddened her to know as soon as she stepped up on that dock the feelings would flood back and she'd be scared again. She pulled at the water working the rubber inner tube around so she could grab onto the boat and get to shore. Her freedom ended as they closed the gap, she kept her face away from Sandy working on a convincing smile. Finally, she turned to her and gave her that smile, "Good ride today."

Chapter Five

10:15 A.M. September 1, 1995

Walt walked into Art's home office and sat across from him. He smiled and crossed his outstretched legs. When he brought his eyes up to Art's he shook his head. "We don't have a clue who that woman was. Not one."

Art knew he referred to the body found on Grape Ave. He got up and walked to the side table, turned and glanced at Walt. "Coffee?"

Walt nodded and said, "Hold the sugar, I'm cutting back."

Art poured the steaming brew, enjoying the fragrance of a fresh made pot that filtered through the room. "No sugar? My you are taking the doctor's orders seriously," Art said as he handed the mug to Walt. "I'm glad your tests came back with only a bleeding ulcer and not cancer."

"Me too, I was scared stiff at the thought. Now I have to lose fifty pounds, and the doc wants to see some progress by my next appointment in four months. I'm not out of the woods yet. If I can't get this weight off I may have to have surgery," Walt said. "I haven't a clue how to change my eating habits. With this job, there's no habit. It's catch it when you can."

Art nodded, poured his coffee and carefully set the mug in a cleared place on the desk. "Losing weight won't be easy." He sat gently to protect his arm. "If I understand," his right hand moved the pictures covering his desktop, "this woman was shot twice, center mass. She fell in the crosswalk, on a clear day, in broad daylight, and no one saw or heard anything?" He rose up with a studied expression. "Except the shooter," he said as he sipped.

The men stared at each other as they sat in Art's den of an office. It seemed clear to Art they were spinning their wheels and getting nowhere. He began noticing the walls of his office. Everything looked like it could use a coat of fresh paint. He wondered why he'd think of that right now and knew the answer as soon as the thought presented itself. Art had nothing toward solving the case so his mind drifted. Art let his attention move to the oak bookcases he'd filled with books he hardly ever opened. He owned them because they were classics and some teacher or librarian, he couldn't remember which, had impressed upon him, while young, that a well-rounded man knows his classics. Art had read one or two and that about covered his well-roundedness. His police scanner and computer and printer were the newest equipment in his office, and they were four years old. He guessed he had time to do this work, just didn't have the desire. Forcing himself back to the subject of the homicide he brightened. "Well there's some good news."

Walt smirked. "Yeah, and what would that be?

"We have over sixty thousand suspects."

Walt snickered, "Well, I'll start calling all of Lodi in for questioning."

"When will forensics know anything?" Art pulled one of the pictures around on the desk. "She seems like a nice middle-class person. Someone must be missing her. No one has called in a missing person?" Art's brows moved together and the lines in his face deepened as he set his jaw waiting for Walt's answer.

Walt shook his head. "No," he said. "It's cold," Walt held the mug with both hands and sipped.

"I sure would like the info on the directions of the shots, they could tell me where that shooter was and how far away from the victim at the time of discharge." Art made eye contact with Walt as he spoke. "We know that she died there on that spot, the blood evidence at the scene shows that." His finger pointed, "These pictures are proof of that. She fell with her head pointing toward Oak Street, her foot toward Grape Avenue. That puts the shooter south and west." He shook his head. "I would really like to know where that shooter positioned himself for the fatal shot," he said tapping the photo with his index finger.

"What makes you sure it was a man?" Walt asked setting his mug on his knee and his mouth drooping open.

Art looked up, "You think it might have been a woman?"

Walt gripped his lips tight together as he nodded, "Well, let's say Adele observes someone taking off with her purse. If you were Adele wouldn't you want to draw a bead on the S.O.B.?" Walt said his eyes wide.

Art narrowed his. "So, Adele sees this woman with her purse. Maybe the victim entered the house and took the purse?" Art paused, "Adele grabs her gun. What? Did she have a rifle sitting handy by the door?"

Walt bit his lower lip and said, "You think it was a rifle?"

Art answered, "I don't know, I didn't get to look at the wounds, the body was draped when I arrived. There were too many people standing around, and I didn't want to give the newspaper any fodder. According to these pictures, Adele would have had to race past the woman and raise the rifle and fire to hit the victim and drop her where she ended up."

Walt nodded knowing what Art meant. "I think we are spinning our wheels until we have some foundation. Right now, I have men covering the surrounding area asking questions. I have someone talking to Adele just to find out what she was doing that day. She's a looker. Those red nails out to here." Walt indicated a large distance from the tips of his fingers. He moved his focus to Art. "They wouldn't fit the trigger area on most firearms. Especially if she were to grab one in a hurry," Walt said.

Art nodded, "Did you notice if one of her nails was missing when you talked with her at the scene?"

Walt shook his head. "They were all intact."

"Cross her off our list of could be's. No matter what we think of, we come up with no lead. This damn case is colder than a block of ice." Art reached up and drove his fingers into his wavy red hair and combed from the forehead to the back of his skull where he scratched a moment.

Walt blinked several times. The room radiated warmth this September morning. He yawned, "We didn't find any shell casings at the scene. If I didn't know better, I'd say the place was vacumed before we got there."

Art crossed his ankles and sighed, "That makes me think sniper, someone shooting from a van. Find the vehicle and we find the residue and maybe the casings. That is if this isn't a professional job and this guy isn't fastidious."

Walt finished his coffee and set the mug down. He sat back and let his eyes roam to the ceiling. "You might be right. That makes sense." He brought his eyes to Art's. "If that's the case we probably will never see this vehicle." He shook his head while an expression of distaste filled his face.

Art watched Walt's facial expression as it turned sour and knew how he felt. He reached for Walt's arm, allowed his hand to press down for a moment before he said, "No one likes cold cases. What we are going to do is start at the beginning over and over until we unravel the mystery. You and I will work together. This one won't get past us, trust me, Walt."

Walt tried a sick grimace, and the two sat quietly as the unsaid word 'But' lingered between them.

"No if and's or buts, Walt. We will solve this crime."

"I hope so. Any chance for a warm up?"

Art got up and carried the pot to Walt's mug and filled it to the top, "Oops, too full, do you want sugar?" He waved his hand, "Forgot for a second on the sugar."

"No, it's fine. Leave it." Walt reached for the mug and repositioned it to his section of the desk, setting it on the mug-rug Art had placed there earlier. "I'll let it cool a bit. "He sat back looking at Art. "I haven't any idea where I can start at the beginning again and find a new thread to pull. I've gone over this from every direction, and there's nothing."

"There's something, there always is." Art turned to the photos again. "I keep thinking there's a clue right here in front of me and I am just missing it. I've looked at these pictures from every angle. I feel sure we are going to find someone that knew her is our killer. That's where you have to pull at the string Walt. All the people she knew."

"I've got that under way and I should have the report in a day or so. You'll see it as soon as I get it."

"That would be good." Art finished his coffee and raised his wrist to read the time. He knew he had to get going but he didn't want to kick Walt out abruptly especially when his old partner needed support. "We will get the guy Walt. We will I know it in my gut."

"Well you sure were right on the Nelson case, you said you were going to hold that emerald in your hand

and you did. If you hadn't found that ring I don't think you would ever have solved that case."

"I hate to kick you out but I've got to get going.

"You got a hot date?"

Art hid his grin, "You could say that.

Chapter Six

5:16 P.M. September 1, 1995

Art selected a new pair of blue jeans and a nice cotton shirt with a faint check print in light blue. Not being a connoisseur of all things clothing he had listened to Melissa when she told him to go casual. Deck shoes and a baseball cap spelled casual to him. She had told him to wear his leather sandals instead of the deck shoes, so he had. He'd spent time on his hair and mustache. His hazel green eyes twinkled as he appraised his appearance. At last, Art splashed some cologne and slapped his cheeks. They stung as he studied the mirrored image of himself.

"That's as good as it's going to get." Art said to no one as he reached out, snatched up his side arm, and slipped it in his holster. Patting the piece twice to reassure himself that it was secure he dropped his trouser. Art looked around, grabbed his jacket and keys and headed out of his room.

"Melissa," he called.

"Yes," she answered entering the landing near where he stood.

"Well?" He waited expectantly. She eyed him up and down her lips tightly closed as she decided.

"How do I look? Do I pass inspection?"

"Turn around," she said. "Umm, you don't resemble my dad," she said. Melissa straightened the arm sling strap to be neater around his neck.

His eyes softened at the care in her expression.

"You're fine. Now don't stay out too late. Remember I'll be waiting up."

"Like hell you will," he said. "This isn't my first rodeo."

"Yeah, but how long's it been since you rode a bucking bronco?" she asked as she turned away. "You go and have a good time, just be yourself."

A quizzical expression flooded his face. "You think Amanda's a bucking bronco?"

She called over her shoulder, "I think you don't have a clue about dating. You are a dinosaur, Dad."

The sound of her voice, or was it the way she said it concerned him and he yelled, "You okay?"

Art stared at the empty doorway.

"Yeah, why?"

"Oh, nothing, just checking that this was alright with you. My...dating?" A blush spread over Art's cheeks.

"It's totally cool," she said as she ran back and hugged him.

Art started down the stairs and stopped. His palms dampening as the enormity of the evening ahead settled on him. His only hope was that Amanda would be as twisted in the gut right now as he felt. Then he realized that she, being a psychiatrist, wouldn't feel nervous one bit. She'd be looking at this clinically. God, he hated to be under a microscope.

"You going or not?"

He turned, "No just making sure I had everything."

"Just checking, I'm going down for a soda."

"Okay, honey." his mind on his inner thoughts as he answered her. Something about last July changed all that. He had a sense of urgency about his life, about

29

Melissa's life. On a level he rarely went to, he understood raising Melissa without a mother in the mix was complicated. Melissa was scared, and he understood why. He didn't have a clue how to help her. His theory had always been if it's not broken don't fix it. Well, it got busted. Got wrecked on his watch, and he didn't know how to put it all back together. He'd seen to it that she had someone to talk to about her fear and he guessed it was going okay. Melissa was going to her appointments that was the best he could do for her. She just didn't want to talk about it to him. He shook it off and redirected his thoughts to this evening. I am not going for Melissa; I am going for me. "I'll see you later," he said as he winked and went down the stairs and crossed to the door. Art turned back to her.

"Be yourself. Isn't that what you always tell me when I have to do some tough thing?"

He nodded, "Yeah." Art went out and closed the door behind him.

They had agreed to meet at the winery, so Art drove from the city into the countryside passing vineyards heavy with fruit. It would be a good year for grapes he thought. He started over a small, wooden bridge that made a hollow sound as his car crossed. As he glanced down he glimpsed a trickle of water flowing over the rocks in the mossy creek. It had been especially dry this time of year. The vineyard wasn't far now; he could see the turn in as he came out from under the tree covered canopy shading the bridge. He braked, turned the wheel and swallowed nervously. The numbers on the heavy ornate wrought iron gate matched his memo. Art realized the gate was at least twelve feet tall and he liked the grape leaves of wrought iron decorating the expanse. Slowly he brought the car past the gate and to a parking place. He could see that everything about this place was top drawer.

He could feel it as the tires crunched pebbles and he maneuvered into a parking spot surrounded by shaped hedges. Art hoped in his heart that he would arrive before her. He planned to sit as though the world were his oyster. Let her see him. But that didn't happen. She was there, and he stopped in his tracks when he saw her.

A waiter stood a foot away talking to her. She raised her chin to answer him and the afternoon light made her blonde hair shimmer and her face radiant. His heart soared. She is stunning. Now aware she had dressed beautifully in a deep emerald green summer dress made his choice of jeans and simple shirt seem right out of Hicksville. He ran his hand over his jeans when an uncertain feeling landed squarely in his stomach. Art felt like running, yet was still drawn forward by some unseen force. As he took the next step his leather sandals squeaked.

She spotted him. The face that had been radiant now glimmered like a thousand spotlights shown down on her, or from her. Her smile broadened to welcome him and the message of love in her eyes for him was magic. Somehow his feet moved above the ground, and he floated to her unaware of his movements.

His voice sounded deep and sexy, "Hi," his grin widening as he came to stand before her. She rose up, caught his eye, holding his attention a long moment, forcing voice control, in a husky breathless voice, she said, "Hi." Her hand found a place in his, and they remained in place, toe to toe and eye to eye. No one else was in the world now. So much passed between them, yet not one word was spoken as their fingers slowly intertwined, and they felt the warmth of each other and savored the moment.

Out of the corner of his eye, he saw the waiter heading their way with a glass of wine on a tray. He set it down on the table with a napkin and stood straight. "Would there be anything else?"

Amanda turned from Art, directing her attention to the waiter. "Yes." She glanced toward Art. "What will you have?"

"The same," he replied pointing to her glass.

With a nod the waiter backed away as birds sang and the evening took on a peaceful note. Somewhere stringed instruments played softly, and their eyes locked on each other as they sat. "I almost chickened out, I mean, I'm too old to be dating."

"I know how you feel, but we've got something worth exploring don't you think? I've been drawn to you since we first met." Amanda's hand circled the tall thin glass stem and the red wine spun slowly around just before she tasted. "I like this."

"What kind is it?"

"It's Petite Sirah."

Art's wine arrived. He acknowledged the waiter as he set the glass and napkin down.

He picked up his glass, they tapped with a sharp clink and tasted. "Umm...that's good."

Three hours passed as they sat talking about Art's work and hers. They spoke about their hopes and dreams for their lives. They covered topics of disappointments and their preferred manner of handling them. While they chatted, they finished off a bottle between them. Stars twinkled, and a cool breeze picked up. It seemed to break the mood for Art. "Let's take a drive."

She grinned and nodded, then took his hand and got up. "I've got a bit of a buzz."

Art waved the waiter over and he paid the presented bill. The night seemed soft to Art, the air light and clear and he had a general sense of happiness that probably was a buzz, but he chose to ignore his good sense. He took her hand and they walked as though they had years to get back to their cars. "Where would you like go?" he asked as they strolled.

"Wherever you say, sir."

As they approached their cars, Art pulled gently on her hand, "Is that your car?"

"Yes, mine's in the shop, that's a loaner."

"Let's take mine." He moved to the rider's side of his car and opened the door for Amanda who sat without a word. They drove around the country side chatting like old friends. Finally Art's stomach rumbled and he saw the time was getting late. "You hungry?"

"Famished."

He drove to Pine Street and parked. As he pulled the keys from the ignition he felt comfortable, all the pre-dating tenseness gone. Their being together seemed normal. He jumped out of the car, remembering his damaged arm after the movement and opened the car door for her. She gave him her hand and he thought, I'm never going to let it go.

Her eyes were on his and he didn't want to take his from hers. There was someone interested in me. As interested in me as I am in her. That astounded him.

Chapter Seven

1:10 A.M. Septermber 2, 1995

Art's hand encircled the large metal handle of Bill's Bar and Grill on Pine Street and he jerked it and held it open for Amanda to enter, then followed her into the dark, cozy neighborhood tavern. As his eyes adjusted to the low light, he spotted two men sitting at opposite ends of the bar with their heads bent over their drinks. Leading Amanda, he showed her a booth and they slid in opposite each other. Music floated from the jukebox in the corner, and the scent long history hung in the air.

Before he could say anything to her the barkeep arrived and Art told him they were hungry. The man turned and pickup two menus and handed them to Art. "Stoves closed now but I have some cold sandwiches left. They looked the list over and they ordered roast beef. The waiter turned away and both called out, "And coffee, regular."

Amanda placed her elbows on the table top and covered the left hand with her right, "You were telling me how you became a father," she said as her chin rested softly on the back of her hands. As she locked her eyes on his, the corner of her lips rose.

Art moved his head giving the expression of, oh, I see what you want to know, and he began, "I met Melissa's mother, Evelyn, when I was thirty. I was head over heels for her, and we were going to get married." Art rolled his head and dipped it toward his shoulder. "I thought." He sighed. "We got pregnant, unexpectedly. She didn't want children, and that was the end of our romance. I begged for Melissa's life, and she gave in providing that I never involved her in the raising years." Art looked down at the table, rubbed his hand over the surface and said, "I never have."

"You've done a wonderful job raising her Art. I've seen the two of you over the years. She's well rounded and level headed. Everything you are," she said almost in a whisper but loud enough for him to hear.

He looked around the room for no reason and every reason. His voice deep, low and aching as he said," I almost lost my daughter last July. It was that close." His eyes took on a stern set. "On my watch."

"You feel responsible for what that person did to you and her?"

"I think I am responsible. I should have known more about what she was doing. She was seeing this guy, I don't know for how long, and I didn't even suspect." Art brought his fingers to his chest and poked them into his breastbone. "What does that make of me?"

Their sandwiches arrived and the coffee. Both of them pulled their coffee cups around to a better place and tested for heat. Amanda picked up and ate a potato chip. "This tastes so good after all that wine. I didn't think I could eat this much. Now I want to wolf it down. I haven't had a roast beef sandwich for such a long time," Amanda said. "Art, I am having such a good time."

"I am too."

"Surprised?" she asked taking another chip and chomping down on it.

35

Art watched her eyes widen. "No, no not at all. Well, yes, I guess if I am honest with you. I didn't think I could get the hang of this dating thing. It should be for the young. At my point in life I'd expected to be settled down," he said and let his words trail off.

"When I took Melissa out of that hospital fifteen years ago I believed I could do everything, be everything. I thought I would not make mistakes with her. I thought I knew enough to do a great job of turning her into a worthwhile adult," he said.

Amanda lifted her chilled sandwich to her lips and said, "You have done that Art. You are too hard on yourself. Life is made up of mistakes."

He picked up his sandwich and studied its contents then said, "She's scared. The lights are on all night long; she won't close her drapes at the bedroom window. The window is open all night. I don't think she shuts her bathroom door. I see these things, but we don't talk about them, and I'm not sleeping. I'm watch dogging her.

"If I'd let her she'd spend all her time on the Mokelumne River. It's as if it draws her. She's being my mother worrying about me and this damn arm. This tragedy has taken my life and turned it upside down. Walt is head of my department temporarily until I can get back full time. If I can get back. We are working a case now, and I have to wait for him to make the calls and give me info. He has to come to my home so we can meet. I hate this."

Art took a bite of his sandwich and one of her chips. She moved the plate closer to him.

"Tell me about you. We've been talking about me all the time," Art said.

"Oh, now there's a riveting subject," she said wiping her mouth. "Well, I finished high school, became a model for a cosmetics company," she wobbled her head, "then I grew up and got my degree." She sipped her coffee and raised the cup to the bartender who nodded and came around to refill.

"You never married?" Art asked.

Her mouth relaxed into a serious frame. Some time passed before she took in her breath and answered him. "I did marry when I was in my twenties. Doug was in the Army, and he never came home. I lost touch with him. I waited a few years, long enough to claim him as dead. Those were painful years for me. Then after a while, I decided he wasn't coming home. His family didn't know anything either. So, I moved on; that's when I dived into my education. That loss became the driving force behind my choosing psychiatry as my field. That whole experience messed me up. It messed all of us up. I wanted to do something about that.

"Hear that," he said.

She tilted her head as though to train her ear. The music in the bar lingered in the background, and she finally made out the tune. "Oh, I know that song. I like it. One of your favorites?" she asked.

Art shook his head. "I was listening to you. I heard the song in the background, and I thought: That's the way I feel, my heart my whole being pulsates with that song. Can you hear the base cello? That one low string, as it's plucked it beats with my heart," he said.

Amanda sang the words softly, ending the last syllable low and sad.

"You've got a pretty voice," he said.

"Do you like to sing?" she asked moving around in her seat to look more toward him. She took the spoon out of her cup and placed it on the saucer.

"Guilty, I sing in the shower mostly," he said.

The lights dimmed, and the bartender announced the last call. Art scanned his watch and said, "It's 1:30 in the morning."

M.L. WEATHERINGTON

They moved out of the booth, paid their bill, bid the bartender goodbye and walked out into the crisp morning air.

They stood out on the sidewalk taking in Lodi in its quiet hours. Art held her hand, "Just look at the stars. Now isn't that beautiful."

Her head turned upward, and as it did, it brushed his good arm and sent electricity through him. Her fragrance joined with the night air and he wanted to remember it this way forever. Slow with reluctance they moved as one to the car and Amanda sat. He closed the door and walked around to the driver's side and got in and started the car.

They drove back to her loaner car; she got in the driver's seat and rolled down the window. Art leaned in to kiss her lips and she didn't back away. "When can I see you again?"

"Not till next weekend."

Art's voice sounded in agony as he said, "That's seven long days away."

She grinned, "I like a man that can count."

Chapter Eight

2:45 P.M. September 4, 1995

A rt noticed the grating, deep, rhythmical sound of the ceiling fan as he entered Doctor James Wexford's outer office. Dust lay on the end table holding several older magazines piled on top of each other. He almost touched the dust with his finger ready to write the date, but he stopped short. His eyes spotted a cobweb draped from the frame of a picture of poppies. It had been there so long it seemed to have collected its share of dust.

Art chose one of the black leather-like office chairs with stainless steel arms and legs. Useless, he thought scowling at the fan. Not one bit of cool air came from the worthless thing. He cringed and twisted his neck each time the dull squeak sounded from the ancient fan. Everything got on Art's nerves and right now this place ranked at the top of his list.

He needed help; he knew how badly. Melissa needed help and needed him to be there for her. He stayed, even though he wanted to walk out of this dump. His nose caught the trail of smoke from a lit cigarette somewhere close. This guy smokes. This isn't going to work! I'm trying to quit.

A large man with heavy stubble and somewhere in his late fifties walked through the doorway. "I'm James

M.L. WEATHERINGTON

Wexford; it's two-forty-five, so that makes you Art Franklin, Amanda's friend," he said as he extended his hand.

"Come on in." His hand indicated that Art should follow. "This is my man-cave," he said as they walked into the room.

Art didn't get a chance to tell him that he needed to be somewhere else at the moment and would need to reschedule. He was thinking along those lines as he walked into the room and saw the messiness from the outer office continued in this space. Doctor Wexford wasn't a neat freak.

An oak writing table took up the room. Two chairs, both the same type low backed office chair, huddled on each side of the desk. Bookcases filled neatly with publications lined one wall, sharp contrast to the messiness of everything else. Two windows covered with wooden slat shutters loomed at Art. It caused him to look into the light, and it cast the doc's face in dark shadow Against the other wall stood a well-used personnel entrance, Art took in all the dirty fingerprints on the edge of the door. as he sat down across from the doc, who now stood inches from Art, the doc's legs leaning against the desk his arms crossed as he studied him. Art felt the heat of that stare.

"Amanda tells me you're stuck," he said.

Art looked up into his face, and in the dimmness saw a slight smile. Other than that, the face seemed calm and quiet, a sense of peace Art could only remember. A feeling he would like to have back. Therefore, he thought, I've got to do this work. "Yes," he said. "I feel stuck."

The doctor walked to his chair and sat down. The blinds displayed striped-sunshine over the doc's body and the top of the old wooden desk as he put his elbows on the desk, knit his fingers together and leaned forward. "Tell me why you feel stuck?"

40

Art shifted his eyes down and a rush of air escaped him. Trying to formulate words he studied the floor tiles of mixed grays and blacks and the wax build up. Nothing sensible would come to him and anxiety built until he said, "I don't know,"

"Take your time. Tell me what you do for a living." Doctor Wexford said his voice soft.

Art moved his hurt arm, using his right hand to adjust the arm sling. "I got stabbed," he said as an explanation.

The doctor nodded.

"I work for the L.P.D. as Lieutenant of Homicide. Been doing that job for the last five years. Worked my way up." Art looked around the room for any distraction. He didn't see anything. The doc just sat there letting him do all the talking. At what rate? He hadn't asked. Did it matter? No. He needed the help.

"Were you hurt on the job?" the doc asked.

Art was quiet for a long moment. All he heard was their breathing. He looked for the ashtray, but none was in view. Still, the smell lingered. The pocket on the doc's light blue golf T-shirt held a cigarette lighter, according to the shape. I bet the ashtray's in a drawer. Art wanted to satisfy his curiosity. Then he said, "Yes."

In a reassuring voice Doctor Wexford asked, "Want to tell me about what happened?"

Art dropped his head and shook it in reply. "Why can't things be like they were when I was a child?"

"How were they when you were a child?" the doc asked.

"Safe," Art said. "They were safe; I could go outside and play and feel safe." Art looked up anger flashing in his eyes.

"You don't feel safe going outside now?"

"Not me. Melissa, my daughter," he answered his voice flaring in sharp anger.

M.L. WEATHERINGTON

"Tell me about your daughter."

"Do you have children?" Art asked. He watched the doc, noticing that his hair was uncombed and a mess although neatly cut around his neck and ears. The doc was a contrast in himself. Art found an interest in this man. How can he let things around him go unattended for such a long time? He wanted to ask, but they weren't on a first-name basis, not yet anyway. Art wasn't sure he wanted to be. His judgment of who the doc was as a person was still out. He's tough, and Art liked tough people. They wouldn't easily bend to another's point of view, and Art admired someone with ideas and thoughts that could challenge his beliefs

Doc Wexford's voice, quieter and devoid of emotion, sounded monotone, "I did." A long pause quieted the room. "I lost my wife and little boy when he was just three." He paused again his face a mask of pain, "I missed my wife and son so much. For a few years, a bottle filled the void." He cleared his throat. "It didn't work, so I quit the bottle and got a degree in medicine and a doctorate in Psychiatry instead. That was twelve years ago. Somehow helping other people helps me."

"I like helping other people too," Art said studying the doc's face. He'd heard the hurt in the words the man used and knew this man would understand how he felt. "I am sorry," Art said.

The doc nodded, "Call me Jim." He opened his drawer, took out a pad of paper, a pen, and a business card. "Art, I think we can work together. If you agree, my fee is two hundred an hour. My next opening will be this time next week, and I am sorry to say," the doc tilted his head, "here again. I have to tell you, I've hired a handyman to renovate my house. I have no working bathrooms or kitchen right now. I'm sleeping on the floor in one of the bedrooms. As soon as my place is finished, I will have an office we can use. Until then I've borrowed

42

this place. It was old Doc Pelly's office years ago, and the widow just shut it up." He tore the note off the pad and handed it to Art. "If you want the appointment, give me a call on Monday. You're the only one I see right now since I am doing most of the contracting work at my place." He wrote the date on the business card and handed it to Art. "No charge for today, this was a favor for Amanda. I owe her. She's responsible for my being here today. She pushed me to stop wallowing in self-pity and get my degree."

Art took the note and business card from the doc with kind acceptance and an understanding for the Doc's loss. "I'll be here." He admired the man and his accomplishments and he felt certain warmth toward Amanda for helping her fellow man.

The doc showed him out the personnel door and Art learned it let him out of the office and into the breezeway of all the other connecting offices in the complex. It became a thoughtful way to lead people back to the parking lot without showing to the world which office they'd just exited.

Chapter Nine

3:10 P.M. September 4, 1995

Art's foot slid closer to the glossy navy blue pots as he watered the Pink Martha Washington geraniums blooming by the front door. He looked up as Walt brought his car to a stop in the driveway. Walt came around the front of the car carrying a new manila folder, and Art knew he had something on the Grape Ave case just by the crisp way he shuffled along. A tickle rumbled through Art's stomach as he made this connection and he couldn't wait to find out what.

Directing the stream of water into the pot before he looked up he grinned at Walt. "What's up? I know that look, want some coffee?"

"No, I'll take a rain check," he said. "We have an interesting outcome on that shooting on Grape Ave. That woman's body looks to be the identical twin sister of Adele Blandford."

"Really? How'd you come to put them together?" Art asked, leaning forward, his eyebrows furrowing as he turned the faucet and it squeaked into off. "Come on in." They walked into Art's office.

"I took a walk to the coroner's office and looked at the body myself. If I hadn't seen the Blandford woman that afternoon, I would swear that she was lying on that slab."

"So, how'd the sister take the news?"

"I thought you might want to accompany me when I tell her," Walt said.

"Oh!" Art nodded. He moved his arm sling strap to adjust it then he reached grabbing his jacket off the chair.

They were a couple of blocks away when Art asked, "We still don't have any suspects? There's no information we can go on from Painless? When's he going to release his coroner's findings?"

Walt shrugged indicating that he didn't know and changed the subject, "How did your meet with the shrink go?

"Just a get acquainted today. I might see him again. He's an interesting guy, a contractor. He's remodeling his house himself," Art said.

"How good can this guy be if he's moonlighting? This his second job? Did he put the hammer down to see you?" Walt asked.

"My sense of him is that he's a fair man. A tough sort. He's not going to get pushed around."

"Yeah, but if he were any good he'd get his house done for him," Walt said then added. "At least that's what I think."

Art turned in the car seat, "So, why hasn't the sister made out a missing person's report?

"We didn't tell her we had her purse at the initial contact. I assigned Oliver to talk to the residents along Grape Ave to see if they had heard anything, and when we were taking down their names, her name came up. Oliver knew something was strange, and he brought her to me to sort things out."

The mystery thickens Art thought as he looked at Walt. "How are you doing Walt?"

"With what?" Walt asked.

"This, my job?"

"Oh, I'm not you, but I'm getting it done."

"What do you think happened?"

Walt slammed on the brakes just as a little boy about three years old ran into the street after a red beach ball.

"That was close." Art breathed out the words while his heart beat faster. A young man ran in front of Walt's car and snatched the toddler and the ball up. As he did Art raised his two fingers and saluted 'well done'.

They idled in place for a moment to let the man clear the street. Walt worked his hands over the steering wheel. "We have nothing. The woman took two shots."

"My thinking it might be a sniper is not far off?"

Walt nodded, "I do. I think she walked north on Grape, probably crossed his sights, and he took the shot."

"In that case, this is going cold, and we may never find her killer." Art thought to himself. That is one big hole in her chest. Makes it personal to me.

"You're not just a kidding."

"There are homes on one side of the street and not on the other. That would rule out the shots not being heard," Art said as Walt brought the unit to a stop at the curb out front of the Blandford house. "This house is just four houses from the crime scene."

The home, white stucco with black trim, looked quiet and peaceful with bright red geraniums in terracotta pots. One elm tree-shaded part of the lawn and boxwood hedges lined the property. "They need to mow the lawn, but other than that the property appears well tended."

Art turned as Walt spoke, "There's no criminal history attached to this property."

"Shall we?" Art's finger released the seatbelt.

"We shall," said Walt and the two left the car and strolled up the walk, knocked on the door. A boy about twelve filled with wide questioning eyes answered the door and looked from Walt to Art and, sizing them up as important, yelled, "Aw, Maw."

Her eyebrows arched in curiosity as she answered the boys call. "Yes, can I help you?"

"Mrs. Blandford, I am Lieutenant of Homicide Arthur Franklin, and this is Sergeant Walter Culpepper of the Lodi Police Department. May we speak with you, please? Do you remember talking with us at the scene on Grape Ave and Oak Streets?" Art asked.

Her expression showed recognition and she nodded and unhooked the door, holding it open for them to walk through. "Nick, get the cat and go outside," she said.

"Aw Maw, do I have to?"

"Now, don't make me tell you again," The woman pointed to the back door as she spoke. Her finger waved up and down as she hardened her facial expression and Nick complied.

The door closed, and Mrs. Blandford, Walt and Art were alone. "We'll sit in here," she waved her hand toward the couch, "Please sit there." She backed up to an armchair and sat gingerly placing her hands on her lap.

Art could feel her concern for them coming into her home. "We have some questions. Could we see your purse?"

Art watched her eyes widen as an expression of shock settled on her face. "My purse? Why do you want to see my purse?"

"Just filling some blanks in our ongoing investigation," Walt said.

Mrs. Blandford got up, her fingers working around each other gripping and freeing the fingers. She's nervous, Art noted as she walked out of the room. As she

47

returned Art saw that the purse resembled the one they had at the station.

Walt asked, "Would you show us your identification, your driver license?"

The snap seemed loud as she opened the catch; she rummaged and brought forth a small wallet.

Art saw the color drained from her face and thought he might have to go to her. She sank down on the chair, looking at the contents of the purse. "This isn't mine," Slowly she brought her eyes up. "You knew that. That's why you're here. You have my purse?" She stared at Art them Walt, "How did you get my purse?"

Walt began humbly. "We took possession of your purse at the scene. It was with the body."

Art watched her eyes. They were those of an intelligent person. Art spoke up, "Mrs. Blandford, do you have a sister?"

She nodded and said, "Adora, she's my twin." She lifted the purse from the floor. "This is her purse."

"May we have it?" Art asked holding his hand out.

Reluctantly she gave the purse to Art. "My sister was the woman killed?"

"You haven't missed her for the last few days?" Art asked, lowering eyebrows.

The woman shook her head. Tears flowed down her face, and she searched her pockets as she answered. "Adora flew into a rage and ran out of here. She always did things like that." Her sad expression expanded as she nodded her head to emphasize her next words. "After a while, she'd calm down and come back. I've learned to let her go do her thing." She found a tissue and wiped her eyes. "How'd she die?" Sobs shook her shoulders.

"It appears she was shot and killed," Walt said as he pulled the driver's license from the purse and twisted his wrist so it could be seen. Art made a one-handed note on his pad. Adora Ann Stumper, age 44, lives in Lodi

California on the west side of town. Art managed the address and closed his notepad placing it back in his shirt pocket.

"Shot!"

Art spotted a box of tissues and pulled one out extending it to her. She snatched it and wiped her face.

"I am sorry for your loss," Walt said.

Art noticed Walt had kept his voice soft while his cop eyes studied her face.

She nodded. "What happens now?"

"Do you have any idea if there could be anyone who wanted her dead? Do you know if she was afraid of anyone? Did she mention any names of people she had trouble with?"

Adele shook her head, "No one. She would get dingy now and again, but no one wanted her dead. What happens now, with her body?"

"We have to finish our investigation and then you can claim the body. We'll need you to identify the body."

"We were so close, why didn't I know she was dead?"

Chapter Ten

2:45 P.M. September 11, 1995

"**H**ow did you feel when you watched Melissa being thrown into the river?" Doc Wexford's voice held a gruff yet tender rendering of his words.

The memory flooded back and Art's brows furrowed. He blanched, took in a breath and darted his eyes around as his long, limber, tanned hands moved to spread the fingers fan shape. He began struggling through a tremor of alto tones. "I had such a sense of helplessness. Emptiness." He paused, "I couldn't breathe. I believed—," tears glistened in his eyes promising to fall as his voice paled to a whisper, "—she was dead." His lips trembled and almost failed to produce, "I'd failed." He looked down seeing nothing but history unfurling before him. Swiftly he wiped his eyes as he whispered, "I failed her. I feel like I could throw up right now just thinking about that day, that minute in my life when I failed her. His eyes flared hate as he locked eyes with the doc. Art's hands trembled, and he studied them as though they belonged to someone else. With a concentrated effort, he wrapped his fingers around the hands to corral them. Art leaned forward in the personnel chair adjusting the green sling that protected his damaged arm, closing the distance between the doc and himself.

"Those are powerful feelings," Doctor Wexford's voice sounded soft. He sat leaning back in his chair, his eyes focused somewhere over Arts head, his feet up, crossed at the ankles on the old desk.

The doc's relaxed and here I am trembling from tension. The two of them talked together yet both seemed lost in their own thoughts. The room quieted, and the tick of the dusty, old, clock caught Art's attention.

"So, what have you been doing this week?" the doc asked, his voice sounding like the answer didn't matter to a hill of beans.

Art took a deep breath glad for the change of subject. "Been working that homicide case from Grape Ave."

"Oh, got anything?" the doc asked, and the conversation took on a more animated beat.

"Not much. I have more questions than answers."

"Um, last week you said something about being safe, or your daughter isn't safe to go outside. Tell me about that," the Doc spoke in monotone, and the upbeat discussion on the homicide died off.

Art looked up at him, and he moved his lips as though to speak, but nothing came out. "I don't know, Jim, it just seems that when I was a kid I could go outside and play. I could stay out all day. My folks weren't scared for me. Now it seems I need to know where Melissa is at all times. She doesn't feel safe. She's scared, and I hate it." Art's voice filled with emotion, "I feel helpless, and I hate admitting my feelings."

"I grew up in the Oregon southwest. We left our keys in the car, our doors unlocked. No one stole. I don't remember a home invasion ever. The drive-by shootings? What's that all about? There must have been a different type of people back then. The golden rule, that's what we lived by."

51

"There are a lot of good, law abiding people in this world today," the Doc said. "I think we hear about the bad seeds..."

"Oh, no Doc. You are naive. You need to come down to the station and see what this world really is like. You'd get your eyes opened fast in just one afternoon. It's an invite anytime you want to come down. I'll give you the grand tour. I'll even let you step into the slammer."

The doc raised his palm as though to stop something. "No thanks, that's one thrill I'd just as soon circumvent."

"You know, we do a lot of good in the community, but it seems no good deed goes unpunished," Art said.

"My, my, aren't you just a bit cynical today?" Doc turned his head toward Art, arched his right eyebrow waiting for his answer.

A bit of a smirk slipped across Art's lips. The doc's lips twitched as he waited.

"You like music?" Art asked.

The doc nodded, placed his left hand up to his mouth and rested his two fingers on his lips drumming them. "Some. Can't stand opera, sounds like a lot of screeching, and it goes right up my spine. What's your point?"

"It seems a lot of songs, the lyrics, are speaking to me these days. That one-, ooh, what's its name? The one about a house not being a home or something like that," Art said. "I keep fixing on that and thinking what if Melissa didn't come home. Everything we've built over the years would be gone. I just want to grab her and hold her," He was getting close to complete openness at the moment, and it scared him. Art took a deep breath and gulped down the fear.

The expression on his face right now did not display all the attributes Art so wanted to possess and he knew the doc saw the fragile state of his inner self and that made him even more disturbed.

Doc Wexford took his legs down and sat forward, "You are scared. Petrified you'll lose your daughter at any moment. You think you have to be near her all the time, that you are the only one who can save her."

Art dropped his head down and nodded a quiet agreement.

"You feel the need to watch over her minute by minute." In an almost whisper the doc said, "Is that something you can do?"

Art's head came up. The thought had crossed his mind. It was not something he could do. Art knew his limits and the normal limits between Melissa and him. There came a sense of peace and calm knowing that everything at the moment was all right. Then the old, cold, calculating fear crept in as though it knew it had a hold on him anytime it wanted. That was the reason he sat in this chair right now letting another person into his private feelings. Art wanted to fight that fear. He couldn't just tell it to go away.

Like smoking. Oh, how he wanted a drag right now. Art could almost feel the cigarette between his fingers; almost smell the smoke taste... he focused on the doc who had his eyes averted to the ceiling and Art swung his gaze to the same point. They sat quietly.

That smoke I smelled the first day I came here, I haven't seen Jim smoke once. "You getting your house in order?" Art asked.

"Ummm. Well, it's a work in progress. That old saying is so true; you fix one thing and two more show right up." He answered with a laugh.

"Got to ask, do you smoke?" Art inquired knowing he was ready to solicit one for himself.

"Me? No. I never did take up that pleasure." The doc answered and took his legs down, standing a moment to stretch. "Why do you ask?"

Art studied his facial expression before answering. "The first day I came, while I sat out there in that sweat box of a waiting room, I smelled fresh smoke."

The doc looked puzzled for a moment then nodded, "That was the handyman I hired. He came by and," he pointed, "I let him out that door, just before I brought you in here."

Mystery solved Art thought as the doc reached across the desk.

"That's it for today. See you next week, same time, same place." He smiled and shook Art's hand.

Art felt sort of kicked free but glad to be walking out of this place. He stepped outside and walked over a wooden bridge that carried him over a moat-like planted area that ran the length of the walk. Very Zen he thought. It felt cool, and the mood struck, and he reached for his phone. He input the phone number, pressed send, and grinned when he heard the connection open.

"Can you talk?"

Chapter Eleven

3:45 P.M. September 11, 1995

"Yes I'm between clients right now, got fifteen minutes. How are you?" Amanda asked.

"On cloud nine," Art said as he strolled out of the shaded area at the doctor's complex and over the cement walkway to the parking lot towards his car. "I'm like some kid again; I can feel my eyes sparkling."

"Isn't that just dumb? Can we be kids again? Art are we too old?" Her voice trailed off.

"No, we're not too old. If we do what Melissa says we should, and that's just go with it. Do you have any idea what "it" is? Art chuckled as though it was a funny joke. He loved hearing her melodic laugh. "Can you meet me at the lake tonight about 9:00 p.m..? I've got something I want to ask you."

Dead silence filled the line, and a terror shot though him for a second, until he realized they were still connected. She hadn't hung up.

"Yes," she answered breathlessly.

Art wanted to say 'yes' to the world, instead he said, "See you tonight." He heard her say "bye" and the call ended leaving Art a happy man.

M.L. WEATHERINGTON

He arrived at his home, walked straight to the refrigerator for a beer. It was early but what the heck, they weren't expecting him at the office. Not these days. He brought the chilled can to his lips and let the cold tartness flow over them and into his mouth. There's nothing like the top of the can. He turned carrying the beer to his office. He set the can down and grabbed the phone, dialing and waiting until Tracy answered.

"Hey, how's my favorite secretary?"

"Missing you."

Art sat down, sipped again, "Not as much as I miss coming into work." He let the second pass, "How's Walt doing?"

"Fine. I think he's on his way over to your place now."

"Oh?"

"Yeah, I got the feeling when he left that you were his destination. Are you taking care of yourself?

Her voice sounded all motherly, part of him hated it and at the same time he loved it, "I am. Did you know I see a shrink?"

"No. When? Do you think he'll..." Tracy paused, her voice raised an octave, "... or is it a she?"

Art imagined her tilting her head like she always did as he listened to her next question.

"Are you seeing Amanda?" Her voice took on that 'I knew it' tone.

"It's a man. I figured you already knew. The news goes like wildfire around there, I know."

"No, I didn't know. Well, it's about time. How's Melissa?"

"Melissa's fine."

"Donuts!" Walt said.

Art spun around holding the phone, and clearly startled by Walt's voice. "Walt?"

"Your front door was open, so I crept in here to see if you were alive or dead. Donuts? They're fresh."

Art laid the phone down and started for the door, but Walt stopped him by saying that he'd shut the door and thrown the bolt. Art turned his attention back to Tracy, "Got to go Gal, Walt's here, and he brought donuts."

"Don't eat them. They're not good for your stomach." Her voice trailed off, "Okay boss, just what both you boys need."

Art laughed as he hung up and reached for the file Walt had by his side.

Walt's smile filled his face and showed his yellowed and browned stained teeth as he said, "It's on the new homicide, a report on the person who found the body."

Art nodded and opened the file, took a sip of beer. "Want a beer?" He knew Walt would turn it down.

"Sounds good, but no thanks. I'm guessing you don't want any of these donuts."

Art held up his can in answer then began to read from the first page. "This reports on, Louise Mead. Louise found the body as she drove down Oak Street after leaving the Veterinarian Hospital on Ham Lane. She was headed home." Art set the beer can on the desk and wandered the office carrying the file and reading out loud. "She saw the body on the ground and stopped her car. She got out of her car and walked up to the person and called out to them. Upon getting closer, she saw blood and used her cell phone to call 911." Art nodded his head indicating that he believed what he read. "She waited by her car for the officer to arrive and parked her car on Oak Street." Art noticed her address and saw that she lived on the west side of town. The report stated she did not know the victim.

None of us know much about this set of twins, Art thought.

The report went on. The veterinarian office was contacted, and Louise Mead's appointment coincides with the statement she gave. The dog was treated and given an appointment for follow-up in two weeks.

"That accounts for her time, so she's not our shooter." Art looked up from the file and let it rest back on his desk blotter. "How is it possible for us to have no lead on this case?" It just fries my eggs to think we can't solve this crime. I don't want that to happen.

Clearly, Adele Blandford did not know about her sister's death. Art picked up the Blandford file and thumbed through it letting his eyes catch key phrases. They were fighting and Adora, yes that's her name, left the premises, and that was the last time Adele saw her sister. It sounds right. That lets Adele out as our killer. Boy, we'll eliminate all of Lodi at this rate. Could it have been someone from out of town? Wait a minute. What's this? Art let his finger run down the vital statistics. Adora was married at one time to Roger Stumper. Where is Mr. Stumper now? He's probably across the country and not our shooter.

"Roger Stumper was married to Adora. They're divorced according to vital statistics," Art tapped the file page.

Walt nodded again. "Yeah, we talked to him. He's got a tight alibi for that day and time."

"He's here in town?" Art looked surprised and pleased.

"Yep. Works as a handyman doing odd jobs. anything he can pick-up I guess."

"A handyman?" Art's eyes narrowed, "We got an address on this guy?"

"Yeah, we talked with him. He's off our radar as of now. Why?"

Art observed his blotter then swung his eyes up at the ceiling, "Well, he could have an ax to grind. Maybe he's paying alimony and is sick and tired of shelling out every month. Maybe he just...I don't know. Just a thought—."

"We've covered that."

Art knew he had, and it was just his need to spin his wheels to keep in touch with his old job.

There was that old feeling cropping up again. He was not needed. "Well, I guess we check somewhere else if Stumper isn't our guy.

"You met with that doc?"

Art studied Walt, surprised at his question. "Yeah, why?"

"Oh, nothing. You seem different, in a good way."

Art's cheeks flushed as he shook his head. "I saw the new doc, but I don't think that's the date with the doc that made the change. It was the date with Amanda that put something back in my heart. I went on my first date in years with her. We went to the winery in Woodbridge, killed a couple bottles between us and drove around just talking until we ended up at a bar on Pine. We ate and talked. And finally, I drove her back to her car. That was eight days ago.

"And you're still on cloud nine?"

"I am."

"It looks good on you."

Chapter Twelve

4:50 P.M. September 11, 1995

Five more hours until he could be with her again, Art couldn't wait. A smile spread across his face at the thought, at once making him feel foolish and at the same time, excited. He had to do something to pass the time so he opened the file on the Grape Ave homicide again.

His drew the photos out spreading them over his desk. There was something in the photos, he couldn't put his finger on it, but he knew there was something. One photo sat right in front of him. Nothing about the picture was outstanding. Nothing was different than usual crime scene shots of the body in its final position. Her body sprawled where she'd landed, a pool of blood surrounded her. Those shoes, red soles, my eyes keep going to them. Does Walt have a maker identified yet? Then he realized he was picking at straws. Why? Would it make any difference who's the maker of those shoes? They are not the killer.

Something about that particular picture drew him, and he couldn't figure out why. He yawned, shrugged his shoulders and gathered the pictures together again and closed the file folder over them. Art walked back to the kitchen with the empty beer can and donut box, shaking his head that he had helped eat every one of those greasy things. Gas building up started a grumbling deep down. Oh great, that's romantic, to be sitting with Amanda tonight tooting away. With precise precision he tossed the beer can and it sailed across the distance and into the recycling container. A gigantic yawn forced his mouth open wider and wider.

"Hi, Dad."

She startled him and he jumped turning to see her walking into the kitchen. "Hi, what are you up to?"

Melissa shrugged her shoulders as she scanned around the room. She slid her hands across the island counter top and said, "Trying to figure out what to fix for dinner."

Art felt like slapping his forehead. He hadn't thought of dinner at all, wasn't hungry. Guess donuts and beer do that to you. "Hey," as an idea came to him. "Let's go to Rosie's for a hamburger. What do you think?"

They pulled the car into the parking space at their favorite hamburger joint and walked to the ordering window of Sno White on Turner Road. They sat for a few minutes at one of the outside tables waiting for their meal. When it did come, he watched her eyes as they ate, they would slide away from his and across the blacktop road, past the dead and dried California poppies, toward Lodi Lake. He watched her pickup a shoestring, dip it in the sauce and eat it as though she were there by herself alone drawn to the river. He felt like he was in contest with that river and he was coming in a distant second. They ate without conversation and it concerned him. She's messed up, I know. I don't know how to help, but there must be something safe to say. "Melissa?"

"Yeah?" She brought her eyes back, took a shoestring and dipped it into the pool of ketchup she'd made by squeezing the packet of sauce onto her hamburger wrapper.

How are you doing?" He could feel her depression from her expression, her absence. That's what it feels like, she's not here. He held a steady gaze at her until she sat back. Her eyes bore into his.

"God Dad, not here."

61

End of conversation Art thought. Where do I go from here? He'd been chastised; his ears burned hot. "I'm sorry honey; I'm concerned, you seem so sad."

Focus on Melissa, be here now with her. Talk to her. About what? What is safe? "Honey, are you ready for the horseback ride trip?"

"Yeah, I guess." She looked off again and sighed, allowing a monotone reply, "It's an endurance ride, Dad."

Art felt like he had to work hard to keep this conversation alive. "What's left to do to get ready?" His voice sounded like someone else's, bright and gay. It was not at all the way he felt.

"Nothing, Charlie's going to trailer Midnight over. You have to take me in our car. Most of my gear will go in the horse trailer. I'll pack a change of clothes for the days we'll be there. What else is there to do?" She dipped another potato.

Art drummed his fingers on the table frustrated and sad that they were having such a hard time talking right now. "Well, are you about done? I'll get us home, and we can get on with the day." He forced a grin, wishing to be better at being her father right now. That sense of failure loomed like the gas building in his gut.

"Yeah," she wound up her papers, sipped the last of her soda and walked all of it to the trash can. "Bye Rosie," she yelled.

Art heard Rosie's answer, "Bye Miss Melissa, see you next time. They rode home in silence. He went to his room and her to hers. She closed the door, and he did the same. He flicked his shoes off. They tumbled across the room as he stretched out and adjusted his arm to a comfortable position. He let his eyes close. The snore started before two minutes passed.

8:30 P.M.

He jumped when the alarm called to him, sitting up and finding the dial of the clock. Art raised his good arm over his head and yawned. He did feel better for a couple of hours' rest. He showered, and that woke him up completely, his evening meeting with Amanda now his top priority.

Art slapped a bit of cologne over his cheeks and down his neck. He'd changed to clean clothes, jeans and pullover shirt. At that moment, he slipped his feet into his shoes and saw he had twenty minutes to get over to the lake and park.

He paused outside his daughter's door. "Melissa?" He waited for her answer.

"Yeah?" Music came from her room. Her door ajar and her answer slid through that crack to his ears.

"I'm going out now."

"Bye."

"Bye."

He pulled his keys out, locked the front door and headed for the garage. He'd never given it any thought before, but he always left the property from the front seat of his car after getting into the car in his garage. Now he stopped and let his eyes go from one house to the next. He'd never really noticed his neighborhood before. Now he observed with renewed eyes. Every home looked normal, every car where it should be. A few he hadn't seen before were parked out front of some of his neighbors, but that didn't send up any red flags. He felt safe in leaving Melissa alone and meeting Amanda. He clicked the garage door opener and walked to his car and drove to the lake.

He located the table by the lakeside he'd indicated and sat on it waiting for her. The lake drew his attention, and he studied its current and color changes. The evening was gentle with just a hint of breeze that lifted the fragrance of the lake to his nostrils. The moon brightened the area, and he felt pleasure listening to the ducks nesting for the night. The sound of her car door reached his ear, and as he turned to greet her his heart leaped.

"Hey."

"Hey. How was your day?"

"Good, and yours?"

"It's just gotten better." his hand reached for hers, and he felt the softness and the tender firmness as she let her fingers circle his palm. At just that moment he wanted to lean over and kiss those lips. He almost did. Instead, he looked into her lovely soft eyes, smelled the fragrance she liked to wear, and he closed his eyes to drift in the presence of her. They stood that way a long moment caught in the sensations of their feelings.

"You wanted to ask me something. I've got to tell you, Art, since you said that earlier I've thought of nothing else. I know I shouldn't probably tell you what I am thinking, but, well, what the hell." Her hand gripped his good hand tighter.

"Mysteries are not up your alley, huh?" He laughed low and gripped her hand with a gentle squeeze.

She smiled up at him, took her other hand and pressed against his good arm with a good-natured banter.

"Okay, I'll get right to it. Will that make you happy?"

"Yes."

"I wondered if you would consider taking a little trip with Melissa and me. She's in this horseback ride thing that is coming up. Its three days long, and we would be over by the ocean. We, you and I, would be taking day trips around the area, and we'd be with her at night. We'll stay in motels. You'd have your room." He saw her pleasant reaction as soon as she realized he didn't expect her to stay with him. "There's something else too. Melissa's birthday is coming up. I wondered if you'd help me plan a party."

"Oh Art, I'd love to plan her party with you. How old will she be? Do you have a theme picked out?"

He shook his head. "I haven't a clue. That's my chief problem. I can't seem to get anything right these days. I don't know what to do." He let her hand go and turned a bit toward the water. "I am pretty sure there will be no blow-up jump houses anymore."

"Well, what birthday is it?"

"Her sixteenth."

"A sweet sixteen birthday. That's got to be the theme."

"Sweet is not up my alley."

She turned to stand right by his side facing at the water. "Relax, I've got this one. I'll need a list of her friends you want to ask. And a budget. How much do you want to spend?"

"I've always spent about two hundred dollars on her parties."

"Well, open your wallet, my dear man. A sweet sixteen party will cost a bit more."

Art spun his head around and down to her face, "How much more? I'm on a cop's salary and disability right now. I don't want this getting out of line."

"It won't. You just need to spend a bit more to make it real nice."

They stood silent a long moment listening to the breeze moving the leaves on the oak tree. Somewhere on a distant road a siren sounded and died out.

"Great, now how about the horseback weekend?"

"When is this affair happening?"

"You'll go?"

"I didn't say that." She cocked her head. "I've got a speaking tour coming up, and I'll be away for about a week in October."

"Oh," he said brightly, "I think we'll be going around the second week of September."

"Let me check my calendar and see if it works out."

"Wonderful. I'd love to have you come. I think if we could get away from here we might find things a bit easier."

"I think you might be onto something." She rose on her toes and pointed. "Did you see that, I think it's an otter? Watch right there where the moons shining on the water." As she brought her head around to Art, he turned toward her. "Listen to the crickets."

Without a clear thought and following his inclination, Art melded with her and let his lips find hers. Sinking into their softness and yielding to the sensation, he slid his good arm around her and brought her to him. As he allowed himself to float deeper into the feelings, her arms encircled him and happiness filled his heart. She met him more than halfway. After a long moment they parted, so close their breaths brushed each other.

"Wow!"

"That about sums it up," she said sliding her hand into his.

Chapter Thirteen

5:45 P.M. September 12, 1995

Art found Melissa working at the prep counter. "Hi, honey." Grabbing the refrigerator door and pulling it open, Art extracted his first cold beer for the day. He took a drink and told her about asking Amanda to join them for the trip to the coast. Art sipped and waited for her response. He didn't have long to wait.

The knife glided up and down steadily chopping green onions then slowed as she brought her eyes up, "You asked Amanda to go along on the trip to the coast, the endurance ride?" Melissa stopped, her eyes narrowing. "What's she going to do out there?"

He held a gulp of beer in his mouth puffing his cheeks, swallowed hard as a stab of fear caught him and he said, "I don't know, the same thing I'm going to be doing, cooling my heels and waiting for you."

She studied him a long moment, nodded her head and went about cutting up some red peppers. She added them to the greens. Two ripe tomatoes rested in her hand, and she rinsed them off and diced them into small squares. She rummaged through the drawer in the refrigerator and brought out a red onion and some celery stalks. She worked at the vegetables, chopping them and

67

adding them to the others. Then she opened a new bottle of Ranch Dressing and poured it over the top. "I guess it will be okay for her to come along," Melissa modulated her tone. "It could be a long day for you."

Art sighed. He set the beer down and picked up the dishrag to wipe up a spill she made while pouring the dressing. He tossed the dishrag into the sink and said, "I thought we'd investigate the area while you were riding."

Melissa stopped working; her hand left the bowl of salad and went limp on the counter top. "You're going on a date with her?"

He brought the can down, looked at her. Did she not like this idea? Did she not want Amanda along on this trip? Great, now that I've asked Amanda what am I going to tell her? "You'd rather Amanda didn't come along?" He watched for her reaction.

She turned, "No, Dad. Not at all, it's great. It's just going to take me a little time to get this idea around in my mind. Your date the other night must have been good? You never said anything about it."

His eyebrows raised and a grin played at his lips as he settled his eyes on hers, "I got the hang of riding the bronco again."

"My dad, the cowboy," A pleasant expression preceded her next remark. "I like Amanda. It's okay that she comes. In fact, I'd like it. We could get to know each other better. "She stopped working and asked, "Guess what's for dinner?"

Art noticed no pots were on the stove, nothing else evident. "I don't know, what are we having?" He sniffed the air, "It smells wonderful."

Melissa moved over to the Crockpot and lifted the lid. "I've got pork roast in here to go with homemade applesauce Nicole, and I made at her house the other day. She told me how to make the roast, and I've put potatoes and carrots in there too."

Art stepped closer and leaned toward the open pot and sniffed, "Oh, I love pork roast and applesauce." He stood back up. "I'm so hungry. When do we eat?"

The phone rang. They stopped dead in their tracks like it was expected that every time they were about to eat together the phone cuts them off at the pass.

"Not again."

"I hope not." Art lifted the receiver. "Hello?" He turned away from Melissa as soon as he heard Amanda's voice.

After listening to Amanda a moment, he turned back to Melissa, "Honey, what's the date of the endurance ride?"

"Tell her September eighteenth, nineteenth, and twentieth."

Art smiled and said, "Melissa says..."

"Okay, that works for me. I can go." Her words came breathlessly into his ear. "Now, what do I need to pack?"

Art hadn't thought about packing yet. She was way ahead of him now. "I guess, pants and sweaters, walking shoes." He turned to Melissa, "Honey, did the requirements say anything about clothing?"

"Dad it's the coast. We could get fog. It could rain. Layer, that's the secret. That's what I am planning." Melissa moved the salad to the table and turned to the crock pot.

"Mel says to layer, says we might get fog and rain."

"It's still hot here in September. I haven't been to the coast in the fall, so I don't know what to expect." She paused a moment, and the line went silent. Then she continued. "Art?"

"Yes?" He lowered his head and turned away from Melissa as though it would make it easier to talk just to Amanda.

69

"It's like, I know this is going to sound silly. All this, you and me, it's just like some song says about the feeling of love. I haven't felt this way for years, forever, if I ever did. I always thought that stuff fluff and silly, and now I am feeling just that way and scared to tell you that, but driven to find out how you are feeling?"

Art directed his sheepish grin to the floor as he felt flooded with the joy her words brought.

He asked Amanda. "What are you doing this weekend?"

Art waited for Amanda's answer. She explained that she had a busy weekend. She was going out of town on Friday and coming back on Sunday. He brought his lower lip up over his mustache and rubbed the hairs down. Clearly, he would be on his own this weekend. He didn't have any idea what he was going to do with himself. All he wanted was to be with her. Finally, their conversation ended, and he hung up, allowing his hand to linger on the receiver longer than necessary.

"Trouble with the rodeo?"

"Huh? Oh, no sweetheart. Amanda's going out of town this weekend, and I was just thinking. That's all, just thinking."

They had a pleasant dinner together, talked about light subjects and each managed not to tick the other off. Both felt the evening was a success, but neither mentioned it to the other. Instead, they cleaned up the kitchen together. Melissa wiped down the counters as Art gathered the trash in the basket and headed outside to put it in the trash container

He moved down the side of the house toward the area where the containers waited, walking over stepping stones that he'd put down after buying this house. They were dark gray in the dimmed evening light with grass growing in the between areas. His foot felt the lump of grass as he passed by. Almost to the trash container he heard a sound and felt air movement as something came close to hitting him.

Thwack!

A startled fear flooded through him as Art dropped to the ground, moaning that he'd bumped his bad arm, but overlooking the sickening pain as his eyes scanned around him for the shooter. He pawed at his leg and reached his weapon.

Thwack!

That one was closer. He crabbed around pushing with his toes believing he was turning into the shooters line. He had to see who it was. The walkway to the street was clear as though no one had ever walked there. His eyes sighted down the barrel as he scanned his close by areas and then the far. Nothing seemed out of the ordinary. He was hemmed in by the hedge on one side and the house on the other. The shots had to come from the front, not the back. He heard the back door crack open.

"Dad?"

He swung as far around as he could as his body mixed with the household trash. He yelled, "Get back inside!"

She walked closer to him. "What's wrong?"

"Get the hell inside that house! Call the police and Walt. Tell them to get over here now." He heard her feet slap the paved stones running to the house as he brought his eyes around to the direction the shots must have come. Could they see him? Why would anyone be shooting at him?

Art squirmed around to get to his feet. If I were going to be dead, I'd be dead already. Art rose to his knees, placed the palm of his hand on the side of the house, pushing while holding his gun, his eyes seeking any movement. Every dark shape caught his attention. anything that didn't look like it belonged in the area he studied until he could accept it felt right.

"Dad?" Melissa stood in the doorway, the light from the service porch over her head flooding out onto the cement porch.

"Turn out that light. Get back inside and wait for me. Did you make the call?"

"Yes!"

Arts shoes smashed trash as he got to his feet. He heard eggshells crunch, and he cringed as he was trying to be quiet and not give himself away. The light from the kitchen flowing over the stepping stones went out as Melissa shut the door and he was once more in the dim of the evening. His ears perked-up for any sound, on the ready to turn that direction and put a bullet in someone taking aim on him. Minutes passed, his breathing lengthened and slowed. The danger seemed over. There was a part of Art's brain that asked, was it over?

After what seemed like an hour he heard vehicles pull up. He moved toward the front edge of his house and peered around the edge.

He walked out front. No one was outside except for Walt and himself and a squad with two officers. All the houses looked normal for this time of day. There were no strange cars parked nearby.

"What's up?" they asked as they reached Art. He told them he'd been shot at, and the two younger officers began a search.

"Art clarified to Walt, "Someone took a couple of shots at me on the side of my house. I was taking the trash out, and I heard the slugs sail right by me."

"Who the hell would be firing on you?"

Art shook his head, and the two waited for the officers to join them. They came up with nothing. After taking a report and chatting for a few minutes, they finally left bidding Walt and Art goodbye.

Art held the arm sling, his arm a dull ache now. "They don't believe me."

"Well, if someone is shooting at you eventually they'll turn up."

"That's a comforting thought. Would that be before or after I'm dead?" Art indicated that they should walk back to the house and so they started down the side of the house and over the trash to the back door. "I can't be upset about this in front of Melissa; I don't want to scare her any more than she already is, okay?"

Walt nodded, and sharing a wizened look between them as they walked inside.

Fear radiated across her face and clearly from her wide eyes as she asked, "What's happening?"

"Just someone shot off some firecrackers," Walt said.

Art shot a look at him, "You'd think they'd save them for next year."

Melissa's eyebrows leveled out and added to the motherly appearance she now gave both of them, and they knew she didn't buy it one bit.

Chapter Fourteen

11:15 A.M. September 13, 1995

Sunshine and white clouds filled the morning as Art poured his first cup of coffee. He hadn't slept much last night. He rubbed his jaw and felt the rough stubble and the yawning tears seep on the outer edges of his eyes. Melissa still slept. At least he thought she must be as she has not come down this morning.

Art sauntered out by the pool and into that wonderful fall day and let the heat of the morning drape over his shoulders. Slowly he rotated his head and felt the vertebrae move and heard the crack as the bones adjusted. During that time, he decided to call Walt and get some help proving that bullets did fly his way. He hated to think the guys were laughing at him over some fireworks. The department would be in stitches over that, and he didn't want to be the butt of any such jokes. Art went back inside and used the kitchen phone to call Walt.

A couple of hours later Walt and Art worked along the fence line by Art's house, moving the vines and searching the board fence. "It would have had to hit someplace along here." Art kept turning toward the front

74

of the home, looking along the side of his house and the trash cans sitting against the fence near the back door. "I was just about there by the cans when I heard two shots pass right by me. If anyone did aim at me, they would have had to be somewhere at the front of the house. The slugs must have hit this fence. They hunted and searched, moving heavy vines that gripped and held tightly together, not giving an inch. As fast as Art or Walt's hands would open an area of leaves, it would close up.

"I think you're going to have to cut these vines off this fence if you want to see any holes. These things are thick."

"Yeah, you're probably right."

Art and Walt took a step back. Art shook his head and looked at the ground. "I know what I heard, and those bullets hit something and that something had to be this fence."

Walt grabbed and held handfuls of leaves so Art could look the fence over some more, "Got any idea who would be shooting at you?"

Art moved his hurt arm out of the way while bending down and scouring the little bit of fence he could see. "Not a clue. Oh, maybe we should get some gloves. A couple of spiders just scurried off."

Walt let go of the leaves and allowed his eyes to rove around as though he was thinking of something. "What if our sniper was on to you, not wanting you to solve this case?"

Art stopped hunting holes in the fence, turned more toward Walt and grimaced. He brought his lips tight together and said. "I don't see that at this point. This arm has me out of the office. Why would the Grape Avenue Sniper think I could, or, would be the one hunting him or her?"

"I don't know. Just a thought." Walt hunched over like always, said he'd like to get inside and have a cup of coffee.

They turned, went back inside and Walt sat at the table. Melissa spread butter on a piece of toast at the kitchen island. "You figure anything out?"

"No. You be careful going out of this house, Art warned."

She had her mouth on the toast ready to bite. She removed the bread and said, "Oh God Dad, don't get all freaked out."

"Melissa, I don't know what happened last night or what it means in the long run, but I do know I want to know where you are all the time for a while. Humor me okay?"

She nodded agreement, let her eyes roll. "I'm going to the river today just to sit and read for a while."

Art twisted his neck to see her, "I'd rather you stayed home today."

Her face clouded, and she blurted out, "Oh, God Dad, let me breathe. It's awful around here. I can't take it anymore." She slammed the knife she'd used into the kitchen sink and stormed out of the room. Her white sneakers were squeaking with each step. Her toast partly consumed lay on the island counter next to the butter dish.

Art hung his head, reached for the coffee pot. "You wanted coffee?" As he waited for Walt's answer, he continued to set a saucer and cup on the counter.

"Yeah, that'd be good." Walt watched Art, expecting an explosion at any minute.

Art poured and brought the cup to Walt. "I'm alright, don't worry."

Walt sat back, pulled his cup closer and stirred the steam around. He tapped the teaspoon and set it on the side of the saucer. "You going to have a cup?"

"Huh?" Art peered at the back door. "Yeah, yeah." He got another cup down and poured coffee for himself. "I can't get it off my mind, and that just pisses me off."

Walt gingerly began, "Could it be something else you heard. You know you've been not yourself lately. You've said it yourself that you see a shrink because things are bad since... Well you know what I mean."

"I know the sound of shots, and that's what I heard. Someone had to have been shooting at me. If it were the sniper, I'd be dead. He wouldn't have missed. It had to be someone toying with me. Or, do you think it was just someone randomly firing off a gun and the two shots just happen to sail down that pathway, right by me. Where did they go? I've got to get back out there. After this cup, I'm getting a pair of shears, and I'll open some of the vines. They probably could use some cropping."

Slipping to the side of his chair Walt leveraged his body up, "Well, I will leave you at this point. I've got to get back to the office."

"Still nothing on Grape Ave?"

"Not one lead." Walt took his cup to the sink, poured out the half the cup of coffee and set it on the counter. "I thank you for the coffee; I'll catch you later." Walt moved toward the door. "I'll go out the back way."

"I'll go with you. I want to get those shears." Walt and Art walked to his car; Art bid him goodbye, and he headed for the gardening section of the arranged garage. He took hold of the shears and realized he couldn't cut anything with his left hand. "Damn!"

He put the shears back and felt sorry for himself as he walked out of the garage and back into the kitchen. It's not a good time to try to talk to Melissa. She thinks I am trying to ruin her life. I just want to keep her safe. Why doesn't she get that? He walked to the sink, looked down at the one knife covered with butter lying in the sink. The stainless-steel sink gleamed. Melissa was a better housekeeper than me. She keeps a better kitchen than I ever did. That thought didn't make him feel any better either. What kind of father am I? Now someone's drawn a bead on me, and no one believes me?

At that point, Art didn't know what to do with himself. He felt lost, and it made him mad. He needed work, and this damaged arm was jerking him around.

Art reached for the phone, took his little book out of his back pocket and found Murphy's number. "Hey, it's me." Art sat down in the chair before he went on. "You off today?"

"Yes."

"Are you busy? Could you come over here and cut some vines back for me?"

"I'm with Willy right now. She made me cookies, and we're having iced tea and cookies." It sounded like Murphy chewed as he spoke." In about an hour I could come by. Would that be okay?"

Art grinned at the thought of that little feisty old woman, Wilma Concord. She's become Murphy's grandma ever since that summer night. He let his mind go back there, and he grimaced when he remembered how brazen Raymond McNamare had been. "Yeah, come in an hour that would be great. Oh. Bring me a cookie." He hung up and thought he'd have to twiddle his thumbs.

Moving from the kitchen to the garage Art began doing his exercises. He'd use the hour picking up and putting down a five-pound weight in his right hand and trying to squeeze a ball in his left hand. Didn't sound like much, but it would have Art sweating in no time. Somewhere deep in his mind, he felt his left arm not responding. It hung like a lost friend at his side, heavy, useless, and needing to be lifted by some other force than his muscles. He put the worry away and worked on himself listening to the music playing from his plastic radio sitting on the workbench. He needed a slow rhythm these days. He still felt young and vital. The department must see that in him, so he worked the five-pound weight up and down, his eye on the clock, his mind on the shooter.

Chapter Fifteen

1:35 P.M September 13, 1995

Murphy maneuvered his car down the block as Art stood on the grassy parkway next to a fruitless plum tree, a variety hosting dark-purple maple-shaped leaves. A smile worked across his lips as Murphy pulled up and stepped out of the car, "Here's your cookies, Willy sent you six. They are good. Almost ate them on the way over, but I figured if Willy ever got wind of it she'd have my hide nailed to her front door. She thinks you're something special, and she says to tell you she hopes you get well soon and to get back to work. In her words, not mine, 'stop lollygagging around.'"

Art chuckled and said, "That sounds like Wilma." His hand wrapped around the napkin-covered paper plate Murphy handed him. It felt nice for someone to care about him. He didn't have much of that going on in his life these days. Except with Amanda, he thought. Art lifted the rainbow-colored napkin and savored the aroma of almonds and vanilla. The vine chopping could wait a little longer, "These do smell good. How about some coffee and we'll make these history?"

"Sure," Murphy said. He left his car at the curb and followed Art into the house.

Art brought the cups and sugar and cream to the table, he said, "Did you notice the vines growing over the fence? That's what I need help with. Someone took a couple of shots at me, and I need to find the slugs or the holes."

"Yeah, I heard." Murphy sat down as Art poured coffee. "Who'd be shooting at you?"

He shook his head and said, "I haven't a clue. What kind of cookies are these?"

Murphy shrugged, I don't know. I didn't ask her. She bakes them, and I eat them. I never asked her anything about them." Murphy gulped his coffee and asked, "Anything new on your arm?"

Art finished his cookie before answering. "Not much. They keep telling me it will take time." They finished off the cookies and Art pointed toward the door and outside with his head. Murphy nodded, and they rose to get to work. "The shears are in the garage. This way."

Murphy worked at clearing an area and they both studied the wood for holes.

"Damn." Art murmured, his stomach sinking in discouragement. There had to be bullet holes.

"I don't see anything." Murphy picked up the shears, but Art stopped him.

"This is just a lost cause."

Murphy put his foot on the hose box housing of the rolled-up garden hose testing it for his weight. Finding it serviceable, he stood on the plastic container and looked over the fence. "What if the shell went over the fence and over there?"

Art watched Murphy's body strain to peer over the fence. "That would mean the shooter would have had to be lying down to get that trajectory." Art turned around seeing the walkway going along his garage to the front of his house and across the street to the neighbor property. It didn't make any sense to him. If anyone had been on the ground, he wouldn't have had time to get up and leave the scene without him seeing movement. Art had acted quickly, dropped to the ground and searched all the areas. There had been no one. His mind replayed the scene and the walk area to the street was clear. The street light lit everything out front, and he would have had an unobstructed view of anyone shooting down that alleyway, an area no more than ten feet wide. Perplexed, Art sighed.

Murphy got down, took the shears back from Art and said, "What if the shots went lower than you thought? There were two shots? How far apart were they?"

Art's thoughts circled back to the moment he walked out the door. He went back to that position. He felt the trash basket in his arm and began to walk through the events.

"I walked from the house. The first shot came when I was about here, then the second a moment later. I dropped the trash and hit the ground right about there." His finger pointed to a place on the ground about two feet from the main trash containers lined up on the fence near the garage door.

Murphy looked around, "Was your garage door open as it is now?"

Art shot a look at the garage personnel door. I don't know. It could have been. I was working around the house that day."

"You might want to keep things locked up."

Art nodded in agreement. "Sorry this is happening right now and I drug you into it. This arm keeps me from doing so many things for myself. You never give it a thought until you don't have the use of part of your body just how much you count on that whole body working at peak condition." Together they walked to the street and at the curb. "Thank you, Murphy, for coming over and giving me a hand. I do appreciate it." He placed his good hand on Murphy's shoulder, "We'll get the son-of-a-bitch." Murphy nodded as he walked around to the car door. Art waved `goodbye to the exiting car as Melissa came out of the house and joined Art at the curb.

"What was Murphy doing here?"

Art turned and gave Melissa a hug. "Helping me cut some of the vines off the fence. I'm still looking for those slugs."

She nodded. "Why didn't you ask me to cut the vines?"

"I didn't think of it, honey. I don't want you doing that kind of work anyway." He squeezed her to him with his good arm. "I thought you would be going to Midnight to practice for the endurance ride."

"Yeah, I will."

"Do you still want to go to that event? You don't have to if you don't want to go."

She peered down at the ground, "We'd lose all that money. No, I'm going to do it and soon. In fact, I'll go out there now. I've got about three hours before I need to be back. Nicole wants me to babysit for her tonight. She's got a concert at Hutchins Street Square at seven."

"Okay, that sounds good." He leaned away from her, "How about if old dad here drives you out to the stables, and I'll come get you when you call?"

"That would be tight."

Chapter Sixteen

3:09 P.M. September 13, 1995

The smell of used straw hung heavily in the air. Midnight's hooves clopped on the hard-packed floor and sent an echo to Art's ears. The horse nickered as Melissa dropped his lead, and she walked over to open the tack box. Picking up a brush, she ran it over his body. Satisfied she put the brush away and placed the saddle blanket on his back. She lifted the heavy saddle with ease and placed it over the horse's back and Art spoke without thinking, "You heft that with ease, you astound me sometimes."

As she worked at readying Midnight, Art followed Charlie from one stall to the next. Stealth movements of a dark gray cat as it wandered over the top of the hay bales piled just outside the doorway of the barn caught Art's attention. He followed the old boy's slow movements until he disappeared. Probably a mouse hunt.

Art looked back just as Melissa picked up the reins and moved to Midnight's side. She leaped easily to the stirrup catching the ball of her foot. Her leg straightened and raised her body until she swung her leg over the saddle seat and let herself settle on the big horse's back.

While he watched his daughter, he spoke to Charlie. "Charlie, I want to tell you how grateful I am for all you did when Melissa was missing. I am sorry I haven't said anything before this or done anything to let you know how I feel."

He watched as Melissa trotted the horse out of the barn and the sun patterned over her head, shoulders and the horse's back changing Melissa's hair to fire red and the dark black of midnight's coat to shine with each muscle movement. She opened the gate and entered the arena, closing the gate behind her. Art turned back just as Charlie forked up used hay. "You enjoy this job, don't you?" A nod was Arts answer.

Art liked the man and enjoyed the easy-going manner he displayed. He moved away to another area he needed to work in, and Art followed. "Charlie, I'd like to do something to help you."

"No need," Charlie said swinging his hand in protest as he grabbed the rake and worked the area in front of the stalls. Art moved his feet to accommodate the rake. Art allowed Charlie to move away realizing he felt embarrassed at being thanked this way. Art needed a new tack. Reaching into his back pocket he pulled his wallet out and flipped it open. Fingering the bills and choosing two one hundred dollar bills he extracted them from the others and folded them over. Closing the wallet, he slid it back in his pocket.

"Charlie, I want to give you this to pay for the time and fuel and care you gave Midnight when he needed it so much." Art held the bills between two fingers and extended them toward Charlie.

The cigar stopped moving, and the face grew still as Charlie leaned his weight on the top of the rake handle. "Mr. Franklin, I figure taking care of my horses and customers are my job. I am pleased to help you and Miss Melissa."

M.L. WEATHERINGTON

Art's hand hung out in the air the two bills waiting. The two men looked at each other. "It would make me feel better if you took this Charlie. You were there when I needed you when Melissa needed you, and we'd like to thank you in this way." Art began to feel like his arm should be someplace else. He hoped Charlie would take the money soon.

A cracked and weathered face with gentle eyes settled on the bills. Charlie took one hand off the pitch fork handle, reached and took the money. His eyes said thank you just a second before they shifted to the sod at his feet.

Charlie was a proud man, and so was Art. Humbling himself done, Art turned his attention to Melissa. He strolled to the arena fencing and hung his good arm over the top rail and watched his daughter handle a huge black beast with ease and flair. Everything seemed fine as she came around the curve and he waved a goodbye to her. When she acknowledged with a gesture of her own, he turned and retreated to his car. Turning the car around, he headed for Lodi, kicking the dried dust on the rutted dirt road into a cloud obscuring the stable in the rearview mirror.

At home, Art felt drawn back to the side yard and the area by the trash cans. His good hand rubbed along the house as he studied it for any marks that might explain a bullet's passage. The house needed painting. Why hadn't he noticed that before? His eyes narrowed as he considered every detail of the area. The grass grew a bit too tall along the fence line. The gardener needs prodding, he thought. After circling the area from the side of the house wall down to the back fence, Art stopped by the neighbor's fence, a six-foot section of weathered redwood. He continued along the fence to his garbage area where the cans stood on cement stepping stones. He'd laid these pavers ten years ago after a very wet winter.

Everything appeared unfazed by anything other than age and weather. No apparent gunshot damage.

"Damn!"

Just to humor himself he let his body back down right where he thought he'd dropped on that night. He crabbed around, fighting his bad arm all the way while studying all the different places someone could have been if they were to get a shot off his direction.

It came down to the same facts every time. Someone would have had to been standing at the opening by the edge of the garage. No one was there that night. How can that be?

Art got up, dusted off his knees and his back side from the dirt that clung after wallowing around on the ground. He checked his watch. It was almost time for his appointment with the doc. A part of him wanted just to forget it. That's the coward's way out, and he knew that as soon as he thought it out. I'm not a coward and not about to start being one.

Art set his jaw and headed for the bathroom. Pulling the brush through his wavy hair settled him. He liked the feel of the stiff bristles moving against his scalp. He checked his mustache, picked up his tiny comb and moved it close to the hairs just under his nose. They looked well arranged, and he wondered how that was possible when he felt so disarranged. He tilted his mouth in a self-satisfying smirk and set the comb down on the bathroom counter.

Art had to go, or he would be late, and that was not the way Art wished to be remembered. His punctuality had always been a mark of his nature. His fingers wrapped around the edge of the closet slider, and he eased it open and pulled his gray jacket off the hanger.

Down the stairs he sailed for his meeting with Doctor Wexford.

M.L. WEATHERINGTON

He stepped into the outer office and could hear male voices in the other room. Art sat down. In just a moment, the door opened and Art rose as Doctor Wexford appeared in the doorway.

"Hey," Jim said as his arm sailed out and circled the air back to his body, "Come on in." He walked back into the small office and took his place behind the desk. "How have you been?"

Art glanced at the other personnel door and wondered who just went out. He would probably never learn that answer. "It was an interesting week." He paused. "Someone took two shots at me as I was taking the trash out of my house." He looked to see how Jim took that news.

Jim's eyes narrowed, he pulled his jaw down and a bit to the left and centered eyes on Art. Disbelief ran all over that expression, and it wasn't lost on Art.

"Who in hell would take a shot at you?"

Art shook his head as his eyes locked on the docs. He sighed, as his upper body lifted and slumped. "I don't know, and I can't prove that it ever happened."

The doc sat forward, elbows on the desktop. He fanned his hands out. "What do you mean you can't prove that it happened?"

"I heard the slugs hit something, but I can't find what. The officers came that night and searched everywhere, but they didn't find anything. They think I'm nuts. Murphy, that's one of my guys, came over this afternoon and helped cut some of the vines away from the fence so I could find the slugs or the holes they made. Nothing. I can't find anything."

The doc had a quizzical expression and stony eyes, "What makes you so sure that someone shot at you?"

Art flared, "I know what I heard, and I know that sound whizzing by me at high velocity."

Jim sat back, a look of disgust played across his face. "You heard a backfire. That's why you can't find anything."

"Jim, I know the sound of something flying by my body and the sound of a gun's report. I heard both. I hit the ground on the first one and the second shot wasn't far behind. It wasn't a backfire." Art stood up glaring at Jim.

"Calm down; there has to be an explanation to all this." Jim took his usual position by leaning back in his chair and looking at the ceiling. "Tell me what's been happening this week, besides those shots."

Art looked at him, chewed on it a moment and sat back down. "Nothing much. Same old thing. I am going to my therapy for my arm, and that's about the same. They keep telling me to be patient. That's all. I am patient. There is nothing I can do. I have to have help with everything. Melissa is cooking and cleaning now. I do have some ladies coming in to do the regular house cleaning every two weeks, but that hasn't changed. What has changed is that I cannot do the regular father jobs. She has to do most everything."

"How does she feel about that?"

"I don't know; I haven't asked her."

"Does she seem angry? Is she acting out about doing any of the jobs?"

"No, not at all. In fact, Melissa seems to like cooking, and she's good at it, better than I ever was. One of our friends is teaching her a lot about kitchen stuff, and she's a fast learner. She made pork roast and applesauce the other day. It's so good."

"Well, it sounds like something's going right for the two of you."

Art smiled, "More than a little right. Mel likes Amanda. It seems Amanda, and I enjoy each other's company. She has agreed to come to the coast for the endurance ride weekend."

"That coming up soon?"

"Yes, it's right around the corner, and Melissa is with the horse practicing right now. When I leave here, I'm going to pick her up. She's babysitting this evening."

The room quieted as they sat in silence. Art shuffled his feet on the tile floor. The doc put his hand behind his head and closed his eyes leaning his neck back against the chair, "Sounds like you are doing all the right things." He opened his eyes and brought them to Art who joined him in a stare. "Anything you want to say?"

Art shook his head. There seemed too many things going around in his head. He felt happy one minute, pissed off the next.

"Keep it up and let's meet on our regular day and time."

Art looked down at his watch and saw with surprise that forty-five minutes had slipped by, and he rose and shook the doc's hand.

Chapter Seventeen

11:35 A.M. September 14, 1995

As Art opened the door for Walt he glimpsed the neighbor's lawn service had just finished mowing. One man walked a blower along the concrete walk. The sound reverberated in Art's ears, and he knew how happy he'd feel when they shut it off. He smiled at Walt as he moved out of the doorway and let him enter. He showed Walt into the office, and they sat down.

Walt pulled a manila envelope from under his arm. He cracked his neck as he held it out to Art.

Glad for the information Art grabbed the file from him and opened the flap. His fingers sorted the pages until Art found the coroner's report. He pulled that out first thing and he read through to the end. Art upended the envelope and the photos taken of the body came sliding out. As he sat he began arranging the pictures, letting his eyes move over the images. They came to rest on her face. "She had a sweet peaceful face," he said. He noticed the soft lips closed in death. They seemed lifelike as though she might wake up. He felt sadness for this woman as he settled on her eyes. Shut as though in sleep, he thought. I've seen that same look on Mellissa's face when she slept. A goose bump chase ran over his arms as he thought about that thin line between life and death. He studied her face in detail. A peaceful expression on her face gave him a hard time thinking that she could ever yell at anyone. Her sister said she often went on a tirade and stormed off in a huff. Art frowned at her picture as he realized this face was not letting on to the world the pain and shock it had endured while lying on the pavement, her life ebbing away. He had a hard time getting over that her makeup appeared freshly applied.

He pulled another photo to the top and laid it over her face picture. It showed the exit wounds on the front of her chest just under her chin, and a second one on the other side as though paired up. He studied two gaping holes looking as though the flesh had ruptured leaving the meat dark and lumpy like cottage cheese but red and black. The skin around the jagged hole darkened out in shades of red and purple where the blood pooled under the skin. Art saw the notations about the size and shape of the wounds on the coroner's report. Even though he knew precisely, he leaned closer and looked carefully at the size and shape of Adora's body in relationship to the wounds

He sat back. His hand moved silently dropping the fingers of his good hand into a bowl of popcorn, circling a few grains and bringing them to this mouth. Art absentmindedly ate. This is one serious shooter. He used the kind of shells that tear and rip. He didn't intend for his victim to survive.

Art fingered a few more popped kernels and ate them. It's a military shooter with military ammo!

The thought that a professional killer was at work chilled him. We may not be able to catch this shooter. He brushed his hands together letting the salt grains drift to the wastebasket just under his desk. Art glanced in the bowl and saw a few un-popped kernels and dumped those and set the bowl back down on the desk.

Sitting back in his leather chair, he gazed at the far wall even though he didn't see a thing in that area, he saw the scene. This killer knew this woman. I'd bet my life on that fact. This is personal. Well, that narrows the field down. I'll get Walt to let me see the list.

He reached into his desk and pulled out his personal and very private recording log, a red spiral bound book with lined paper just like any student used. In bold black Sharpie permanent fine point ink, he'd written 'The Franklin Logs' on the outside front cover. Upon opening the book to the first page, he penciled in Adora's name and August 31, 1995, as the date of death. Even though he was no longer in charge of homicide at the station, he still felt like she was one of his. Especially she was his if he could figure this case out. He looked at his list and smiled at the last one, Samuel T. Nelson, and tapped his finger on the number twenty-one the number of days it took to close that case. There numbered just seven homicides in his book. Adora would be the eighth when it was solved. He held the book on edge and saw the unused portion of pages waiting for some entry. He hoped he would not be able to go to a second index page. If he was in charge, he wanted homicide crimes in the low percentages, so far, so good.

He brought his bottom lip up over his mustache and pulled down smoothing on the hairs. An unconscious mannerism he'd done since a boy and watched his father do it with his mustache. Could he solve this case? He knew he was as good at problem solving and putting out fires.

These days it pleased him to think he could still do something and do it well since he mostly felt useless. Now he had something to do. Now he had Adora, and she needed him as much as he needed her.

"Dad?"

Art raised his head, "Hi honey, come on in." He didn't move the pictures. Melissa had seen horrible pictures before. Not that he meant for her to see them, but it was part of his life, and she was going to be around. Having secrets from her didn't seem the right way to treat this problem. So, for the last year he'd been sharing with her hoping that his explanations would help her understand that people are not always nice to one another.

She examined the holes in Adora's body and shook her head. "What did that to her?"

Art cleared his throat and got ready to explain. How much explanation he'd have to give he was about to find out. "Just speculation on my part, but I believe now that the shooter was using a rifle and military ammo."

She looked at him with a quizzical face, "You mean some soldier shot her?"

Art's eyes widened as he leaned his head on his right shoulder and shrugged, "I'm not sure of all things yet, but what I feel is that it was a shell used by a military because of the pattern of damage left on the victim. That's what is called a wound profile. The profile tells me the maximum disruption that a given bullet can be expected to cause on soft tissue. Most ammo used by regular citizens won't do this much damage. They would just drill right through small on entry and a little bigger on exit."

"I get it." Melissa moved the photo so she could see Adora's face. "Is that all?"

Art shook his head, "Only the beginning. I'm waiting for forensics to get back to us with all the testing completed so we can narrow our search for the scumbag who did this to her."

She smiled at him, "You are going to take care of her, aren't you Dad?" She noticed the notebook, "What's this?"

He shut the book and put it in his top drawer. "It's a record I keep of homicides I work on."

She smiled at him, "My Dad, the scorekeeper."

He nodded and answered, "Something like that."

Chapter Eighteen

11:15 A.M. September 15, 1995

Driving on Highway 12 West toward Mendocino this morning with his two girls in the car put a grin on Art's face. They were headed for the endurance ride for Melissa and a weekend for Amanda and him. Art roamed his attention from mirror to mirror and back to the two-horse trailer Charlie was pulling a car lane ahead of them. It amused him how the horse's hips kept pace with the bounce of the trailer. His eyes turned to passing vehicles and to the golden fields that ran to the hills. Mount Diablo to his left reigned majestic against the fall sky. Art took in a deep breath of the clear air and smelt the occasional scent of burnt diesel fuel. His hand moved down a bit on the steering wheel as he glanced over at Amanda.

At that second, he felt Melissa press at his seat's back and he turned to see her. Such a serious expression on her young face he thought. Her eyes were plastered on Midnight. He pulled the rearview mirror down a bit so he could see her face better. Somehow, the years have sailed by and she's no longer my little girl, that's the face of a young adult. He felt surprise at the realization.

"Dad, I can only imagine how happy Midnight's going to feel just to be with other horses and going along without cars in the way."

"I bet he will."

Amanda turned to her, "I think all living things like their freedom."

"I do too."

"I think dogs and cats bond with people, but I didn't know horses did too. How long have you had Midnight Melissa?"

"Over a year now, this is the first time we've gone anywhere like this and I know I'm excited, what must he be feeling and thinking?"

"He's probably hoping the hay keeps coming. Did you see how much Charlie put in the trailer's feed trough?" Art said.

"Yeah."

"How far is it to the campsite?" Amanda said.

"Its 201 miles, and about four hours. I think we've gone about a quarter of the way."

"We go through Petaluma, don't we?"

"Yeah."

The two girls were talking now about Lodi and events that were taking place in town and Art settled back listening to their voices. The road noise and their female voices soothed him. The time passed and he sat up as soon as he spotted the last sign he needed, "There's Little Lake Road."

"The ranch shouldn't be too far ahead."

"Boy, its way out in the country." Amanda said.

Charlie turned the trailer off the winding road onto a dirt path and moved over ruts, passing under a sign that announced the Bent Horse Shoe Ranch. They pulled across grassland, coming to a stop in an open meadow ringed at a far distance with trees. A gust of wind whipped through the open car window bringing the scents of pine and ocean.

"We're here honey."

M.L. WEATHERINGTON

Melissa craned her neck as she looked around, "Oh Dad isn't it beautiful?"

A male rider on a dark blue roan came trotting over to them and Melissa leaned forward.

The man waved his drovers hat. "Nice to have you with us," he said staying on his mount. He pointed with his left arm toward the tree line to the west, directing their attention that way. "See that stand of trees over there? We've chalked out camping sites. Pull your trailer into an unclaimed one and set up camp." Then he pointed to the other end of the field. Art and Charlie turned together. "See that big tent over there? You can finish registering there and get your number and placement. You'll need to set up your vet checks and other stuff too. You'll find out when you get there." He allowed his torso to lean back in his saddle and his horse backed up, "I've got to get back so I can get the next trailer that arrives. Just check at the tent for anything you need." He tipped his hat politely, nodded, and in the same movement he galloped off.

"We just met the Marlboro Man," Charlie said with a droll voice as he sauntered back to the cab of his truck and got back inside. He pulled forward toward the campsite area.

Art took Melissa's arm and headed for the car, they got back in and Art followed the trailer tracks. He noticed the sun, high overhead and decided that they were now facing eastward. Sparse growing grasses made the ground appear patchy. He turned his attention to some scattered trunks of cut down trees, dark sentinels stuck up in the field.

The brakes squealed on Charlie's truck and Art stepped on his brakes. Art cut the car and walked to meet Charlie.

"Guess you need to tell me which spot you want and I'll back her in there for ya."

98

"Melissa?"

She ran to her Dad.

"Which one of these sites do you want?"

"I guess one on the end so we don't feel crowded."

"Okay Charlie, you heard the lady. Back her up and drop her."

They drove to the last marked out site and Charlie parked and began opening the trailer's back gate. After Midnight had backed out of the trailer, he went for the dried clumps with relish.

Art watched Melissa tie Midnight to the trailer. She then jumped up on the pickup truck and helped Charlie pull four bales of hay to the edge of his truck bed. Together they rolled the bales off and they dropped with a heavy thud on the ground.

Art winced, Melissa lifting those heavy bales. I can't help even with that. They rolled a large barrel of water to the edge of the truck bed, and Art noticed Charlie motion Melissa out of the way as he horsed the heavy weight to the ground. He undid the spring locked top and removed it, sloshing water over the side. Midnight nosed the water and drank.

"Is Midnight going to eat all that hay?"

"No." Charlie, his usual unlit cigar hanging from his lips set his teeth to hold it tight as he said. "He'll probably eat about a half of the bale. The others are straw bales and furniture for you, so you have some place to sit out here." Charlie strode to the back of the pickup truck and took five-gallon containers of water setting them on the ground. "Miss Melissa, you drink from these jugs okay?"

"Thanks Charlie."

Melissa placed the water under the trailer so it would be out of the sun then busied herself pulling the straw into a seating arrangement, making the place home.

Art brought his hand up and rubbed his elbow and upper arm just behind the green sling trying to ease the ache that started up. As he did he heard another trailer entering the grounds and he turned to see the Marlboro Man trotting out to meet the rig. "Ah, good someone else is here, Melissa won't be alone."

Charlie walked over to Art and shook his hand. "I'll be heading out soon. You call me when you are ready for me to come pick the old man up."

Art nodded and let Charlie's hand go. "Thanks Charlie, this has been a big help to me."

After they waved goodbye to Charlie and Art saw that Melissa was settling into her digs he called her over. "We're going into town to check it out and find places to get food and some rooms. We'll be back in about four hours. You going to be okay by yourself?"

"I'm going to be just fine, Dad. Midnight and I are settling in, and I'll ride him over there to check in. We'll be going on our first introductory ride soon. We won't be back here before eight tonight. We start about five, I think the brochure said."

Art looked at his watch. She'd be back in about six hours. He glanced around the campsite area and said, "You know I'll be right back here if you need me don't you?"

"I know," she said. She walked them back toward their car, kissed Art on the cheek and hugged Amanda.

Art and Amanda waved, started the car and turned around heading for town. Art's eyes bore into the rearview mirror where Melissa's image shrunk with each wheel turn. His hand gripped the steering wheel with force.

Amanda's hand lay gently on Art's arm as she spoke, "She'll be all right, Art. She's looking forward to this event and it looks like it's pretty well organized. See the tent over there? There are people here, so she's going to be okay."

He nodded agreement and swallowed hard. Art turned to Amanda, "My little girl is growing up and not needing me anymore."

Amanda grinned at him, "She'll always need you, Art. What's important is that she wants you."

Art nodded and dragged his eyes from hers to study the vast area ahead of him. As they left the camping area and passed under the sign at the entry, he said, "Let's go see what we can discover."

Amanda's giggle sounded like that of a school girl as the car made hardtop and picked up speed.

Chapter Nineteen

3:37 P.M. September 15, 1995

Gravel spit out from the tires as Art rounded a tight turn and he let up on the accelerator to gain better control of the car. They rode along a country road about five miles when the next curve brought them into Little River, population 117, elevation 90 feet. The town spilled down a slope to the beach and the rolling waves greeted the shore and their ears.

"Boy, isn't that something?"

"Art, let's eat here. This place is just oozing with charm."

"The streets are narrow," Art craned his neck in search for a likely eating place, "How about that place."

"Looks good to me."

Art turned the tires into the curb, pulled the keys and got out. Then he walked around to the other side and helped Amanda out. The salty air set the mood for them as they took each other's hand and sauntered toward the door.

A clunk followed by a squeak accompanied Art's opening the door into an old turn of the century building He saw a long wooden bar ran the length of the room.

102

Behind the stools nestled up to that counter ran a walkway leading to the dining area through a doorway on the back wall. "This way," he guided her. Amanda moved into the dining room. They chose a seat at a wooden table covered with a heavy white cloth.

A few other people were seated. Art pulled the thick napkin from his water glass. The words of the song just loud enough to hear comfortably played in the background and the idea to dance with Amanda came to him just as the waiter stopped by their table. They both asked for water and a glass of house wine.

Art reached his hand across and took her hand in his, he stood, "Dance with me?" She rose and he led her to the small dance floor.

She placed her hand gently on the sling near his shoulder and put her other hand around his neck, moving until he felt her fingers find the vertebra at the back of his neck. Instant warmth flooded through him and he pressed on her back to guide her to the slow jazz piece. The melody ended almost as soon as they started to dance and he stopped to walk back to their seats. They'd made five steps when the Righteous Brothers rendition of Unchained Melody filled the room.

He stepped into a rhythm with the song's beat and the words he knew so well took on a special meaning for him. His heart melted, and he guided Amanda back under the lights. His hand rubbed over her back, the touch filled with warmth and tenderness. She moved closer, her head just under his chin and her blonde hairs caught his stubble making him smile with pleasure. The smell of her favorite fragrance floated everywhere, and he felt dizzy in his feelings now. The singer's voice was pleading with the same words and emotions Art felt. How could the singer know what I am feeling? His eyes sailed around the room, he saw everything, everyone and remembered nothing. This woman controlled his whole world, and he was happy. Art was keenly aware of her nearness as she moved back from his body. He looked down as her eyes came up to meet his.

The song's words burned into him, the word 'hunger' echoing in his mind.

Their eyes focused on each other's, searching back and forth.

It felt to Art no words needed to be said at that moment. He knew how she felt, and he knew she understood him. In that instant, they had become one. His heart beat faster. Tears burned to be let free. He gripped his lips together tightly then freed them. Amanda raised her chin. Her lips were there. All he had to do was bend his neck to reach, and they connected without his willing the movement. The song lingered in the background, asking if they still belonged to each other. She is mine. Art's lips pressed harder into that sweet softness. They held together a long moment and eased apart, her head slipping by his cheek, his face snuggling into her hair and neck. He felt the warmth of her, the life of her. The singer's voice pleaded his very desires as Art felt flooded with emotions. Art snuggled deeper into her shoulder and smiled as her head pressed closer to his cheek.

Art allowed those feelings to take over and carry him along, certain in his position with her. In that minute, he knew now deeply he cared about her and what she wanted. A protective sense grew within him and about how he looked at her. She was no longer just a woman. She was his. She was significant to him, important in a special way like Melissa.

Goose bumps raced over his arms as the reality sank into his heart. The world just transformed for Arthur Franklin, and he welcomed it with open arms. He felt he could sigh, drop his shoulders and relax for the first time since...he couldn't remember when.

SIDESWIPED

She reached upward on tiptoes and breathed into his ear, "I love you."

His head came down and snuggled with hers, and he whispered, "I love you," back to her with all the love and warmth his shaky voice could carry.

"So, now what do we do? I think we've quite made a spectacle of ourselves out here on the dance floor all alone. Everyone's watching."

He gazed down at her. "I don't care. Let them watch."

"We could eat?"

"We could." He scanned around the room checking out what the other diners were doing. Some seemed to be watching while others were busy with their thoughts. "That's what we came to do, so let's eat."

Amanda turned to his side; he slipped his arm around hers and guided her toward their table. The song resolved to an end and pulled at Art's heartstrings. The singer's voice rose in a falsetto so pure, so sweet, it moved Art to wonder if Amanda felt the same. As they walked, he squeezed her hand, and she squeezed right back. She sat back down with his hand on the back of her chair.

Amanda, tears filling her eyes, said, "Would it be cruel of me to tell you what we are feeling is simply a chemical reaction? We're just two bodies that recognize the complete connection we have."

"Oh, you're one of those who take all the fun out of things." Art sat adjusting his arm sling and grinning at her. "I suggest we go with it and don't ask questions, or look back. Are you with me?"

"All the way."

"Good, let's pick something from the menu." Art picked up the menu and wiped his glasses positioned them and studied the listing. "Looks like a steak sandwich would be the easiest. How about a steak for you?"

Amanda shook her head, "No beef for me, I'm a chicken girl. I think the grilled chicken salad for me." She put the menu down. "And coffee."

"You had a roast beef sandwich at the bar. So, you don't like beef?"

"Watching my girlish figure."

Art nodded understanding, "I'm going to order a sandwich to go for Mel."

Chapter Twenty

5:40 P.M. September 15, 1995

After they ate, Art and Amanda drove to the coastal road and parked the car near a high cliff. The roar of the ocean called to him as he came around the side of the fender and met her as she closed the car door. Her hand went into his, and the warmth of the touch filled him with a soft, sweet feeling. Gently he squeezed so as not to hurt, but to say I am here and always will be. As he did a fresh wind picked up and tousled his red hair. It felt wonderful, as though Mother Nature ran her fingers through his hair and told him, 'This union is my choice for you.' At the same time, he smelled the sea fragrance and Amanda tightened her grip. He took in a deep, fulfilling breath. They strolled toward a pathway at the edge of the cliff where they spotted the gray wooden stairway winding down to the beach.

Caught up by the sea air, the sound of the seagulls calling, and the ocean rushing over the sand and boulders to the beach far below gave Art the sense that his world was fresh and new. A strong breeze pushed at his face and shoulders as he asked, "Do you want to walk down?"

"No, too full. I'd have to come back up, and that looks like a steep climb from here."

Art positioned himself behind her and placed his good arm around her for protection. He stood that way with her as though they were in complete tune with the surroundings, an intricate part of life's beat. The surf crashed into the land again, and Art thought. What if I bring Amanda into my life right now? If someone is shooting at me would I bring trouble into her life? Maybe I should figure that out first. As he rationalized Art almost decided to protect her by calling this off before it went any further. I should. It would be the adult thing to do now. But, and it is a big but, I've always put off what I've needed for Melissa's good. She's growing up. I have only one life, and it's getting shorter every moment. Amanda is perfect for me. She makes me happy. This is my time now. I feel that Amanda and I are so right for each other. Suddenly Art jerked. If someone is targeting me, it's time to find out whom, and why?

"What?"

He turned down to her face, a face being brushed by her hair as it was blown first one direction and then the next. She tried to manage it with her hand, but it was useless. "Oh, nothing just a thought crossed my mind, and I was surprised by it coming right then."

"Tell me about it?" She snuggled back against his body and sighed.

"Nothing to tell."

"Hum."

Now Art couldn't wait to get home, and that wasn't about to happen until Melissa was ready to go home on Sunday afternoon. He'd just have to put his idea out of his mind until they were in Lodi.

"I hate to end this, but we need to check into our rooms. Then I need to see Mel, and how her days went, and give her the sandwich."

They lingered at the edge a few minutes longer without speaking. Then they turned back to the car.

Instead of them being two separate people now, they began acting as one.

Amanda spotted a sign in front of The Gull House, a homey bed and breakfast, and pointed, "Honey, there."

He swung the car into the parking space, and they went inside the white wood sided building to the check-in counter. Art paid for the rooms. Deciding to stay while Art went back out to Melissa, Amanda pulled her suitcase and took the key from Art. He gave her a kiss on the cheek. "I'll be back. I don't know when. I need to be sure she is alright and get her to come back here to sleep tonight."

"I understand."

"Bye."

"Bye."

Art brought the car into the area where Melissa and Midnight had set up camp and parked. Art was pleased to see all the nearby sites now filled. Many sounds from talking to horses pawing the ground and nickering met him. Midnight stood tied to the tailgate of Charlie's horse trailer, his nose to the ground as he foraged for clumps of grass. A paper bag rustled in his hand as he made his way to the bales of straw Charlie had left, Art dropped down on one. He watched his daughter pull the horse's black tail hairs through a comb. The smell of fresh air and the aroma of horseflesh gave him happy thoughts. "You have a good ride this afternoon?"

She looked up and gave him her big toothy grin, "Awesome, it was great Dad. Midnight went well. It was just to get us familiar with the trails around here and with each other."

Art nodded and leaned forward to rest his left arm on his knee. "The night's nippy."

She finished bedding Midnight down, picked up her tack and put it in the box of the trailer, then shut the door and twisted the lock. Melissa slid her hand between flakes of alfalfa hay and pulled one free. Walking with it back to Midnight, she pulled it apart and dropped it on the ground. Midnight's nose wrapped around a bit of the flake as she placed the hay before him. He pulled, nickering thanks as he managed to separate some of the flake. Melissa came to stand by Art.

He gave her a hug and said, "Now that you've taken care of your responsibilities how about my taking care of one of mine?"

Melissa knew exactly what he meant, but she played along, "Which is?"

"Feeding my daughter." He glanced down and picked up the brown paper bag he'd carried. "Are you hungry?"

Melissa's body lowered as her knees bent, and her hands shot out waiting for whatever he had for her. "Give!" she demanded. "I'm so hungry. The hay is beginning to look good."

"Well, I think I've got just what the doctor ordered. How would you like a steak sandwich, some," he wagged his head, "probably soggy fries, and soda?" He brought the sandwich out from the paper bag and gave her the capped off soda and straw. "The fries are in the bag."

She took the food from him. Melissa made a place on the bales for her dinner. She plunked herself down, brushed off her hands which looked dirty. "There's nowhere to wash up out here. I suppose that was the way it was for cowboys hundreds of years ago." She opened her steak sandwich, smelled it and fished inside the paper bag for the fries. She looked up and straight at him, "No ketchup?"

"Oh, I didn't think of it honey, sorry."

She jerked her head to one side and blinked both eyes to say never mind. Without waiting another second, she chomped into the sandwich. "Hiss is so 'ood." she mumbled.

"Don't talk with your mouth full," Art said. Her cheeks puffed out like a chipmunk's as she ate. He enjoyed seeing her eyes sparkle like that. He felt so proud of her right at that moment that he could bust. He wanted to tell her about his feelings for Amanda and a little about their dinner tonight, but he didn't. He just watched Melissa enjoy her food. It wasn't long before she sucked on her straw and made that drying up sound crushed ice and sodas can make. She took the straw out of her mouth and said, "I made all gone."

That statement took him back through the years when she would get a reward for eating all her dinner and telling him she'd made all gone. "I don't have anything else. That's it, no reward."

She breathed deeply, looked up into the sky, and after that, over at him, "You're reward enough Dad. Thank you for letting me do this. I needed to get involved with Midnight again and get back to my regular life. This event has helped a lot." She leaned her body against his, and he cradled his unencumbered arm around her.

They sat together looking up into the night. Several moments passed before she said, "Can't see the stars very well, too much light around."

The crickets rubbed their legs in chorus with each other as father and daughter listened to nature's melody and just let the night be. Midnight's throat rumbled, and he snorted as he chomped. One of his hooves slapped the ground as he moved.

"It's getting cold." Art pulled his jacket to cover her arms.

"Yeah."

They stayed on, not wanting to disturb the feeling that they enjoyed.

"I haven't felt very good about myself Dad." She waited for him to say something.

He didn't, just hugged her tighter.

"I'm sorry I didn't tell you about Ray when I met him. I didn't think it meant anything, or I didn't know what was happening. I just need you to know..." She swallowed and sniffed. "I just need you to know that I never meant to hurt you."

His lower lip slid up over his upper, caught the mustache hairs, and pulled them down like he'd done a thousand and one times before. "Honey, I know that. That guy was a predator and a killer. He never had your best interest in his mind, never."

He felt her nod.

"I don't think I will ever get married Dad." Her voice sounded hollow.

"Oh, yes you will. Someday, not anytime soon, I hope, but you will meet the right person. When that happens, it will be okay with you."

The camp settled down to quiet as the other attendees and their animals slipped off to sleep, and they lowered their voices so as not to bother anyone.

"How do you know the right person?" she queried, her head turning to look up at him.

"That's a good question. Pumpkin. So many things are going to come your way, and you are going to have to pick, and sort and use your slide rule to figure out your path, but this I can tell you." He shifted his weight, and she moved to sit up facing him, the light from the lantern sending shadows over his face making it more a mask. "Know what you like. Make sure you understand where you draw the line. Once you've done that you can find the right person because he's going to want the same things you do, want to set the same standards you do. He's going to want the same lifestyle you do. It will just fit." Art thought about Amanda and how he felt that way with her. "If you find yourself at odds with someone you think might be the right person, that's probably a red flag you should pay attention to."

She slipped back to leaning against him and he to wrapping his arm tighter around her waist.

Life seemed to be changing for both. He ventured into unknown territory, "How have your sessions been going? Are they helping?"

Melissa raised her shoulders, her voice flat, "it's okay I guess. She asks me how I feel and things, and I tell her I don't know. Mostly, that is. But, Dad, when it was happening, I felt scared. The fear took over, and I couldn't make clear decisions like you always told me. You said if you're ever scared about something to get busy, work it out. Dad, I couldn't do anything but lay there. God, I don't know how long. I couldn't move. And I sure couldn't think. I was so scared of where I was, how to get free, or, if I'd ever get free. Then when I went into the river, it felt so cold, and I got stuck in those roots. The water lapped and lapped at my nose, but it never hurt me. I felt like the river saved me."

His eyes glistened as he tightened his lips. One armed he hugged her to his side and held her gently, rocking their bodies back and forth in the smallest of movement. Gathering his courage, he spoke almost in a whisper, "Thank you for telling me that." He squeezed her. "I love you, baby, always will and I am proud of you. Always believe that."

He quieted, and they listened as somewhere near them, a man snored rhythmically. Art lowered his voice to a soft whisper, "You are doing all the right things. We'll both get through this mess."

She wrapped her arms around his forearm that held her to him. "Yes, we will."

"I've got rooms for us in town. What say we go get some sleep?"

"Dad." She sat up squaring herself. "I can't leave Midnight here alone. This is my watch. He's important to me."

M.L. WEATHERINGTON

Art studied her a long moment. He nodded. "You have a sleeping bag?"

"Yeah, two of them."

He nodded again, "Let's roll them, babies, out.

Chapter Twenty-One

2:50 P.M. September 17, 1995

They arrived at Lucky Horse Shoe Stables just before three p.m. Sunday afternoon. Art reached the ground first, followed by Melissa and finally by Amanda. All of them yawned and stretched. Art's body was so tired and drained from the weekend's non-stop activities, yet happy and content.

Charlie parked the horse trailer around back. He unlocked the trailer door and walked to the window, stepped up on the railing and swung the door open. He reached in and untied Midnight and coaxed him to back out.

The horse felt for the earth with his hind leg, allowing the other leg to follow. Once he had firmness under his foot, he backed out to the edge and onto the ground. "Good Boy," Charlie picked up the lead rope and led Midnight to the arena. The horse went down and rolled coating his hide with dust. He stood and turned to Melissa as she came into the arena her hand extended, a low nicker greeted her as Midnight's head stretched forward.

"Hey, Charlie? Is the stall ready?"

Midnight bent his agile neck, pricked his ears forward, stretched his nose and took the offered vegetable from Melissa's hand.

"Yeah, it's ready. You can bring him in now."

Melissa encircled his forelock and led him into his stall. Charlie lifted a fresh flake of alfalfa into his trough and Midnight enthusiastically moved to the feedbox nickering all the way.

"Charlie, do you think Midnight liked this weekend? I mean, do you think horses care about things?"

The unlit cigar came out of Charlie's mouth and into his hand as though he'd spit it out, "Miss Melissa, of course, horses care. They're just like us. They have feelings. I think Midnight had a great time. The question is— did you?"

"Oh, yes, Charlie I had a blast. We didn't win anything. That's okay. I learned a lot and I would love to do it again next year." She placed her hand on his shoulder and said, "And, thank you for taking Midnight and bringing him back home."

The cigar went right back into its normal position in Charlie's mouth as a slight bloom of embarrassment reddened his cheeks. He rubbed the mane by Midnight's withers. Then Charlie patted him twice. "I've got to finish feeding." With that, Charlie nodded to Melissa and left her stall.

Art and Amanda waited for Melissa to finish putting Midnight and all the tack away. She came running to them, and they all piled back into the car and headed home.

Art pulled the camping gear and suitcases out of the car trunk and set them on the driveway.

Melissa gave Amanda a hug and a kiss on the cheek. "I had a really good time, and I'm glad you came along."

"I had a good time too." Her eyes caught Arts fleetingly then centered on Melissa's. "I wouldn't have missed this trip for the world."

"Dad, I'm going to go shower. I think I have as much dust on me as Midnight, and I didn't roll in the dust. Just look at my new boots."

All attention swung to her feet.

"You can't even see the design."

She picked up their bags, leaving Amanda's, and headed for the house.

"Bye, honey," Amanda said. They watched as she entered the house and the door shut. "She's a great kid Art." Amanda started to pick her bag up, but Art put his hand out. "I'll carry it out to your car I want to talk to you a minute."

She nodded, and they moved down the driveway to her car. She opened her back door, and slid the suitcase into the seat.

"We need to get started on her birthday. I'd asked you for help and wondered if you could still do that."

"You bet! I am looking forward to working on that project. You better get me a list of the names of her guests. And, most importantly a budget, what's it going to be?"

"I am thinking," he checked to be sure they were alone. "Five hundred. Does that sound, right?"

Amanda nodded. "That should be more than we need. Do you know where you want to hold this party?"

Art used his body and shoulders to point at this house. "Right here, I've got the pool and big backyard. I have a boat. What are you thinking of doing?"

She gave him a sly glance, "I've got a few ideas. Let me mull a bit longer now that I know the venue and the budget. Does she like or not like something that I should know about, so I don't foul things up?"

Arts expression showed that he couldn't think of anything that she didn't like. "Mel loves chocolate cake, the deep dark kind with fresh walnuts in the frosting, and French vanilla ice cream." He gave it some more thought, "She loves fresh strawberries."

"That gives me some ideas. What do you think of a high tea?"

Art shook his head. "No clue. What's that?"

"You know, like a queen."

Art did his best to recall anything he knew about being a queen. He squints and tries to see Melissa as a queen. It wasn't happening for him. Instead of raining on Amanda's parade he shrugged his shoulders.

"It'll be great, you'll see." Amanda stood on tiptoes, pecked him on the cheek, let herself back down to the ground. "I've got to go. Talk to you later?"

Standing on the curb he watched as the tail of her car left the curb and wished she wasn't leaving. Swinging his attention to across the street to the house next door to Judy and Irma's his eyes narrowed. The White's house had a for sale sign. They must have put that up while we were gone. He thought about that for a moment and then crossed to the side of his house by the garage and the walkway to the trash cans.

The idea that had struck him while standing on the edge of that cliff and looking out over the sea and the infinite horizon flooded back. He hurried to see if he might be right. Back to the fence he went. His hand moved some of the vine and leaves. There it was a large knot hole. What if? He dropped the leaves and headed for the garage and his small set of binoculars.

Back at the knot hole, Art bent over and tried to see through the opening made by that hole to identify where a bullet might have gone. Art turned the focus wheel until one tree came clear.

Art stood up, walked around the house to the poolside and positioned himself even with the knot hole; he turned his back on the fence and directed his gaze at that tree. Bringing the binoculars up to his eyes, he adjusted them and began the search inching up the trunk of that tree until he felt certain in his gut that the tree was the answer.

He had to get over there. Knowing the area, he knew with his arm in a sling he couldn't maneuver that terrain. Art went into the house and called Murphy and told him to come over and that he'd find him around back by the pool, so Art walked around the back yard checking out what he needed to do on the property and watched his clock. It seemed Murphy would never get there.

This had to be right. Even if they found a bullet in the tree over there it didn't prove that there was a second shot. If he could locate one shot, he could find the other. The one would vindicate him in the minds of everyone who doubted him.

The pool filter system cycled and set a hum as Murphy came around the side of the house. Together they centered their attention on the pool vacuum working the bottom at the deep end.

"What's up?" Murphy said.

Art pointed to the trees on the other side of the river. "I believe you're going to find a shell in that tree, the one with the crooked top."

"It's about three hundred feet across the water, and sixty feet from where we are standing to the river edge." Murphy turned and looked at the fence, the shell could travel fifteen hundred yards, "Okay, I'll head over. Got my tools and my trusty camera in my pocket. If I see anything I'll snap it for you."

It took Murphy twenty minutes to get into position. Art remained in his back yard with his binoculars trained on the tree watching Murphy. Ten minutes passed when Murphy signaled. He took a couple of pictures and used his knife and dug the shell out. Finally, his hand went up in the air for Art to see.

Five minutes later Murphy left the tree and disappeared into the brush and Art waited for him to come back. Art did a little jig as he went back into the kitchen, stopped in front of the refrigerator and removed two chilled beers. He took them back out to the pool table.

"What were you doing over there?" he asked as soon as Murphy came around the side of the house to the backyard.

The young man grinned and said, "I thought I might find the other shell, and I'd get it too. But..." Murphy shook his head and shrugged his shoulders as he dropped the ballistic evidence in Art's hand, "No go."

The two men considered each other's eyes and a silent message passed: there was a shooter. Art twisted the bit of metal around. It was clear that that slug hadn't been in that tree long.

Chapter Twenty-Two

10:55 A.M. September 18, 1995

Melissa stepped with care on the carpet of Amanda's office aware that Amanda was a woman of dimension and quality and Melissa Franklin wanted to emulate her. That Melissa was young and impressionable hadn't crossed her mind at all, she just simply wanted to be the woman she was meant to be. To date, her modeling had been her father and Sandy's Mother, Meredith. Neither of them were anything like Amanda Burtoni. She had style, and glamour, and well, Melissa couldn't think right now, her mind was taken up by the surroundings she found herself in the moment she stepped through the door. Her eyes sailed around as she smoothed the hem of her cotton print dress, at the same time she clutched the golden heart-shaped pendant around her neck.

"You're here. Good. Sit here Melissa." Amanda swept her hand gracefully in an arc ending with her finger extended toward a high back chair next to a white linen-cloth covered table.

Melissa moved toward the chair and sat. She brought her eyes to the two stemmed glasses standing near a bowl of white roses. Off a little rested a frosted pitcher. "Thank you," Melissa said.

Amanda took her seat and picked up the pitcher. "Would you like some lemonade?"

"Yes, please."

Amanda poured and turned to Melissa, "Honey, your dad asked me to help plan your birthday. I'm thrilled to do that, and thought it would be best to get you involved in the planning. What do you think of that?"

"I don't know."

Amanda picked up a small tray of sandwiches with the crusts cut off and set them in front of Melissa. Then she lifted a small plate painted with roses of every red and pink color an artist could choose, she chose a sandwich and placed it on the plate and set it in front of Melissa.

Amanda's office was very nice, and Melissa let her eyes roam the room, and she was pleased to see that Amanda liked the same color values she liked. Acting the lady very much now, Melissa took the dainty glass up and sipped. "Thank you. I've never seen anything like this before."

The two sat quietly for a moment sipping lemonade and tasting the sandwiches. Finally, Amanda put her sandwich on her tiny plate and turned more fully toward Melissa.

"How do you like the sandwich?"

Melissa smiled back at her and said, "This sandwich is so nice. Mostly around my house, it's 'cook up, dish it out and clean it up.' To take time like this to make everything look so, well, like a picture takes talent. And this sandwich is wonderful. What is it?"

Amanda reached for the plate of sandwiches and moved it closer to Melissa. "It's a deviled ham. I'm glad you like it." Gracefully her hand indicated Melissa should take another.

Melissa reached for a second one and studied it over. "So, you chop up ham and mix it with pickles and onion and mayonnaise? I love that they are so small, one or two bites and you're done." She turned to Amanda as she asked the question.

"That's it in a nutshell." Amanda lifted her sandwich allowing her little finger to circle like a hook. "A proper tea allows you to care for others in a special way. There are pretty dishes, flowers and you dress up. What do you think?"

Melissa furrowed her eyebrows, "it's okay."

"I'd like to pass some ideas I have by you for your approval. But, before I get started with my ideas, let's talk about your ideas for your sixteenth birthday. Do you have any thoughts?"

"No," Melissa shrugged, "I haven't given it any thought." She looked expectantly at Amanda. She lifted her lemonade and sipped, her eyes on Amanda.

"Would you like to have friends over?"

Melissa nodded.

Amanda moved the sandwiches closer to Melissa, "Okay. Let's start there. How many?"

"Well, how many can I have?"

"That's a fair question and one I'll have to run by your Dad." She took another sandwich herself and bit the tip off. She chewed a moment, cleared her mouth and said. "I'll ask him this afternoon. Why don't you give me a list of the friends you'd like to invite and that will give me some idea of what to include?" She took her glass up and drank. Quietly she set the glass back down. "What kind of birthday party would you like?"

Melissa shrugged again, not knowing what she should answer. "I don't know. It's in September and hot. We could have a pool party."

"How would you feel about a high tea party turning into a pool party with lawn games and dance that night under the stars?"

"What's a high tea?" Melissa said.

Amanda grinned and patted her hand. "It's just a fancy meal served in a special way and featuring tea as the beverage. It's something the Queen of England does from time to time."

Melissa picked up her sandwich, "With this kind of food?"

The kid was sharp and that pleased Amanda. She smiled and nodded to Melissa. "Yes, and so much more. Like clotted cream and scones. The menu options are limitless." Amanda shifted her weight and crossed her legs. "What would you like me to call you Melissa? I've heard your dad call you Mel."

Melissa looked at her. "Mel is fine or Melissa, whatever you want. And what shall I call you?"

A surprised look came on Amanda's face, "I guess Amanda works for me."

"Okay," Melissa gazed up at her, "I think a high tea would be fine, I don't know what my friends will think. Are they going to be warned?"

"Warned?" She turned to Melissa, "At what?"

"Well, I don't know what my friends will think about, you know, being all hoity-toity." She curled her little finger, and giggled.

Amanda laughed too. "We've got two weeks to plan this, so if it's okay with you, I'll get started."

124

4:30 P.M. October 1, 1995

The two weeks flew by since Amanda and Melissa met in her office. The day of the party arrived steamy hot, cloudless. No breeze plied the air, and the birds were looking for refreshing water to bathe and drink. Flies filled the air annoying everyone. Laughter and squeals filled the backyard as young bodies ran, jumped and flew into the air to slam into the pool.

Art sat under the shade of a backyard tree, fanning himself watching Amanda work at making sure the party went off as planned. She and Melissa got along well together, and he was heartened to see them working together. Melissa seemed happier since their talk out in the meadow on the coast that night. Art thought about that day, and then turned his thoughts to today.

The day started with them having breakfast at IHOP. Melissa loved the pancakes there, and Art liked the coffee. Amanda seemed to be a good sport and had oatmeal, orange juice, and coffee.

After that, they went home to meet the caterers and have the lawn furniture placed in the backyard pool area. White awnings hovered over white tables, and Amanda saw to it that the most beautiful set of dishes were used. Tiny sandwiches with the crusts cut off waited on fancy plates, and an array of fruits artistically placed added color to the table. Large bouquets of pastel toned flowers decorated the center of each table using Melissa's favorite aquamarine as the contrast color. Amanda had acquired several ornate teapots, and they sat prominently on each table.

The cake had arrived an hour earlier and placed under an arch trellis covered with pink roses. The three-tier cake was a showpiece, and Art wondered what that cost. He'd given her five hundred dollars to work with, and if she'd pulled this all off within that budget, he'd be amazed. Melissa was happy, it showed on her face, in her whole body and how she moved. A woman was making her happy. It was almost a shock for Art to realize that. He knew right then and there that Amanda was the right woman for him and Melissa.

It seemed like a mountain shifted off his shoulders. He sighed and relaxed. Things were coming together in his life. He was glad that he'd met Doc Wexford who was helping him through some tough self-doubts issues and felt relieved that Melissa was better.

Art moved to see the young people playing in the pool. He adjusted his sling, so it didn't pull at his neck.

"Well," Amanda came to sit by him, her eyes on the kids as the party moved into the pool stage of the party timing. "You think they're happy?"

The yelling and screaming and water flying from the pool had Art smiling and shaking his head. "God only knows but, by all evidence, it appears the party is a big success."

"It's been fun Art. It has." Amanda leaned back in the lounge chair relaxing. "They're still children, aren't they? I mean they dress the part of an adult, but their very continence is that of a child, still unsure of themselves. That shy look on their faces and the tentative hand movement is evident. Their bodies haven't matured yet. The young men haven't bulked up."

"Innocence." Art said, "You're looking at innocence." He turned and looked straight at Amanda, his face a mask of concern, "That's exactly what I didn't want Melissa to lose."

"You're afraid she's lost her innocence?"

"Just look at her, can't you see it?"

Amanda studied the girl, "Melissa asked if Sandy could stay the night, I told her I'd ask you."

"They are best friends. Yeah, it's okay." Art thought how nice it would be if Amanda stayed the night too. He didn't even let the idea go beyond his private thoughts. He sat up, "Is there anything you need or want? You must be out on your feet. You've been at it since this morning."

She closed her eyes.

He admired that sweet, peaceful face.

"Not a thing, I am enjoying listening to the kids and sitting here with you." She sighed, "Awe it's such a warm night. The sound of the river is lulling—. You sit out here often?"

His eyes moved around taking in all that she was saying. It is nice here, and it is a happy night. As soon as that thought crossed his mind, he hunted for Melissa.

Art spotted her in the gaggle of kids. Her mouth was wide open in laughter. "Amanda?"

"Hum," she answered.

"Where do you see us going?" Art turned. He wanted to see how she answered this question. So much hinged on her answer.

She opened her eyes, turned her head so that their eyes locked together. "Art, I have not been this content for a long time. I have not belonged as much as I feel I belong with you and Melissa, here, right now." She sat up, her eyes glistening. "I see a lifetime with you. I want to be a part of your life, of Melissa's life."

Art took her hand in his, "Amanda, I see things clearly for the first time in my life. I can't imagine you're not a part of my life and Melissa's—there's on big question I need to ask. Do you want to have children of your own?"

"Yes, I do."

"We'd be getting on if we started a family at our ages."

She nodded her head, "We wouldn't be alone. Lots of people have children in their thirties."

"I'm almost forty-six."

"I know," she said. Amanda sat up and took his hand in hers, "It'll work out. I don't think a family is a whole family without welcoming new members."

Art nodded and turned his head to look more fully at her.

One of the children did a cannonball into the pool, splashing water that sprinkled down on them. "I guess we should quiet them down before this gets out of hand." Art said.

"Let them be for a while," Amanda placed her hand on Art's arm and he sat back.

Chapter Twenty-Three

9 A.M. October 2, 1995

The steaming coffee met Art's lips just as the rental truck pulled up in the driveway. He was glad to see them come on time and he lifted the mug in salute to the two men as they stepped to the ground. They were there to remove the rental furniture and the umbrellas, the large table and the folding chairs, the dishes and the glasses, cups and saucers. Art watched them clear away the remains of the party and at the end one man handed Art a form to sign.

He walked them back to the van and waved a goodbye. As they were pulling out of the driveway, a woman's backside came into view. She hovered over the interior backseat of the cab parked at the curb in front of his house. A curvy leg stretched, and he couldn't help but look. She hauled out a small crate. At the same time, the driver worked at unloading three suitcases from the trunk. Art was more than interested.

His eyebrows wrinkled, and his expression turned into one of curiosity. He stood there in the empty driveway. Finally, the woman turned toward him. "Arthur! I certainly didn't expect you to meet me at the curb."

He blinked, his eyes went wide, and his mouth hung open. He managed, "Evelyn?" Art's gaze went from painted face to her black pumps in the blink of an eye.

"Yes darling, it's your Evie!"

Her small feminine hands fluttered as she spoke. Everything about Evelyn was animated. Her short, tight, black skirt pulled wrinkles across her hips as she moved.

"Evelyn?"

"Yes, dear man." She said glaring straight at Art. She stood by the suitcases and the crate sitting on the sidewalk, the driver of the taxi waiting. Suddenly she closed the distance between them and planted a kiss right on Art's gapping mouth then patted his cheek with cold fingers. "You don't seem happy to see me," she said, backing away setting her mouth in a pout and giving him a petulant look.

"I didn't know you were coming."

Her short and springy haircut sailed out as she turned this way and that. "Oh, my. I guess I got here before my letter." Her hand flapped toward him and down as though to dismiss, "Well, never mind, it's no matter. I'm here now, and we can go on from here. Where is she?"

"Where is who? Melissa?" Art was off balance and trying to get his mind around the fact that Evelyn was standing in his driveway. "She's inside. We had a late night last night. We celebrated her sixteenth birthday, and it went late. She's got a girlfriend over, and they are in the kitchen making pancakes."

"Art," she swung toward the taxi driver, "pay the man. I'll be inside," she pointed at the house that seemed connected to the driveway, and Art nodded indicating that it was his house.

He turned to the taxi driver and wondered what the heck was happening. Evelyn went inside his house as he walked over to the driver and paid the sizeable bill. This weekend was beginning to get expensive. He picked up the crate and walked it to the porch and came back for the suitcases. It took him three trips to get them up to the doorway.

Art found all three women in the kitchen. He noticed the shocked look on Sandy's face, as she seemed paused in time with a fork in her hand. Her mouth was open as she plastered her wide-open eyes on Evelyn.

Evelyn's arms opened wide as she stood in the kitchen near the island. "I thought it time you met your mother. So here I am Melissa, in the flesh."

Art walked quickly to Melissa's side and said, "Honey, this is your mother." Art felt the room go silent as Evelyn was introduced and Melissa took in the information. No one seemed to breathe and finally embarrassment filled the air.

Melissa put the spatula down, extended her hand, "How do you do?"

Evelyn smiled broadly, "Get over here. Well, I understand you are celebrating your sixteenth birthday." She leveled her eyes on her daughter. "My, but you did get Art's red hair, didn't you?"

Melissa grabbed a strand of her hair and looked at Evelyn unsure what to think.

"Never mind, I'm here now, and I can rectify all that."

Sandy's eyes had stayed on Evelyn in her curiosity. They now shot to Melissa's face and sailed over to Art's.

Art was beginning to remember how this woman worked, always getting her way. He wondered now how he could ever have seen anything in her. He remembered he was young. He stepped between Melissa and Evelyn, cutting off her view of Melissa. "Melissa is just fine the way she is."

She moved around Art as though he was a feather to be brushed aside. "There's always room for improvement. Every woman knows that. Am I right or what?" She picked up Melissa's hair, some on both sides of her head in each of her hands as though weighing the hair.

Melissa, her mouth shut tight didn't move a muscle while her eyes were riveted on her mother's face.

Evelyn lost interest in her hair and took a step back. "You're going to be tall like me dear. Good." She turned from Melissa to Art. "What in the world did you do to your arm?" And in the next breath, she said, "Where are my things?"

Art turned toward the doorway, "They are on the porch."

"Well, let's not have that, get them in here. Where shall I stay?" She looked from one to the next, ignoring Sandy completely.

Art managed to collect himself and finally said, "We can put you up in the spare bedroom." He turned to Melissa, "Can you get her some sheets and towels? You know what she needs." Art turned to Evelyn, "You'll have to make your room up yourself as you can see I'm not able to help you right now."

"Not a problem, just show me the way, Oh!" She rushed from the room and came back carrying the crate. She extracted a fluffy whiteness with big dark eyes. "Happy Birthday Melissa," she placed the puppy in Melissa's arms, "What are you going to name her?"

Art couldn't believe his eyes. His mouth gaped. He'd never allowed an animal in their home as their lives had been too hectic. He and Melissa were rarely home, and a puppy or kitten just didn't work out. He'd have to cut this off at the pass. What was Evelyn thinking? Before he could say a word, Melissa sailed across the floor to Sandy. They cradled the puppy, kissing her and falling in love. Art hung his head. There are too many women in this kitchen.

"Melissa, we have to talk about this." Art took a stand. It appeared clear from the start that none of them heard a word he said.

Evelyn shut him down over speaking in a voice that grew louder with each syllable, "Art you can't take my birthday gift from my daughter. That's just cruel."

The puppy had that sweet broad-eyed look with curly hair and floppy ears. Melissa was sweet-talking the animal when she stopped, looked up at Evelyn and asked, "What kind of dog is this?"

"It's a mix of poodle and terrier. She'll be a small dog. Isn't she so cute?" Evelyn reached and caressed the puppy's head. "Well, have you decided? What's her name going to be?"

Melissa held the pup out from her, made her lips stick out as though to kiss her. She spoke baby talk to the puppy that looked back at her with such love, "Her name is Daisy." She turned to Sandy and held the puppy for her to love and pet. The two girls were deeply into the pup, and Art just stood there lost, his shoulders drooping, the last sip of coffee stone cold.

Finally, he found his voice, "Evelyn, let's go into my office and have a talk." He took her by the elbow, and she turned keeping her eyes on Melissa and the pup. "I'll be just a minute, honey. Then we can get me set up. Take good care of Daisy." Art held tightly to her elbow and pushed her to his office. His eyes shone with fire.

"What the hell do you think you're doing? How can you come waltzing in here, take over and disrupt our lives?" Art moved like a cat around his office. He could feel her eyes were on him the whole time, saw the cunningly grin. She could care less. He saw that, and it inflamed him.

She took in her breath and said. "Live with it. You exist in a fine house and by the looks of it... You survive well. You haven't done that on your measly salary. You

133

enjoy this lifestyle because of the money I've poured in all these years. So, if I decide to come and see my daughter and to give her a gift you will have nothing to say about it." She, like a cocky rooster came up on her toes and glared into his eyes for effect and delivered, "You got that?"

It was true. He couldn't live on the river's edge in Lodi on his salary alone. Her words cut and hurt. He was trying so hard to find his feet again, feel good about himself. He'd done that with Amanda. Now he was rethinking. He enjoyed the police force. It fit him. The pay wasn't great, but the helping other people suited him. He was good at his job. What else could he do? Art adjusted his sling again.

"You got that? Did you hear me?" There came a force into her gaze as she defied him.

He glared at her. "You can't come in here and take over. This is my turf. You show up unannounced and think you can run things because you and I have an agreement. That agreement ends when Melissa becomes an adult and not one minute before. I expect you to honor it to the letter."

"I'm here now, let's see what Melissa wants."

"There's nothing to do with Melissa, Evelyn. It's what I say."

"We'll see."

Chapter Twenty-Four

9 A.M. October 2, 1995

Art's eyes were blurry from lack of sleep. He yawned long and hard, worked his dry and pasty mouth. He stumbled down the stairs and into the kitchen. Scooped enough ground coffee into the filter, added water, and pushed the red button. A grumbling sound started right up and brought the fragrance of French Roast sailing into the room. He sniffed the fragrance deeply as he pulled down his preferred mug and waited.

He poured the mug an inch from the top and filled the rest of the space with half and half. To top it off, he stirred one teaspoon of sugar into the creamy mix. Art experienced the steam like a sauna to his nose and cheek. He circled his lips around the mug and drank the top. He waited then frowned at the mug. The coffee didn't help this morning. He couldn't imagine his life being any more messed up. His mood continued to decline as the clock clicked off the minutes. He stepped out the back door and sauntered to the boat dock.

Evelyn had arrived like a tornado. She'd taken over their lives. How long would she be here? He hadn't yet asked. Why was he not asking that question? And, is it good for Melissa to have her here? He didn't know. He stood on his dock watching five mallard ducks and a white goose sail past his boat's stern quacking as they went, their world in order, or so it seemed to Art. I'd like to jump in and paddle away with you. The large goose turned his head and eyed Art, as though to say, you'll have to clear that with me, buddy.

The coffee did seem to be opening his brain cells. At last! He turned and looked back at the house. It was quiet as though slumbering with four females sleeping in this morning; Melissa, her best friend Sandy, Evelyn, and a fleabag. What was the name, ooh, yeah Daisy?

What was Evelyn thinking to bring a puppy with her and just dump it on me? What kind of trouble would that pup cause?

He sipped his coffee. He hadn't thought of Amanda one time since Evelyn showed up. Why was that? Because Evelyn's a steamroller, it would be much better when Evelyn packed up and left town.

I don't want her here. He chuckled. She needs to go and the sooner, the better. His fingers circled the slug in his pocket that Murphy dug out of the tree. Would Melissa be in danger? The thought dogged him. Out of nowhere, he thought of Yvonne Tango, Inc. His shoulders came up as he saw his path forward.

Art was pissed, that someone was shooting at him and that the guys at the station didn't believe it for a minute. He would pay his favorite P.I., Yvonne, a little visit and soon. It was not something he wanted to talk about over the phone.

He turned as the back door opened, and Melissa came outside in her bathrobe carrying the pup.

She was baby talking to the little thing again. He looked up to the heavens. Evelyn should have brought a stuffed dog He watched as Melissa picked the wiggling puppy up and cuddled it close to her cheek. She turned and headed back into the house. He raised his chin, his lips set tightly together, his eyes narrowing as he reasoned. It is not going to be easy getting rid of that mutt.

When Art went back inside everyone was up and doing their thing. They ate breakfast and went about their day and Art closed his office door behind him. He spent hours poring over the recent photos again, fully aware that he'd need to close that file if the fire-horse, Evelyn, came marching into his office, he didn't trust Evie one bit.

The clocked ticked off 1 p.m. as he grabbed the phone on the first ring, "Good, Walt, I'm home, come on over." Walt told him he was out front of his house so Art walked out of this office, and out to the curb to join him. "Hey, I wanted to tell you that Melissa's Mother is here and she brought a puppy for Melissa. You can wipe that smile off your face for starters," Art said. "Come on in." Walt said he'd just come to give Art a file and that he needed to get back to the office. After a moment he said he would come in. Art smiled, he knew Walt was curious about Evelyn. The two went into his office, and he closed the door. "Can I get you anything?"

"No, thanks." Walt took a chair close to Art's desk chair and handed Art a file. "We've got lab reports on the trajectory of the shots."

Art looked pages and pages of information over. "We've got a sniper. The son-of-a-bitch was sitting in a vehicle right in front of the school. The victim was walking away from her sister's house. Probably mad. She didn't see anything coming her way. She was just hurrying along and bam!" Art turned to Walt, "We got anything?"

Walt shook his head. "Nada."

Art nervously worked at his mustache, "Then this is personal."

"Yeah, that's what I think too. So far, we've come up empty on everyone we've interviewed.

"Then go back to the beginning. Start over again and this time, ask some different questions."

Walt nodded agreement. "We do know that the shooter used military ammo."

"Yeah, I figured that out by the wound. So that should narrow the field considerably. Someone trained by the military, maybe even someone trained as a sniper. It shouldn't be too hard to find that person from her field of acquaintances." Art sat back in his chair and looked at his old friend. "You need to get someone on the ballistic evidence from the line of flight. It's probably in one of the houses on Oak Street. You're going to get this perp."

Walt smiled and nodded. "I already did that. We have the evidence bagged and tagged. I hope so. Unless..."

"What?"

"Unless this was a contract killing, if it were, it wouldn't matter what questions I ask. We're going down the same garden path."

"Not necessarily." Art reached into his front pocket and tossed the spent slug to Walt who, although clearly surprised by Art's movement, caught the missile in mid-air. "Murphy and I figured out where the slug went that was fired at me the other night. That came from a tree across the river. I'm still looking for the other one."

Walt looked at the shell, moved it around in his hand studying it a long moment. "Well, this isn't military ammo."

"No, so I think it is safe to say it's not the same shooter, which means to me that it's not a contract killing. It's personal."

Walt stood, "Well, I'd like to stay, but I've got work to do so I'll get along. Maybe I can wrangle up a dinner invite and meet Evelyn before she leaves."

Art nodded, and accompanied Walt to his car. He stood in his driveway watching as Walt turned the corner and went out of view and, as he did, another shot slammed past him. He reacted immediately dropping to the ground, his one good arm taking the brunt of the weight, his knees bumping into the cement hard enough to bruise. He was out in the open and nowhere to go to save himself from ambush.

Nothing happened.

There were no more shots. After a long time, he got up. He was the only one outside. Art moved to a parked car and glanced inside for anyone hiding. He moved to another vehicle and did the same. It was empty. He moved to the houses and checked the bushes. When Art finished he had been on every surrounding property and nothing seemed out of place.

Someone had their crosshairs on him. Could someone be shooting at him from a window? Would they have been able to shut the window and he not hear it? He had to think this through. He was about to go back into the house when the girls, all of them accept the pup, come rushing out of the house.

"Dad, oh, Dad." Melissa ran to him her face glowing, her eyes sparkling. "We are going with Mom."

Oh, it's Mom already. When did that happen Art wondered. He nodded and watched as a taxi slid to the curb, and they all jumped in and off they went. He felt glad to have them drive away and out of the target area. "Where...are you going?" The words sailed off happily into the air, unheard by anyone else.

Why didn't I ask? What's wrong with me? It had him ticked off so much so that thinking about someone shooting at him got shoved aside. Sending his mind spinning. He adjusted his sling, the arm still aching from the jolt to the ground. He bit his lip waiting for the pain to subside and while he waited for that his knees stung. He guessed he'd scraped the skin off when he hit the ground. His body was taking one hit after another. One thing he'd noticed was that he was not nearly as agile as he used to be. I am getting old. He closed his eyes and grimaced at the pain from his knee. Getting old! God, don't go there.

Chapter Twenty-Five

2 P.M. October 3, 1995

Art turned into the apron and drove onto the lot. Choosing a spot under a tree it made him happy that the front seat would be shaded while the car was parked. He saw Yvonne's car in its assigned spot. A few other vehicles were parked nearby, but for the most part, this parking lot was empty. That further pleased him knowing that he wouldn't be interfering in Tango Investigation business if he popped in for an unannounced visit.

He pushed hard on the door to releases the suction the weather-stripping produced. When it was half-open, he called out, "Yvonne?" The heavy smell of pine met him as he proceeded. Yvonne must have mopped the floor recently. He moved past the front desk now empty and cleaned off except for a phone, notepad, and pen. Art came to a post. He wrapped his hand around it as he looked around and to the right. Yvonne's salt and pepper head raised up from behind her desk. Their eyes caught, and he knew she recognized him, "Okay if I come in?"

She nodded a curious look on her features. Her lips were set; her clean face devoid of makeup, her hair combed back from her forehead and her piercing brown eyes merely dots on her face.

He grinned at her, and she spoke, "You said you'd never need my services." Her mouth, lips tightly closed, slid off to the side as though appraising the man before her. "That has to be the reason you're here."

Not much got by her and Art liked that about Yvonne. "That is correct!" Art said slipping into one of the two orange personnel chairs placed across the desk from Yvonne's. "I have learned that I can change my mind on some things." He beamed; a red flush to his face brightened his freckles.

Yvonne put her pen down, sat back as her eyes hooded over and her lips curled. Never known for being talkative, she laced her fingers together and waited.

Art reached into his pocket, pulled the spent slug out and tossed it to her. She followed its flight with her eyes and swiftly caught the flying missile as it entered her airspace. She stared at it and turned her head so that he saw only her right eye. The look told Art she wanted more information from him and not to feed her a load of crap.

He nodded toward the hand that held the evidence, "That was dug out of a tree across the river from my house. It was shot at me."

She seemed interested. However, Art knew Yvonne was not an easy read. He waited for her to say something. Finally, it came.

"And this should concern me how?"

Art looked down at the floor; she wasn't going to make this easy. He chewed his mustache again, oblivious of his habit. "The guys don't believe I've been shot at. They think I am making it up probably to stay connected with the department since I am on disability and can't go to work." Art tensed up and sat straighter as his expression changed to one of despair. "I don't know if I am the only target. There's my daughter, Melissa. Her girlfriend

Sandy spends a lot of time at our house. And, Melissa's mother, Evelyn, just showed up." He spread his hand out raising his wrist and extending the fingers to express his next words. "I don't know which way to look or who to protect." He fingered the sling and her eyes focused on the green cloth.

"You want me to find the shooter?" She brought her eyes to his. The room went silent as they studied each other. It became a staring contest to see who would blink first. After a long moment, Yvonne dropped her shoulders. "I shouldn't do this. It's against my better judgment." She reached for her notepad. "Spill, give me everything."

Art sighed and settled into his seat. "I was taking the trash out. I didn't look at the time, but it had to be about seven as it was dim outside. I was almost to the cans when I heard the shots zing past me."

"Shots?"

Art nodded, "There were two."

"You have only one slug?" She rolled the spent shell around in her hand.

"I haven't found the second shot."

She nodded. "Who would want to take a shot at you?" She looked down at her desktop waiting for him to answer.

He shrugged his shoulders in answer and his eyes widened, "I have no clue."

"I'm sure there are plenty of people who might want to shoot you. I've given it thought myself." She twisted around in her chair and looked squarely at him. "Anyone just get out of prison? Maybe some family member righting a wrong? Some old friend wanting to get even?"

He shook his head. "No. Nothing that I can think of."

"Well, what kind of detective are you? You waltz in here after..." Her eyes fixed on him in such a searing stare, "...four years ago you said that I couldn't make a Private Investigator Business work."

"What can I say? I was wrong." Art held his hand out in supplication.

She pouted her lips and looked him up and down, nodded and said, "I'll get on it and find the son-of-a-bitch." She brought her eyes to his. It's gonna cost," She looked straight at him.

Art sat forward and reached around for his back-pocket. "I expected that."

"You're on disability?"

He nodded.

"Well, I'll keep it reined in as much as I can."

Art pulled the envelope from his pocket. He'd withdrawn a thousand dollars from the bank on his way over. It waved up and down as he directed it toward her and let it fall to the desk in front of her. "That should get you started."

Yvonne looked down at the envelope, picked it up and raised the flap. She pulled the hundreds out and fanned them. She nodded, "This should cover coffee and donuts." Yvonne's gaze drifted up settling on his, "Just an observation, this person is not a very good shot. I mean, if they shot at you twice and missed. It looks to me like you're porking up and a pretty good sized target."

"Thanks a bunch. I was shot at three times on two occasions. I was shot at just a little bit ago today in front of my house when I was saying goodbye to some people. The shot was fired just after the taxi pulled away from the curb."

Yvonne's head twisted, her eyes narrowed and pierced, giving her a look of analysis. "You are standing at the curb, and you didn't see anyone?"

"I didn't. I looked around right away."

"Anything happening in the department? Any old memories sticking their head up now with a vengeance on their minds?"

"Walt's got a homicide, looks like a sniper, appears personal."

"This isn't military ordnance."

Art looked at the hand she held up. "No, it isn't."

Yvonne squared herself in her seat, placed her elbows on her desk picked up her pen and rotated it slowly; "You don't see a connection?"

Art's fingers touched his lips; he brought them away and tapped them gently twice. He shook his head, "None."

She sat formally in her chair, her expression serious. Her eyes moved around as she thought, and her head nodded to her internal conversation. Finally, she stood, walked around the desk and gave Art her hand. He took it, and she grinned. They had been friends while she was on the force and Art had always liked her.

"You were right to bring this to me."

He looked her over to see how she was getting along and was pleased to see that she seemed healthy, maybe even rested. "How's your back?" Art said.

Yvonne grimaced and rolled her tongue in her jaw, "I have my good days and my bad. Don't have a clue what it's going to be until after I have the first cup of coffee in the morning."

Art grinned and laughed "Don't I understand that." He remembered how gruff she could be until she had that first cup in the morning. It was noted around the department that you didn't want to cross her if she hadn't had her caffeine. He couldn't think of anything else to say to her and she never was one to carry on a long conversation. She was the strong silent type. Their conversation was over, and they both understood that so together they walked toward the front door, and Art

M.L. WEATHERINGTON
noticing the front desk chair empty he turned to Yvonne, "Where's your girl Friday?"

She swung her gaze to the empty desk, "Lessie? She's out on the job."

Chapter Twenty-Six

11:05 A.M. October 4, 1995

Art slipped this key in the lock and opened the front door. The house was dead silent as he stepped across the threshold. It dawned on him that there was a puppy somewhere in the house, and he'd better find it and make sure it gets outside and soon. As he moved through the rooms, he saw the mess left behind from the girls getting ready to go this morning.

Where did they go? That he had no information on Melissa or her whereabouts pissed him off. How could he let himself get so embroiled in what was happening that important stuff like Melissa seemed to be slipping through the cracks? There's the cage. His hand wrapped around the handle and Daisy whined.

Art walked out of Melissa's room, down the stairs and into the kitchen heading for the back door. He moved outside and placed the cage on the ground. Slowly he opened the cage door, and the pup bounded out, loping happily over the grass and stopping to squat.

Art felt pleased that he'd managed to dodge the potty problem for the time being. If he hadn't said it before, he'd make sure it now would be the new rule of Art Franklin. No doggie is pottying inside the house. He leaned over, scooped up the fluffy ball of fur and held it to his chest. He opened his mouth to explain to the pup the house rules when he heard...

"Art!"

He spun around and grinned broadly, "Amanda."

She strolled to his side and let her hand pet the pup. She peered up into Art's eyes.

Art bent pressing his lips on hers feeling the tender warmth of their connection.

Through the kiss, she asked in monotone, "Where'd the pup come from?"

"Come on," he leaned down and placed the pup back inside the cage, "let's go inside, and I'll explain everything to you. Not that I know all that much, but I will share what I do know."

Amanda let her hand slip around his hurt arm by his elbow and walked side by side with him to the back door. There she opened it and let him, and the cage, enter first. He put it down on the floor.

"The morning after you had left, I was saying goodbye to the caterer. As his truck pulled away, a cab stopped at the curb and out of the car comes Evelyn Colby—, Melissa's mother."

He pointed to the pup, "She brought that ball of fur as a birthday gift, along with her three suitcases." Art pointed upstairs, his voice escalated, and he yelled in a run-on sentence, "She has ensconced herself in our guest bedroom." He sat down heavily on a kitchen chair. "Sit."

Amanda sat almost as in a dream, her mouth open as she took in the information. Art ran his good hand over the tabletop watching as his fingers worked their way from left to right. When he'd finished, his voice had lowered, and he'd calmed. He sheepishly looked up, "I have no idea how long she's going to stay or what she has in mind. She's been a powerhouse since she got here."

He waved his hand in the air, and her eyes followed its movement, then returned to his eyes. "I'm thinking how hard it's going to be to get rid of that mutt." They both looked at the cage. "I never allowed a cat or dog or bird for that matter, because I just don't have the time to take care of a creature. Until now Melissa's been too young to trust. And our lives are busy. We are hardly home."

"What about the horse?" Amanda questioned.

"Midnight doesn't live here. That's my concern, I've got to pick up and take off at a moment's notice, and you just can't do that with a pet. They need care."

"I agree with you there," she said. She looked around the kitchen at the general mess but didn't mention the disorder. "Where are they now?"

Art blinked his eyes. "You know, I haven't a clue." He scratched his head running his fingers like a large comb setting his hair in place again. "They all piled into a cab and took off. Melissa was so excited; she called 'Bye Dad' to me as the door slammed shut and the cab took off." He scanned his watch as his face took on an expression of alarm, "Six hours ago."

Art worried about the shots fired at him. He didn't want to tell Amanda about the threat to his life believing that he, and only he, was the target. He worried that she might be mistaken for him by this would-be killer. He had Yvonne and Tango, Inc., on his mind hoping that they would get to the bottom of this shooter business fast. He had Evelyn and her impact on Melissa heavy on his mind, and little room for anything else including the pain from his useless arm. Amanda's warning expression was lost on him.

Melissa is clearly taken by her so how can I compete with that? My daughter is meeting her mother for the first time and on her sixteenth birthday.

Amanda cleared her throat. He turned to look at her, "The mailman handed me this." She extended an envelope. "You don't know where Melissa been for the last six hours?"

Art tore the envelope open immediately. "Shit." He stood and moved away from the island, turning away from her and bending his body in abject anger he said, "Shit, shit, shit!"

"What's wrong?"

He didn't answer. Then he turned toward her, "I didn't pay my car insurance on time, and I have a fee connected to the renewal. He melted deeper into his chair, "That seems to be the way things are going lately just plain out of control. And now with Evelyn here I don't know, she just came in here and took over. I have no idea where they are or what they are doing." Seething anger filled his features, and he breathed heavily.

Amanda leaned toward him and placed her hand on his arm. "Do you trust Evelyn to have Melissa's best interests at heart?"

He nodded.

"You believe that if someone were to come into the room to do harm to Melissa, her mother would step in between and stop the assault?"

"I do."

"Well, then let's start worrying about something when there's something to worry about. Okay? Call your insurance company. Have you ever been late before?"

"No."

"Talk to them. They'll waive the fee. Would you like a beer?" Amanda moved toward the refrigerator, opened the door and removed two bottles of Bud. She held it up making sure he would have one with her.

"I will," he said beaming as he reached out for the chilled bottle. As soon as Amanda opened it, he took it from her. Art lifted the cold glass to his lips and let the icy

150

liquid cascade down his throat. He took a deep breath as he removed the bottle a couple of inches from his mouth, and she did the same. "Boy that hits the spot."

They were about to settle into the conversation when the front door opened, and all hell broke loose with talking and feet shuffling over the tile floor heading toward the kitchen. Melissa's voice carried excitement with her as she hurried, "Dad?"

"In here honey," he called setting the beer on the counter. Amanda did the same, and they watched the doorway for Melissa.

She rushed into the room, "Hi Amanda. Dad you're not going to believe this." Her face flushed a bright red causing the freckles to pop, her eyes sparkled with excitement and her words ran together. "Oh, Dad. I know what I want to be now. It's all so clear." She turned to her mother who entered the room. Evelyn fussed with three large shopping bags, tossing them upon the counter.

Evelyn's appearance had changed Art noticed. She'd been to the beauty parlor and now had her hair even shorter. Streaked, they call it he thought. Should I trust her? Does she have Melissa's best interests at heart? I don't know.

"Here," Evelyn said, "you'd better take these upstairs, so they don't mess up the kitchen. It's getting tight in here."

Mel grabbed up the packages and ran upstairs as Evelyn finished moving around the room. She took center stage and ended up right across from Amanda. Evelyn's brows arched and a cynical stare froze on Amanda. "And who are you?" She leveled her head tipping her chin downward so that it appeared she was staring with both her eyes from just under the upper eyelids. Her freshly polished French manicured nails pointed directly at Amanda.

Amanda stiffened, understanding that Evelyn meant to be the House Bouncer, ready to flex her muscles.

Amanda glanced at Art. His jaw dropped, and he stared at Evelyn but said nothing.

She turned back to Evelyn and said evenly, "I am Amanda Burtoni."

Evelyn's nose tipped up just a bit, "You're the girlfriend?" She stated as she moved around the table to get a better look at Amanda.

Amanda straightened her back even more.

"You bleach your hair?"

Amanda's eyes smoldered. "You dye yours?"

Art stood, "Amanda, I'd like to introduce Melissa's mother, Evelyn." He turned, "Evelyn, Amanda. Make nice!" His voice was firm, and both women quieted as they kept their eyes leveled on each other, a trust issue lingered between them that grew silently and out of sight like cancer.

After a long moment, Amanda said, "Nice to meet you."

Evelyn smiled and said in a boring monotone, "I'm sure."

"Dad?" Melissa's voice carried down the stairs and into the kitchen.

He yelled back, "Coming," he turned to the women; this better not turn into a catfight. They looked like a good match, but he didn't want anything to happen to either of them. Dropping the thought he headed up to Melissa.

Evelyn and Amanda stood as though rooted, sizing each other up. Amanda started, "It must be nice meeting Melissa after all these years."

"What's that supposed to mean?" Evelyn's eyes hardened shoving any room for nonsense aside then narrowed as she leveled them on Amanda.

Amanda shrugged her shoulders, "I meant she's a lovely girl, and it must be nice to meet your daughter."

Evelyn made a circle of the table and stopped close to Amanda, meaning to intimidate her.

The sweet, gentle soul that she was had more steel in her than the blonde hair, soft clothing, and fancy heels portrayed. She rose to her full height and became a formidable wall of a woman.

Evelyn, three inches taller said as she looked down, "You think you're going to move in here. You think you're going to marry daddy?"

Amanda's eyes went wide. "Art and I are exploring the possibility of a relationship."

"Is that what old people call it these days. Exploring the opportunity?" Her eyes were on fire now, and she latched onto Amanda's arm, holding firm. I'm here now, and, Sweet Cheeks, I'm not going anywhere."

Amanda called on all her training to remain disconnected from this brawl that simmered between them. She held her hands at her side. "Remove your hand."

"You a boozer?" Evelyn asked pointing to the two bottles of beer.

Amanda let her eyes go to the bottles. She shrugged as though Evelyn's remark didn't even need an answer.

Evelyn's stare burned into her. "Look here, girlie. He's mine. I am the mother, and that has more weight than a come-to-late-to-the-party old hag that is trying to look young with too much makeup and a really bad, and I mean bad, bleach job."

Amanda took her breath, "You've talked this over with Art? You've worked things out between the two of you?"

"There's nothing to work out. It is the way it is, and it always will be. He's never married. Doesn't that tell you anything? So take your flirty shit out of here and stay out of our lives."

153

"What makes you think you can push me out that easily?"

Evelyn looked long and hard at Amanda and sneered, "Art couldn't have lived here in this house if it wasn't for me. I footed the bill all these years to help support our..., well— shall we just call her, our accident? Did he tell you how we were? Did he? I bet not. Well, I can kindle that fire any time I want. And I think Melissa is all the leverage I need. So it's been so nice meeting you. Have a nice life." She had risen over Amanda and seemed to press down on her even though they were inches apart. "So get the hell out."

Amanda rose; leaving the beer bottle next to Art's and picked up her purse. She walked to the front door and out.

Chapter Twenty-Seven

11:15 A.M. October 4, 1995

Art entered Melissa's room as she pulled a pair of pants from a dark blue bag with white labeling he'd never seen before. She spread this item out on her bed and added it to several others.

"What's up?" he asked taking in all of the new clothing.

Melissa turned to him and gushed. "Oh, Dad this has been the most wonderful birthday ever."

The look in her eyes seemed different, and Art tipped his head as though to question what he witnessed. Chills ran up his arm. His little girl had changed, and it seemed her mother made the difference. It scared him in the pit of his stomach, that he may have made a huge mistake raising her alone. He nodded back at her so she would feel he was listening.

How could he ever discourage those feelings in her? He must not; not today, not ever. "That's wonderful, Sweetheart." Before he could ask where they had been today or anything else about their day, she ran on.

"I know what I want to do with my life now Dad. It's so crystal clear!" She bounced around the room and announced, "I'm so excited. Can you believe it, I know what I am going to do the rest of my life...""

He watched and listened, using his training as a cop to listen carefully to everything being said or done and interject nothing until all facts are ascertained.

"Uh-huh?"

She went on and on saying absolutely nothing concrete for Art's ears. He let her continue until he heard the word 'pilot.'

"Did you know Mom is an aviator? Why didn't you ever tell me? Oh, Dad, she is wonderful. We went to Nevada today."

Red flags flew at full mast as the hairs on the back of his arms raised on end. "You went to Nevada?" What in hell was Evelyn thinking?

She rushed on. "To a location where they are making a film, I got to meet Rocky Palatino." She bent her body giving him the expression, "Do you believe this? Rocky Palatino, you know him, Dad?" She slammed her hands into her chest and looked heavenward. "Oh, God, he's better looking in person. I've got to tell Sandy." She smoothed a pair of pants over the edge of the bed and picked up the hem of one of the legs inspecting it carefully before she let it go.

She looked up and straight at him, "I want to be just like her Dad. Did you know that I am old enough to get my pilots license?" She picked up a new pink nightgown and waltzed around the room. "I'm going to fly." She raced back to him, stopping by his side. She looked up into his eyes as he looked down at her, "Do you know what it feels like to leave the ground?"

He stood silently with the fakest pleasant expression while shaking his head.

"It's like..." She searched for her words. "Your stomach stays on the ground while you suddenly go up, and it has to catch up." She swung her body, lifting her arms like wings. "You are way up off the ground before that happens. It's a funny feeling Dad." Her eyes, though directed at him, were not seeing him as they focused beyond him. "We flew over the clouds. They were beautiful. And, the land below looks like a quilt from up there."

Art took in some air, seeming to get some balance, and his senses began coming back. At least that was the way he thought. She's okay and home. I need to change the subject and get this freight train derailed as soon as possible. "Did she buy you all these new clothes?"

Melissa swung her head toward the bed. "She took me shopping in a boutique in Reno. God, what a day. I am tired, going to get a shower. Are we going to get some dinner? I'm starving."

Art nodded, "I can barbecue something, and we can eat leftovers from the party."

"Great, ask Amanda to stay."

"I will." Art backed out of her room, happy that she was so content. All the terror she had acquired from the McNamare affair seemed to have disappeared.

His memories seemed to weight heavier. Their quiet talk in the makeshift stable area that evening over on the coast helped. This day appeared to be just the right medicine for her. That made Art happy but, in a way, it seemed to him like a whole new load of crap was happening, and he didn't have any idea how to handle it now.

He couldn't complain. If Evelyn has helped Melissa get over a trauma that was destroying her life, that is a good thing. Flying her to another state? Now that's just too much, Evie and I are going to have to talk about boundaries. Art started down the stairs, and as he walked into the kitchen he saw Amanda's beer sitting by his and her chair empty. He looked at Evelyn's back as she drank a glass of water.

M.L. WEATHERINGTON

"Where's Amanda?"

Evelyn shook her head as she took a glass of water from her lips. "She said she had to leave."

"Oh, okay," he said, walking over to the counter he snatched up his beer. Art took a swallow and held the bottle chest high between them. His eyes narrowed as they found hers, "We need to talk."

"Yes, we do."

Her masterful voice gave Art a sense of immediate fear that he might just be losing Melissa to Evelyn. He plowed on, certain that he had to to get some order back into their lives. "You took Melissa from this house today without asking me, or telling me what you were planning, or where you were going. You took her out of state."

Evelyn leveled her eyes on his. They were close to the same height, and Art had never intimidated her and still didn't today. "Your point?"

"You can't just take off like that without informing me. That's the point."

A sinister smile grew around her mouth. "Oh." A long moment came between each word. "Yes... I... can!"

Art's eyes widened. He took in air and red bloomed over his cheeks, "No, you can't. Melissa's a child, and you cannot take her out of state." He turned his body as though to block something.

She picked up Amanda's beer, wiped it off with her sleeve and lifted it as a salute. "She's home safe and sound so shut your hole up, Artie."

"Don't call me Artie." He put his beer on the counter. "You came waltzing in here as though you owned the place."

"I've paid for this place each month for years. Don't you think that gives me the right to enjoy my daughter?" Her eyes flared as she spoke, her bottle went on the table with a clunk. Her voice rose in volume, "Don't stand there like some dumb bunny. You couldn't fight your way out of a wet paper bag if you had to. So, as I see it, Melissa has only one parent worth anything right now, and that's me."

Right this minute he wanted to pack her bags for her and toss her fine arse to the curb. "What are you saying?" He followed her as she walked out of the room.

"I'm going up for a shower. What's for dinner? I would think Melissa's hungry, and I know I am." With that, she turned a cold shoulder on him and sailed out of the room.

To Art, the room felt bigger, peaceful without her in it, but messy. He looked around. Where should he start, with dinner, or cleaning this up? He shoved the counter to clean off a section so he could get something from the freezer. He'd have to thaw some chicken. There were some pieces frozen in one of the zip bags. His hand pulled the freezer open, and he shoved items around until he spotted the bag he wanted. There would be enough for three people, maybe four. He put the chicken on the counter and turned to the phone.

Amanda picked up on the first ring, but her voice sounded funny to him. "Hey, I'm fixing chicken and going to put out leftovers how about coming and eating with us?"

She sounded so distant and almost declined, but in the last moment, she agreed to come over.

Art busied himself; one handed to getting everything out of the refrigerator. He ran the frozen chicken through the microwave on defrost. All the work was slow going for him, and he couldn't help but think about what Evelyn has just said to him about him being a useless parent. It hurt. And, there lingered an element of truth that stung like the prick of a knife tip. He wanted his old self back, the confidence, the sharp critical thinking. God, he can't think sometimes.

He walked out to the barbecue pit next to the swimming pool and lifted the lid. He grimaced. It had not been cleaned up from Melissa's birthday. The crud began to flake off as the wire brush caught on something and screeched in protest. Shining stainless steel peaked through in places, and Art knew he'd be working on this for a while. The hum of the pool filter added to his scraping sound. When he stopped for a rest, he could hear the rustling of the leaves in the trees lining the river and the sound of the boat bumping against the wharf. It was his home and had been since he bought it so many years ago. He turned and looked at the back of the house. The wood looked dry to him. He'd have to check that out. Probably the house needed painting. The idea was not well received. He didn't want to paint the house himself, and he didn't want to hire anyone right now, and he sure as heck didn't need another problem.

Amanda came into the backyard area and joined him standing back a foot or two instead of coming for an embrace. Art knew when he looked at her that something was wrong. "Hey."

She made a slight, sickly movement of her lips. Her eyes stayed steady, unsmiling.

Art stepped toward her, and she took a step back, "What's up?"

"I think we need to step back. Give this new..." Amanda paused as though she couldn't think what to say. "...this new ripple some time to work its way out."

"What new ripple? What are you talking about?"

She looked down, her voice lost as she spoke to the ground, "I think you need to give yourself some time, and Melissa needs time." When she brought her gaze up into his eyes, he knew. That sinking feeling that comes when you know you've lost something you wanted. She began walking to the driveway and worked her way down to the sidewalk where she stopped. He'd followed, carrying the heavy bristled brush, mutely devoid of anything useful to say. He placed the handle of the brush in his rib area by his bad arm and clasped tightly, the pain intense. Gently he took her hand, his heart pounding. What could he say?

He knew, the chill prickling his arms as he looked into her eyes. It was there in her eyes. She's done. Walking away, leaving what they had.

Why? Didn't she feel the same as he? How can she just give up? Tears ached to fill his eyes; he held them back, stealing his back, but wanting to tell her he knew there was a place for them, that this was their time. We are a couple. He wanted them to be a couple.

She's pulling back and my chance to heal this is slamming shut. He stood mute.

Why can't I find the words, be brilliant when I need to be? Tears welling as she made three tiny backward steps, her eyes still on his, aware his hand and hers were slipping apart, the warmth and softness of her ebbing away, the tips of their fingers at a final point, sluggishly releasing.

It was as though a weight lifted at that precise moment and his body rocked. Wanting that connection again, Art fought his desire to reach out, take her hand in his to hold on forever. She was leaving, and he mustn't stop her.

Now they were at the curb, almost to her car.

"No," he screamed in his head, "Don't go," but he remained silent. "She's a grown woman; she should make her own decisions. And if she doesn't want me... We have something together. You're a beautiful bird and must be set free to find your way back to me. Someday we'll come together again." All these thoughts he tucked down inside wanting so desperately to say something brilliant. Finally, knowing she was about to leave he managed.

"I love you."

She turned to face him. "I know."

"Amanda?" The word pleaded as the last 'a' was sounded.

He saw her opening the car door. watching as she paused a moment before turning to him. She held her head high, tears glistening, "Take care." Amanda sat in the car and started it up. At that moment, she drove away leaving him with his head down.

Evelyn allowed the drape to drop back in place. The grin beginning as a cunning glint flared in her eye. A picture is worth a thousand words. The bitch had seen her standing in the window, with a towel wrapped around her body and one about her head.

Chapter Twenty-Eight

6:45 A.M. October 5, 1995

Art showered early this morning and now sat at his desk staring at the computer screen needing to know all he could about securing the house. Security doors on the front, back, and garage personnel door. Someone he could trust to come out to the house and install them along with some sort of security system.

The spot on the wall seemed to get darker as he stared at it and thought about Amanda and her sudden departure. Thinking about that right now didn't help the hurt that her walking out caused him. His desk was cleaned off and shone from polish applied just before he sat down to the computer. He liked order, her being gone brought disorder.

Art stopped being OCD at that point. The paint on the walls, under close inspection, needed refreshing. That would make too much of a change right now, and he didn't want anything else to shift off center. Bottom line; everything in its place made him feel confident and competent. He hated hunting for something.

Now he searched for something on the computer using an application that he used at the police department when he wanted an address. He leaned forward, the tension in his neck and upper shoulder areas tightening as his eyes followed the list to the one he wanted. He grabbed a pencil, made a note and closed the program. He folded the paper over and placed it in his pocket.

Art sat back in his chair, rested his head back and found a spot on the ceiling. He listened as music played in an upper room, Melissa's home. This is the sound of home.

Evelyn here complicates everything. She needs to go. He knew he couldn't ask her to leave right now. Melissa's so taken with her. Evelyn is the pied piper, and Melissa completely mesmerized.

His eyes roamed to the right focusing on nothing as he thought. Art tensed as he moved forward in his chair and stiffened his back. His eyes squinted as a thought gelled in his mind. He stood, checked his pockets and found his car keys. Art walked to his office door, locked it behind him and called out, "Melissa?"

She ran to the landing and looked over the rail. Her cheeks were bright pink her eyes shone. She wore that pink nightgown Evelyn bought her yesterday. He grinned at her and said, "I'm going out for a while."

She nodded and sailed back into her room leaving him standing there looking at the emptiness of the landing. I'm feeling a bit like chopped liver he thought to himself. What am I standing here for? Am I not needed here? That didn't sit well with him. It hurt, and he bit his lip with sadness.

Art left the house. He got into the car and backed out. He drove across town to an older neighborhood where the lawns were expansive and filled with coastal redwood trees their trunks massive and the bark craggy, dense, deep, red-black in color. He parked in the driveway and got out following a cobblestone path to the front of the house. The porch, painted shiny gray, had wicker furniture off in the corner ready for relaxing. It was inviting, and Art sighed. He'd like to have a porch, but his house was too new, and they didn't make expansive exteriors anymore.

The lots were smaller in the newer housing tracts these days, the houses so close you could have a conversation with your neighbor window to window. Art rather liked the good old days when the focus on land seemed the priority. He looked at the deep stuffed padded outdoor furniture and imagined sitting there, holding an iced tea and listening to the sounds of that tree as he heard it right now, sighing with the gentle breeze. A bird sang nearby, a joyous sound pleasing to Art.

He knocked, but there was no answer. After a while, he worked his way around back and found Doc Wexford bent over a large wooden table with a table saw and clamps.

An older, potbellied man dug through a pile of wood. His long graying hair was pulled back at the nape of his neck. He had a faded red scarf tied around his sunburned temples and sweat soaked his navy-blue T-shirt.

Art figured him the handyman and he turned his attention to the doc.

Jim twisted toward him, a look of surprise on his face, "How'd you find me?"

Art glanced toward the lawn for a second then leveled his eyes on Jim, "I'm a cop remember. I can find anyone." Then an inner truth came to mind; anyone except the one shooting at me. He grinned to mask that particular inner thought.

Jim pulled a well-used beige scarf from his back pocket and wiped sweat from his face, "To what do I owe this visit?"

"I wanted to run something by you." Art saw Jim nod, turned toward the house and gestured for Art to follow. He did, and they climbed a set of stairs and walked into the kitchen.

"How about a beer?" Jim washed his hands in the ancient kitchen sink and dried them. Opening the refrigerator, Jim's hand wrapped over the tops of two cans of Bud. He gave one to Art and said. "Let's sit out front." He led the way and Art followed through the dining area and the living room to the front porch, and the seating area he'd seen as he came on the porch earlier. Clearly, Jim had his work cut out for him, as the place was a disaster. Jim took the chair to the right and pointed with his can to the chair next to him. Art sat there and both snapped their lids open. He raised his drink toward the doc in toast then he sipped. Jim looked at his. Art shook his head a bit and smacked his lips, "Boy that hits the spot." He leaned back, stretched his legs, and crossed his ankles.

Art saw the layer of sawdust covering Jim and wished he had the use of his arm, and some carpentry knowledge, so he could build something. The arm felt better these days, not so sickening when he moved his arm.

A quiet moment passed, then he said, "This is going to be a nice place when you finish." Art studied the wooden windows and the craft that went into making them, geez, about a hundred years ago.

Jim nodded. "Right now, it seems like a long way off," he said and tasted the beer again.

Art understood that feeling, a sad one where everything appeared out of reach. He sat back comfortably in this chair with this man.

"So, what brings you to this part of town?"

"Jim, I need to secure my house. I wondered if your handyman would want to work for me."

"Roger? We can ask him, but I've got him tied up here now. When do you need to do this?"

Art rose in the chair; set the beer on the flooring of the porch, leaned more toward Jim and began. "Evelyn showed up on Melissa's sixteenth birthday and has steamrolled through our lives ever since. I thought I had a pretty good thing going with Amanda. You know her? Of course, you do. I don't know what I'm thinking." Art shook his head. "Amanda walked out on me last evening," Art looked over at the doc and then over the porch railing to the trees off in the distance, shading the lawn.

He knew hurt registered on his face and in his eyes, and he didn't want to share that with Jim.

Jim leaned forward, pulling his legs in and moving his upper body closer to Art. In a quiet, slow pace he spoke, "How do you feel about that?"

Art's head swung back. His cheeks reddened with emotion. "Don't go all Doc on me now." Art shot back then added, "I don't know."

Doc Wexford couldn't help himself. He was in doc mode now, "Yes, you do."

"Shit, why did I come here?" Anger flashed in Arts eyes as he snapped out his answer.

"To get Roger to work for you, at least that's what you said."

Art sat back, "You don't make anything easy, do you?"

A cagey expression crossed the doc's face, "Not in my job description."

Art listened once again to the boughs of the giant redwood gracefully swaying in the breeze. "I got shot at again."

Jim looked at him, "Again? Where?"

"Out in front of my house in broad daylight."

"You didn't see anyone or anything?"

Art swung his head emphatically, and said, "Nothing."

"What are you going to do?"

167

"Good question." Art picked up his beer and finished it in one long gulp. He shook the can to test it and said, "How long are you going to be working on this place?"

Jim let his eyes rise to the second story ceiling over the porch, "As long as it takes."

Art envied him. The man knew how to relax with utter turmoil all around. "I'd help if I could."

"Thanks, but I 'm doing okay, I don't need to have it done, and it offers me some time to think. I need that from time to time." Jim brought his eyes to Art's, and they held a soft expression. "So do you."

Art stood, handed the empty can to Jim and started off the porch. "Will you ask? What did you say his name was?"

"Roger."

Art nodded, "Roger, to stop by my place." He reached into his pocket and took out his cardholder and handed one to Jim. "Give him that, and he can call me. Maybe we can work out something for my place."

Jim took the card, "I'll give it to him."

"Thanks for the beer." Art walked to the edge of the porch ready to take the first step down. "I like this place it kind of feels like a vacation spot, with the size of these redwoods..., and the smell." He took a deep breath. "It's nice here, Jim."

As Art left Jim standing on the porch, he walked to his car and, as he turned it around, a rifle on a rack in the back window of a beat-up, old, rusted out Ford pickup truck parked in Jim's driveway caught his attention. The cop in him, made him note the license number, a Mississippi plate. It shouldn't be too hard to get the skivvy on this dude. He drove to the next block and pulled over. Art pulled out his notepad and jotted the plate number down for good measure. He'd get it to Walt and maybe just maybe something will turn up and push the hot button.

Chapter Twenty-Nine

3:47 P.M. October 5, 1995

Art pushed on the dark wooden entrance to Tango Investigation, Inc. He stepped through and heard Yvonne and Lessie's muted voices. They were hard at work and he followed those voices to a closed door. He tapped with the back of his knuckle.

The talking stopped, and it was a moment before Lessie stood in the doorway. "Hey, come on in," she grinned at him with her big full-faced smile. He nodded to her and looked toward Yvonne who had that calm, never gonna ruffle my feathers look about her. These two women were exact opposites, and Art wondered how they had found each other and formed a working relationship. However, it happened they were good at what they did and Art was here for their brand of problem-solving.

They were in an interior room with no windows. Walls Yvonne had put up for keeping private information just that. Before him he saw a mystery, board filled with notes and pictures and maps. Art stepped close and recognized his picture pinned to the top. As he scanned from piece to piece, he was shocked at how quickly Yvonne had erected this pool of facts. "When did you get these pictures?" He pointed and looked directly at Yvonne.

Yvonne crossed her arms in front of her, taking a squared stance as though she was barring something, "You seem to think we sit on our butts around here. You hired us. We are on it. End of discussion. And, Buster, don't come in here expecting to run this opp. It's ours so buzz off." She set her mouth hard and gave him a blistering stare.

Art threw up his hand giving her the I-give-up signal. "Just wanted to see if you'd found anything. When in the hell did you get these pictures?"

They were of Evelyn, Melissa, Sandy, Agnes, Art's neighbor, the puppy, Amanda, Judy and Irma, his neighbors from across the street. There were pictures of the mailman, the sanitation workers and one of Walt. Some old mug shots were of people Art had interacted with some time before. There was a picture of Raymond Michael McNamare with the word deceased stamped across his face. His grandmother, Emily June McNamare, and grandfather, Michael Allen McNamare also took up some space on the board. A purple string connected a smaller picture of Art that reigned supreme in the center of the storyboard with the McNamare clan, and all the other photos. There was one of Adora Stumper from the case he and Walt were working on now. His jaw dropped. A square of white paper with a marker pen question mark drawn on it caught his eye. A purple string went from that piece of paper to his picture. Clearly, they didn't know the identity of the assailant. His eyes moved on. There was a picture of Murphy in his uniform. Art put his hand to his lips. They are making connections with people in my life and out of my life. He didn't think he had anything to worry about from the individuals in the mug shots. One was in prison and would be for life. Unless he'd managed to get out somehow, and Art knew he would have been one of the first to learn about that event. They had the slug pictured that he'd tossed to Yvonne the day he hired her. He leaned closer to read about Evelyn.

Evelyn Lynn Conley, age 41, Pilot. Worked the past seven years for ASN Studios. No arrests, no warrants. She had an outstanding debt balance of $561,000 on an airplane. Her driver's license and Pilot's licenses noted there. Her description was spot-on, except there was no mention of her steamrolling methods. As he read, he formed a thought and spoke it aloud without thinking, "You seem to know more about Melissa's mother than I do."

"You can thank Lessie for that," Yvonne said turning toward the storyboard and joining Art in his interest. They stood shoulder to shoulder.

"How'd you get that information, I mean about her being a pilot and belonging to some movie making industry?"

Yvonne tilted her head toward Lessie, "You'd have to ask her about that. She's the one that got the pictures and did the follow-up."

Art looked at Lessie with expectation. Yvonne turned more toward her, and as they waited for Lessie's answer.

Lessie's chin went up as she crossed her one leg over the other and rested on the tiptoe of her tennis shoe. "I have my ways."

"Yeah, and we were just talking about those ways. They are going to get my license pulled if you get caught."

Lessie picked at one of her fingernails and said, "You're just too persnickety. Don't let things get to you. You worry too much. I just don't let things get to me. I figure if you've got a problem, it's your problem and not mine. So, it's not likely to bother me one way or the other."

Yvonne's eyes were steady as she looked at Lessie, "It's my license on the line and your job. Ever think of that? If you don't start worrying about my problems you may be out looking for another job. Do you think you could find one?"

Lessie grinned and looked from Art to Yvonne, "In a heartbeat."

Yvonne put her hands in the air, "There's no reasoning with her. It's Lessie's way or the highway." Yvonne mumbled something and both Lessie and Art looked at her, "Nothing!" She answered their facial queries with sharpness in her voice.

"Look, Art," Yvonne began, "We have nothing yet. But if someone is shooting at you, and they have done it twice, your whole family might be in danger. Until we unravel this mess, I think you should take precautions."

Art nodded. "I am considering some work on my house, and I've come to you to find the son-of-a-bitch, excuse my French," he looked at both of them.

"How often have you been shot at? Let's see if there's a pattern," Yvonne asked.

"Huh, well, I put it on my calendar. The first time was August 28, Monday. In the early evening, I was taking out the trash, so I was almost to the trashcans on the side of my house." Art leaned over toward the layout of his property. Yvonne had the placement of the house and the rooms in the house with the outside backyard all the way to the boat ramp on the river. His finger traced from the back door along the pathway to the trash can placement. His finger stopped just before where the cans waited. "I hit the ground right here."

Yvonne's finger traced from that spot along the pathway to the side of the garage and the front sidewalk, directly across the street and to some bushes at the far end of a neighbor's lot across the street. "It had to come from there."

"I didn't see anyone standing there when I looked that night. I don't think there's room for anyone to hide there, certainly not enough room to raise a rifle and aim it with any surety. There must be a fence behind those bushes." Art studied the spot on her drawing. "But, I will check it out. I'm heading home now, and I'll give you a call."

"And the second time?"

"The second time was yesterday when I walked Walt out and he'd just driven off. A few minutes later the cab with my girls pulled away from the curb. That's when I heard the shot and I hit the ground. Got up and looked the area over." His finger stopped on the board and tapped. "Right here."

Yvonne's finger traced from that point to the bushes, and she smiled a knowing smile at Art. "Nope, you won't."

"Nope, what?"

"You hired us, Art. Let us do our job. I want you to ignore that spot. Be aware of everything around you, but leave that particular area to us."

"Lessie, get everything you can on that area stat."

They were back to work and Art saw he was in the way. He said goodbye to Yvonne and walked back outside to his car and sat down. He had more questions now more than ever as he watched Lessie adjust her sunglasses and drive off the lot.

He followed for the first block but turned on to a tree lined street heavy in shade at this time of the day. He knew where he was going and couldn't help himself. Art drove into the parking lot where Amanda's office was located. He felt better when he spotted her car in its assigned slot. His hand went to his cell. He could call her just to say hi. Thinking better of that idea he brought his hand away, and he looked toward the door to her office. He'd like to knock on that door. No, he'd like to go through that door just to see her. Art looked down, then up, and off to the side. He knew he was acting like a teenage kid.

She'd broken it off. He could not go crawling back, crying that he needed her. He wanted her. He missed her.

Art gathered himself. He wished she would come out of her office, but she didn't, and he had to leave.

Chapter Thirty

4:05 P.M. October 5, 1995

Art's knuckles were white as they stressed over the steering wheel, twisting and turning as though wringing its neck. He couldn't get his mind off that storyboard at Tango Investigation, Inc. He sat in the car in his garage, the images of those people circling before him. After a while, he left his car and walked out front.

His neighbor's house stood directly across the street. Now focused on the house as though a horse with blinders, Art raised his lower lip, caught his mustache.

The older home reigned on the lot it had been assigned, white on white with stately pillars and a tall double door that appeared massive and heavy. Larger than life hinges, hammered of metal and burnished, held the door in place. Snuggly trimmed pines grew in urn-shaped pots standing on either side of the entry. The lines at the outer edges of his eyes deepened as he grinned at the thought of this house at Christmas time. There was no way he could ever get that many white lights on his house. He chuckled as the thought crossed his mind that the house could probably be seen from space on a clear night.

Judy and Irma, her mother, had lived there longer than Art had been on this block. He knew both women, but not well. Not because Art wasn't friendly. It was simply because they were all working and busy people.

Yvonne believed that their property was involved in the shooting incident. He exhaled. He'd decided. His eyes narrowed as he studied the top elevation of the two-story house directly across the street down to the welcoming double doors. The thought nagged at him. Could one of those ladies have it in for him? And if so why?

Yvonne told him to stay out of it and let Tango, Inc., take over. Yeah, like that was going to happen. Art walked across the street, up the walk and to Judy and Irma's front door. He had to see their expression when they saw him.

His hand reached for the doorbell and, with determination, he leaned into the push. It wasn't long before he heard footsteps and the door opened. "Art, how nice to see you."

Judy beamed at him as he replied, "Nice to see you too. How's your mother?"

Judy fixed a wisp of her short blonde hair behind her ear. "Mom's fine. Would you like to see her?"

"Yes, if that is possible."

Judy leaned away from the door, leaving her foot behind to keep the door open. He could see her toenails in her sandals all neatly trimmed and colored silver. She spoke over her shoulder, and after a moment Irma came to the door.

"Hello, Irma," Art said. "Would you mind if I did some looking around in your backyard?"

Irma sized him up, her face wrinkled and stern, her eyes piercing. She narrowed her eyes a moment then said, "You're that cop that lives across the street, aren't you?"

"Yes." He gave her his toothy grin, "I'm Art Franklin."

"You are looking for someone in particular?"

Art was, but he didn't think trying to explain to these two women a very good idea. "I just wanted to see how your yard was laid out to get some ideas for mine."

Irma smirked, "You don't expect me to believe that do you?"

"Well, I'd hoped you would, 'cause I don't have anything else." Art studied her expression. She was hovering on the verge of allowing him access to her backyard, her eyes settling on his green arm sling.

Judy sounded tense when she asked, "Mom, are you going to answer him?"

Irma turned and looked at her daughter, "What? Answer what?"

Judy smiled and looked at Art, "Is it okay for him to look around in the backyard?"

"Yes, well by all means. Look it over to your heart's content." She moved back inside the house.

"Thank you," he said as the door closed. He walked to the garage side of the house and opened the wooden gate that hooked to the side of the house. He strolled down the side of the building to the back yard, sure that these ladies were not the shooter he was looking for.

It was a green expanse with lovely ornamentals growing along the fence line and spreading shade over the lawn. Art moved to the other side of the house. There was a fence, just as he thought. He looked over the five-foot tall weathered redwood fence. On the other side was a pie shaped piece of ground too small to build on and in the wrong place to be usable to the back yard. At some point it had been fenced off and forgotten. Some volunteer trees grew there, and weeds abounded. They had dried a golden color at this time of the year. Art turned back to the inside rear yard area. He peered closer at the ground by the fence facing toward his house.

He studied each blade of grass to see if it had been disturbed by human means. The grass appeared matted in a few places. Someone had been standing there. Art reached over and took hold of the fence. He wanted to move the bushes on the other side of the boards to see if his house and especially the side yard where he works on the trash were visible from this vantage point. It startled Art when the board he put his hand on moved as though free. He leaned over and checked the bottom of the board to see how it was attached and found the bottom of the board free—, the nail had been removed. Art got to his feet and checked the top of the board, it had one nail in the center and it was loose. Art moved that board so that it slid off to this right. He sat back on his haunches and could see the bushes on the other side of the fence. Interested now, he moved to his knees.

Art realized that the bushes grew thick everywhere but right in this one spot. He leaned closer and could see that someone had trimmed an opening and Art could see his house. A cold sweat broke out over his skin. In that instant it had become very real and personal.

There were some leaves in the cutout area but all in all, he could see his house unhampered. He could see down the side yard where the trashcans waited and where he had stood. Anyone would have a clear shot at me from here. No wonder I didn't see anyone. But, if he's had such a fine bead on me why didn't he kill me? He didn't even come close enough to nick me. Art set his jaw. They don't want me dead. This is some kind of warning. That I am not safe? That he has the power over me.

Art got up. Tuesday is our trash pickup day, so this person was here on Monday, the day the first shots were fired and again on Sunday morning when the caterers came. This is someone who can come at any time.

He pulled the board back into place. Art smoothed the grass where he'd been to pick it back up. He wanted to leave the ground as he'd found it earlier. His hand came to his mouth, and he formed a tripod with his fingers over his top lip and under his chin. It must be someone with a body mass similar to mine. I can rule out both these women. They're too small to sit in that space hold a rifle and shoot through that small opening. His eyes looked off into nothingness as he gave it his best. Who could the son-of-a-bitch be? Who would want to do something like this to me? It's just crazy. Not normal at all.

It was time to leave this yard, not get Judy and Irma all excited about something being wrong in their backyard. He took a moment to look over into the part of the yard that was fenced off. It seemed clean except for the overgrown weeds and grasses that grow in the valley. Summer was hard on plants if they didn't get watered and these plants were on their own. Art noticed two oak trees and some sweet gum. They could handle drought conditions.

Art went around to the front door and tapped again. When Judy came to the door, he thanked her, said he had looked around, and wanted her to know he was done. She nodded and closed the door. As Art turned to step away, he heard the yielding click as it latched. He knew they suspected something. The local homicide lieutenant wants a walk about in your backyard just for kicks. He walked back to his property feeling their eyes were on him.

Art headed right for his car. He backed it out of the garage and down the driveway into the street, turned onto Turner Road and whipped around the curve toward the freeway on-ramp, destination, Stockton.

Twenty minutes later, he pulled up in front of the Army Surplus Store and went inside. The building smelled musty of dust, rubber tires, metal, and years of collecting. Rows and rows of leftover gear, no longer useable by our military, filled this place floor to ceiling. He spotted mess kits and helmets. Memories flooded back for Art of his peacetime service in the Army.

180

After searching through most of the store Art found what he wanted. He closed the trunk lid and pulled it by one end and its handle. A salesperson in desert storm fatigues stooped beside him and took up the other end of the container.

The clerk helped him move the heavy wooden footlocker to the checkout where he charged Art and helped him load it in his car.

Art turned the car radio on the minute he reached the street and had to pause to wait for traffic. A light bright jazz piece of tinkling ivory filled the car's interior and his heart. He tapped the steering wheel with his long index finger to the rhythm while he whipped onto the ramp signed Sacramento. The wind brushed his hair and drowned out the music. He closed the window and hummed as his plan came together.

He managed to get the new used locker out of the back of his car and on the garage floor. Art moved on to the next part of his plan. Stepping into the kitchen, he found Evelyn working at the kitchen sink. An apron was tied around her waist, and she looked domestic.

"Hi, honey, I'm home," she said. A bright grin met him as he came fully into the room.

"Evelyn, where's Mel?"

"She's wonderful Art." Evelyn wiped her hands on a striped tea towel and placed it on the sink counter as she turned to him. "I just can't get over it. You and I made that perfect girl."

He nodded in agreement.

"She's bright. She gets things like that." Evelyn snapped her fingers.

"Evelyn, we've got to talk."

Her face changed, hardening her chin and eyes as she leaned back against the sink counter. "Okay."

He looked down to the floor for a time then brought his eyes up. "It's time for you to go..."

"You're kicking me out?" An expression one of surprise and shock spread across Evelyn's face. "Don't you think we should try being a couple again? Think about how it was. Art, we were so good together as a couple, and we owe it to Melissa. Remember? We could be a family. Mel would like that I know."

I don't believe what I am about to say! Art procrastinated. Fully aware giving Evelyn any room at all would not be the best avenue to take with a steamroller, he had to speak. Get it out. "Yes!" He stared right at her. "I want you to leave first thing in the morning."

"Well, that's awfully abrupt don't you think?" She shook her head and questioned him with her gaze.

"I want you out of here as soon as you can in the morning." Art's voice sounded clear, forceful, and certain. He let a long moment pass while she stood mute, staring at him. His heart leaped at what he would say next, "And I want you to take Mel with you.

She readied herself for a fight. It was all over her face and as his words sank in her eyes widened, and she caught her breath, "What!?"

He dropped his shoulders, leaning his good elbow on the island counter top, and brought his mouth as close to hers as he could without walking around to her side. "Someone's taken some shots at me lately. Here at the house. I think you and Mel might be in the line of fire and I want you both out of here so I can work."

She smirked, "I know that look, Arty. You are going undercover. Aren't you?"

There came no answer. "Will you, do it?"

She stared at him a long moment and dropped her gaze, without rising she nodded.

He sized up the front of the refrigerator. A cold beer, the last one for a while sounded awfully good. He reached in, captured a bottle, twisted the top open and headed for a talk with Melissa. There had to be a way to send her off without scaring her.

As he got to Melissa's door Evelyn, carrying a beer of her own, joined him. Art called to Melissa, and she said to come in.

Evelyn walked in ahead of Art and began talking, "Honey, I've got this crazy idea. I have ten days of vacation left. How about if you and I fly to my home in Florida and we take in Disney World?"

Melissa jumped into Arts face, "Dad, can I?"

Art looked over Melissa's head as he gathered her to him and saw Evelyn mouth "ten days enough?"

He closed his eyes and nodded yes.

Chapter Thirty-One

3:43 A.M. October 6, 1995

The led light brightened the space on the nightstand. Art glanced at the numbers, not so much to check the time, but because he'd been on an opp and awake all night. Melissa and Evelyn would leave in the morning and then he'd have to swing into real time action. Over the long dark hours he'd worked out a to-do-list that was daunting. One that would be difficult for a two-armed man, but would fall to him just the same.

He turned back to the darkness, fluffed his pillow and crammed his head into it hoping that he could get a couple of hours before the new day began. A moment later he turned, brought his leg up and tried to find a comfortable place for all his body parts. That didn't work. He turned again, fixed the pillow and sighed.

Amanda... Why did she walk away? Should I go and talk with her? Should I call her? His heart was lost and heavy with loneliness. He loved her. The thought that he might lose her scared him. His lips pulled apart. *I love her.* The clarity astounded him, and now it seemed necessary to see her. He had to tell her.

Reality swung into place. Calm centered within him in the deep dark of the night. First, he had to find out who was shooting at him and make sure no one else was in any jeopardy. He couldn't risk her becoming a target. If anyone finds out that I love her, she might be lumped in with Melissa and that he would not allow.

He looked at the clock again, 3:44 a.m. Only a minute had passed. This is one long stinking night. The house remained quiet, and he listened to any and every sound. His mind turned to the plan.

As soon as he got back here after seeing them off, he would get the handyman over to fix the doors and windows. Next, he'd get the alarm company to get this house monitored. That thought did not sit well with him. He hated the thought of Big Brother looking down his throat. Having the house all censored up just went against his grain and then the possibility of the alarm going off just because of a spider web made him shake his head. He'd heard about that from others and he didn't want it happening to his house. He wanted to be the defender of the realm.

It had become necessary, so he clenched and unclenched his hand as he accepted the fact as truth, a truth that must be acted upon sooner rather than later.

Something slammed into the house. His head turned the suspected direction.

What was that?

He stiffened his attention on the shut bedroom door. It felt as though his ear reached for that sound. Nothing came back. After a long moment, he removed the covers over his legs and slipped them over the side of the bed.

Still the house remained quiet.

Art stood and leaned down sliding his hand to the side table. His fingers slipped on either side of the knob and he pulled. He felt inside for the small flashlight and placed it between his teeth. At the same time, he reached for the Beretta. Gun in hand, dressed only in his underwear, Art moved forward on bare feet to his door.

He turned the knob, and walked onto the landing. The house was dim at this time of the morning. His eyes could make out the staircase banister; he put his palm on the railing and looked down to the foyer then over to the front door. Everything seemed all right. He moved to the stairs and looked toward the kitchen area. One wall kept him from seeing into that room. He started down the stairs, his ears peeled for any odd sound. Nothing. Art made the bottom of the stairs and studied the windows. They appeared undisturbed. He went into the kitchen. A small amount of light played across the counter over the sink and the faucet. Art moved into the back porch. He lifted the curtain with the Beretta's barrel and scanned both directions. The side yard remained empty.

He probably heard the house settling, and that was all. Art realized he felt jumpy, possibly because he was sending Melissa away. That just went against his grain. He wanted to be the stand-up dad, but he couldn't. Someone targeted him and until he knew who and why she had to be safe.

The stove clock made its clunking sound and another minute of his allotted lifespan ticked off. Art grimaced at the darn thing and headed back to his bed. It's almost time. We'll all be up at six. Sure, now that the house was his castle and not being invaded by infidels, he stepped silently up the stairs and past Melissa's room to his. He closed the door, put the gun back into his drawer and left the flashlight on his bed stand. Art lay on top of the covers. The house felt warm to him as he laid his head back down on his damp pillow. He grabbed it up and disgustedly tossed it off the bed. He hated that cold, damp feeling. He had to do sheets for all the beds.

Dread crept in as he realized he had all the work to do as he would be the only one here. Oh well, he said to himself, at least the mutt will be gone. He sighed and turned on his stomach. He liked to sleep without the pillow that way, and he dropped off.

"Hey! You going to sleep all day?

Art lifted himself and tried to drag his lips apart. His mouth was dry, and his eyes didn't want to focus. Someone was in his room speaking to him.

"Do you want breakfast? I'm fixing pancakes. You'll get to clean up the kitchen, because we are running a little late." There was a pause, "Hey, Fathead, are you listening to me?"

"Yeah, I got it." Art sat up and looked at Evelyn through squinted eyes. "Melissa up and ready to go?"

Evelyn nodded, "She's dressed, got her bags downstairs and is ready to go."

Somehow that hurt.

Get over it. He contemplated. This is not personal. She's a kid and Evelyn is opening a whole new world to her, and it is exciting. I get that. But does she have to love it so darn much? How can I ever compete with Evelyn and what she brings to the table? "I'll be right down," he said as she backed out the door.

He considered the shower and decided to forgo the renewing experience and get downstairs to help them with their plans. He donned yesterday's clothes and he trotted down the stairs and found Evelyn lifting pancakes from the griddle onto a stack. "Hey," he said brightly.

"Dad, isn't this exciting? I am waking up in California, and I'm going to sleep tonight clear across the country. Wow, isn't that outstanding?" She came to him, and he slid his arm around her waist.

"It is, honey, it really is." He turned toward Evelyn who removed a pancake from the grill and placed that golden heavenly smelling cake on an empty plate.

"Here, sit and eat your breakfast," she said to Melissa. "Hurry up now, we've got to get a move on."

Melissa left Art and slid into the chair right in front of the steaming pancake. She plunked butter on, and it melted. She pushed the dark container of syrup aside and reached for the maple syrup, which she poured over her pancake.

"How many for you?" Evelyn asked Art.

He grinned and had to admit her pancakes were a perfect size and the same color, not like his that could be oblong and sometimes burned. Okay, he couldn't cook as well as her. "Three for me, please."

"Three it is," and she placed a plate before Art, then shoved the syrups toward him.

"Thanks."

"Will it be okay for Melissa to miss school?"

"It's going to have to be. She'll have to make up her work when she gets back. I'll call in the excuse."

Evelyn picked up the empty plates and Art wiped his mouth with the napkin, "I'll get the car out. You girls ready?"

"Oh, Dad, I wish you were going."

"So do I honey."

Art watched as Evelyn, ever-capable Evelyn, readied the aircraft. He felt equally surprised that Melissa whipped around loosening the tie downs from the moorings. They had everything loaded, everything except the animal carrier with the pup.

Melissa ran to him. "I wish you were going, too, Dad." She kissed him on the cheek and hugged his right side. His good arm surrounded her, and he brought her closer, savoring the sense of her. Tears started and he blinked. Tears came easily these days it seemed.

Melissa pulled away, "I really, really wish you were coming." She backed away as Evelyn returned from the flight office.

"All set," she said. "Oh, Art. Dog's staying with you for now."

Art's head swung back and forth; his mouth opened and out came, "Huh. Ah, no way."

Evelyn picked up the crate and brought it to him. "Take care of it for her Art." She gave him a sneering stare. "It's only ten days."

His shoulders dropped, his head hung, "Evelyn, you don't understand. She can't keep it. She cannot have a dog in our home. I planned on you taking it when you left."

"Oh, Art, you don't mean that. She loves Daisy. It's my gift to her. She can hug and love and remember that I love her too. You just can't be mean-spirited."

He looked at her. It was the best he could do. Art wouldn't want to send Melissa off with bad feelings. He didn't want her upset or angry at him. Not right now. There was just way too much on his plate to add this too.

"The mutt's going to lock up."

"Lockup?"

"Yeah, a kennel. There's a good one out in the country.

Evelyn looked at him, "Give the pup a chance Art, you will love it as much as Melissa does." She kissed him on the cheek, turned toward the plane and raised her hand to wave goodbye.

He watched as they climbed into the airplane and settled into their seats. Evelyn waved once more to him, and Melissa's hand rotated wildly in the window. The plane lurched a bit forward, then rolled smoothly following the line with the front tire. It moved out onto the runway, and just like that it picked up speed, found its place in the air and left Art behind. Immediately he felt the loss of Melissa, they hadn't been apart since last July, not even for one night. He stood rooted to the spot listening to the sounds around him. Lonesome sounds. The wind picked up and brushed against his ear, it tossed

189

his hair and five minutes passed before he budged. Defeated he picked up the carrier and headed for his car. "I guess it's you and me Daisy."

Chapter Thirty-Two

9:15 A.M. October 6, 1995

Art drove the car into the garage, took the pet carrier out of the backseat and carried it into the house. He opened the door to the coop and pulled the timid pup out, her eyes shown like two black marbles. Art didn't know what to make of the dog and by the looks of her, she didn't know what to make of him. Art held her by the scruff of the neck, and the pups legs stuck out as he held his first contractual discussion with the furry houseguest.

"You will not potty in the house! The yard is for that purpose. And not just every place you might want to go. A site will be designated for you and you will comply." Art looked at the pup, and it seemed fixed on him, "You understand?"

Daisy looked at him for a long moment.

Art started for the back-sliding glass door to the poolside yard. He closed the slider behind him using his elbow. He carried Daisy to the lawn and set her down. The pup stood there for the longest moment and began searching out the best place. Finding said place she squatted Art scooped her up and praised her profusely. "Thank you, thank you, Daisy. I felt sure you understood.

You keep your end of our bargain, and we'll get along just fine. Fail once and you'll see the inside of the lockup faster than you can say bow-wow. You got that?"

Daisy wiggled in Arts hand, and he did his best to keep the pup from falling. Giving up on trying to hold her in his good hand he snuggled Daisy in his sling. Art opened the slider and went into the house. "I guess if something came out something should go back in." He set Daisy down and looked for her water dish and food dish. Not finding them, he decided they must have gone with the girls. He turned and looked at his cupboard. His lips curled at the thought of giving his nice dishes over to a dog. He'd have to, at least until he could go shopping, and he was not ready to do that now. He had other more important things to do.

Begrudgingly he took two small bowls from the cupboard and filled one with water. He put it on the floor and Daisy drank. With no dog food in view Art opened the refrigerator, and there was a can of puppy food with a lid on top. He pulled the lid off and figured he had enough for a day or two. But then he wondered how much a puppy eats, and when do they eat? The label gave him guidelines and Art spooned out some cold gelatinized meat and gave it to Daisy.

Taking care of the pup seemed to be turning into a major job for him with one more requirement following the next. He turned to find the pup. Her growling caught his attention. He looked under the table and off in the corner he found her playing with a hot pad from the stove. How'd that get on the floor? Daisy ran as soon as she realized the human wanted to play a game with her. She deftly carried the potholder, keeping just ahead of Art.

Art was surprised at how fast the little white ball of fur could travel, and he with the disadvantage of the sling. The thought that he was moving fast made him realize that he was getting better. A grin crossed his face as he scooped Daisy and the red, white, and blue potholder up. "You look very patriotic Daisy."

Daisy dropped the potholder, it fell to the floor, she had better things to do. Her tiny pink tongue came out and found Art's cheek as he lifted her to look for the pad. The soft touch first startled him and then he liked the feeling of love. Hard as he tried to maintain a strict persona, Daisy melted his heart. Art walked the two of them back outside to the lounge where he sat down to study Daisy. At the end of a long moment, he let his body rest back against the comfort of the lounge pad. He felt tired, and he closed his eyes. The warmth of the sun bathing him relaxed his legs and then his back and finally his neck. Daisy crawled to his shoulder near the sling and cuddled by his chin, crowding Art's neck.

The two slept that way for an hour when Art woke to the sound of the trees along the river rustling. Carefully he opened his eyes against the bright light and squinted toward the water. A strong breeze moved the trees in a cadenced dance against the blue of the sky. Art sighed and reached his good hand to wrap around Daisy's little body.

"Come on girl. I've got things to accomplish." Art headed for the house and put Daisy in her crate. He drew a glass of water and slipped a notepaper from his pocket. Dialing he waited for the pickup.

"Hello?"

Art turned and walked toward the kitchen window over the sink and looked out into the backyard across the pool and to the trees on the other side of the Mokelumne River. "Doc, it's Art. I need your guy right away. Can you spare him for a day or two?"

Doc Wexford was silent for a second and Art's heart leaped with sudden worry that he couldn't get this job done today. "Yeah, I can turn him loose for a couple of days, but no more." He paused again as though he had something to say and Art felt like asking him what it was. Before he spoke the Doc continued, "Hey, I've come across something that just doesn't seem right, and I'd like your input. Any chance you could drop by here anytime soon?"

Art nodded, afterward he realized that the doc could not see his answer, "Yeah. Let me get this place fortified and then I'll give you one hundred percent of me. I need your handyman over here now. I've got to get security doors installed." Art listened as the doc spoke, then he said, "Okay, I'll look for him, Jim. Thanks, I'll send him back to you in a day or two."

When he finished the call to the doc he looked up the number for the alarm company and called.

"We can be at your place next Friday."

"That's not going to work for me; I need the system installed tomorrow at the latest."

"Sorry sir, our technicians are all booked up."

"I'll have to call another company, thanks anyway."

"Hold on please."

Art grabbed the earpiece away from his ear as the music blasted.

"We can make an exception sir. Let me get your information."

Art smirked. It wasn't his intention to strong arm someone, or some company, but right now he had to get things moving.

He put the phone down and slid the phone book back into the drawer as he heard the pickup truck backfire out front. Aw, he thought, Roger's arrived. Art moved to the front door, went outside and saw Roger's hefty body coming out of the red, rusted-out old pickup truck with the rifle still hung in the sling across the inside window. The workman appeared with his long gray hair pulled back from his scrubbed face. His beard neatly combed.

Art walked toward him and extended his hand. They clasped and shook. The worker dropped his gaze to the ground and Art found it difficult to hold eye contact with him. Roger kept to himself to some extent and Art figured there was some back-story.

"I need security doors installed on all exterior entries. There will be an alarm system in place tomorrow. Can you hang three of those kinds of doors today for me?"

Roger shuffled his feet looking down as he spoke, "Do you have the doors?"

"No."

"Let's get the measuring done and we can go to Lowe's and get them. I might get two of them today and have to do the third in the morning." He looked at his watch and then fleetingly at Art.

Art's mouth tightened, he worked his mustache, looked at Roger. "Okay, that will work. How much do you want?"

Roger's rather high voice answered, "It depends, eighty-five dollars an hour if all goes well, but if there're any big unforeseen problems we'd need to talk that over. If all goes well it shouldn't take too long.

"How long will it take you?"

"Again," Roger moved his hands in waves, "Depends on what I run into. An hour a door. After I get all things ready to go. It's more a tedious job of adjusting to get it swinging smoothly."

"You can't give me a ballpark figure or time?"

"Wish I could, but older houses present different problems."

Art was getting nowhere with this guy and the day was growing long. It didn't matter anyway the job had to be done and he really didn't care what it cost as long as he got it done today. "Okay, let's get the measuring done."

M.L. WEATHERINGTON

Roger returned to his truck and brought what had once been a bright red, but was now a red rusted toolbox up the walk. As he joined Art, he said, "Show the way."

Together they walked down the side of the garage to the side door of the laundry.

Roger ran the tape up the length of the door on the left side and then the right. He pulled the tape across the top and then the bottom. He used a square to check the level of the corners and said. "Your door is not square, caused by the house settling. It won't be a problem. I can fix that easy enough."

Art felt glad to hear that. They checked the other two doors and found small problems with them, but nothing that would keep him from installing the new doors. They went to Lowe's, and Art chose the doors, and loaded them in the back of the pickup and headed toward Art's house. The sense of moving ahead pleased him, and he looked out the dirty windshield upon Lodi, a town he rarely got to see from this perspective. "You been in Lodi long?"

He turned at Roger waiting for the answer.

Roger gripped the stirring wheel. "Not long, just working to get the money up to head back home. Won't be too long now. When I finish with the doc I'll be out of here."

"Where's home?" Art watched as Roger twisted his neck to keep his eyes from coming anywhere near Art's.

"Where I park it mostly. I like traveling around. My trailer is waiting for me in Kentucky right now. I'll pick it up and then point to a place on the map and head there."

Art, interested now, turned more toward him and checked out the green printed stripped shirt. He was amused by the suspenders of orange, brown and yellow, bending over his shoulders to the much-faded blue jeans. "What brought you here to our fine community?"

Roger shut up, and Art felt the man change. He had hit a sore point, yet he waited for an answer.

Finally, as Roger drove through a yellow light he said, "I had a job to do."

Art nodded that he understood and wondered to himself what that job might be. He didn't ask as he didn't want to run this guy off with too many questions. So he rode the rest of the way home thinking about Roger and how he connected with Doc.

Chapter Thirty-Three

4:28 A.M. October 6, 1995

Roger worked at hanging the security door on the side entry near the trashcans. Art gazed down the house line and across the street to Judy and Irma's side yard where the fence with the loose board waited. The area was concealed by vegetation and too far away from where he stood to see if anyone was there looking through the manufactured hole in the hedge. Goose bumps raced over his arms with the possibility that someone might be there dialing in the cross hairs right now. Just in case, he hugged closer to his house and hoping with God's will, he was out of the line of fire. Reluctantly he turned his attention back on Roger's work.

He glanced at his watch thinking. It will be dark before he gets this one door up although he held his tongue. After all, carpentry was not Art's expertise. Roger cut the cardboard box open and removed the packaged parts. He took time as he laid out all the parts and accounted for everything he needed. When he finished that process he took the thermos bottle and opened the lid raising it and guzzling for a long moment. Art moved his tongue around in his dry mouth.

Roger removed the white security door from the plastic wrap and tossed it to the side. Roger studied the door over, it appeared okay to him, and he turned and asked if it was acceptable to Art.

Art bent for a better view, and saw it was satisfactory and nodded. The carpenter filled his hand with screws and popped them into his mouth. He stood the door in the jamb area and took one screw from his lips. In a few minutes he'd installed the door.

With relief Art shot a look down the side of the house back at Irma's and Judy's. He backed up to get out of Roger's way and then followed as they walked ten feet over to the next project. This entry opened to this same side yard area. However, the entrance itself opened into a protected area from the street. It faced the back fence where the ivy grew thick and where Art felt the bullets went through. Art relaxed as he was out of the line of fire.

He watched Roger go through the same procedure for the next door.

Feeling bored Art walked back inside, drew a glass of water and drank. As he did he looked out the window over the sink, his mind working a mile a minute. Turning to the phone, he picked up the receiver and dialed the memorized number. He waited.

"Hello."

Art's expression radiated pleasure, lines creased around his eyes as they sparkled, "It's me, Art. I need you to do a favor for me." His eyes followed the kitchen wall to the floor as he listened.

"Okay, when?" Murphy said.

Art's face showed both concern and pleasure in the lines around his mouth and eyes, "Tomorrow, I'll come to your place in a couple of hours to lay it out for you. Will you be home?" He ran his right hand through his hair feeling the waves over the top of his head.

"Yeah."

Nodding silent thanks, he said, "Bye." Art placed the phone back on the cradle and allowed a smile to play across his face. The grin grew larger until his heart could contain the happiness he felt no longer and he yelled, "Yes!"

The puppy yipped, and he walked over to the carrier and put his hand on the hard-cream colored plastic. "I'm sorry, Daisy."

Roger knocked at the back door.

"Yes?" Art said.

Roger turned toward Art, his shirt damp from sweat. "Done for the day."

"What time will you be here tomorrow?"

"Seven-thirty." Roger backed away, mopped his brow again with his faded red scarf as he picked up his old tool box and shuffled his feet down the cement walkway.

Art closed the back door, hearing for the first time the phone. He rushed across the floor to catch the call and Daisy began whining. Damn, he thought as he grabbed the earpiece. "Hello?"

"Dad."

Her voice floated to his ears, and he let everything go, his shoulders dropped. "Hi, Honey." He could hear background sounds and thought he heard a train clacking in the distance. "How's your trip? Are you there yet?"

Her voice sounded rushed and loud at the same time. It made him want to slow her down, but he listened with love and heard the sometimes-unrecognizable words flooding from his daughter.

"Dad. It's so great here. We stopped in Louisiana, and I am at the air museum. Oh, Dad, you should see this place it is marvelous. They've got planes hanging like they are flying. You know the Red Baron? Well, his plane is here too."

She is growing into a fine person. This experience will open her eyes to the world that I might never have been able to do. On the one hand, it made him happy, on the other fear raised an ugly head and settled to stay.

What if she doesn't want this life anymore?

"Dad, got to go. Mom's waving at me." The sound of activity met his ears. "Bye, love you lots."

The call ended and he stood holding the receiver.

Daisy whined.

"Love you too." He hung up.

"Come on Daisy," Art lifted the wiggly ball of white fur from the crate. "Let's take a walk and clear our heads.

Chapter Thirty-Four

10:17 A.M. October 7, 1995

"Hi, Walt, I wanted to let you know that someone took another shot at me."

"When?"

"Yesterday morning."

"And you're just getting around to reporting it to me?"

Art understood that Walt wasn't happy that he called in so late and probably didn't really believe that he had been shot at again. "I knew the guys didn't believe I was shot at the first time and without evidence, I couldn't prove it one way or the other."

"No one else heard the shots?" Walt said. "What took so long?"

"I was busy getting security doors on the house and I have the security company putting a monitor system on my house this morning. "What going on with the Stumper case?"

I've talked with everyone again and asked different questions, but nothing came up any different. I'm still working on it," he told Art.

Cold, Art thought as they talked. He hated when a case went into the bottom dead file drawer. Art chewed on his mustache. Not on my watch, he almost said before remembering it was not his watch right now. "Oh, Walt, Melissa's with her mother in Florida."

"Got her out of there for a while, that's probably a good idea."

"Yeah."

He filled Walt in on everything but his plan to smoke out the shooter. The idea did seem ridiculous even to him and it would embarrass him to explain it to Walt. "I'll be talking to you soon."

Roger had been working for an hour and a half now, and Art wandered out to see what he was doing. The last door hung in place, and Roger swung it to test its balance. He backed away and nodded to Art. "That's the last."

"You did a good job." Art took hold of the door and swung it back and forth. "Looks really good. Come on, and I'll write you a check."

They walked into the kitchen. Art opened a drawer and pulled out a checkbook. He looked at Roger, eighty-five an hour at four hours is three hundred, agreed?" Roger nodded and stood with his feet apart and his arms crossed in front of him.

Art could feel he was not at ease and he wondered about that sense of him as he wrote out the check. "I make it out to Roger....?" Art waited.

Roger looked up, cleared his throat, and said, "Stumper, Roger Stumper."

The hairs rose up on Arts arms. His eyes shifted as the pen halted in the air a hair's breadth from the check surface. "S.T.U.M.P.E.R." Art spelled aloud.

"Yes."

Carefully, he finished the check, tore it from the pad of checks, closed his checkbook and paused before straightening up. He turned and glanced at Roger as he handed him the check. "Thank you."

He followed Roger to the back door and something drew him to walk outside with him. Art watched him gather the loose tools and close his toolbox. Roger picked his things up and started to walk away. Art followed him back to his truck. Roger shook his hand at the curb, left him and slid behind the wheel.

Art leaned into the opened window on the rider's side of the pickup truck, "Okay if I give you a call if I find anything else I need to be done here?"

Roger threw his elbow through the open window, resting his fingertips on the left side of the steering wheel and smiled, "Yes, that would help. I don't expect to be here too much longer, but while I am I could do some work for you."

Art let his eyes roam. The floorboard area on this side of the truck was filled with different items. He hadn't paid attention to them when he rode to Lowe's with Stumper earlier. Art spotted a box that looked like a cover for shells. "You a hunting man?" Art grinned and directed Roger with his eyes to the rifle.

Roger's eyes flew to the rifle and back to Art's fleetingly. He looked over the wheel through the windshield, "When I can." After an awkward pause between them, Roger nodded.

Art slapped the doorjamb with his hands and said, "Okay. Thanks so much." He stepped back and let Roger drive away.

A keen eye followed that red rusting Ford as it lumbered down the street. There's a story there. The hairs rose on the back of his neck as he walked down the side of the garage by the trashcans and into the house. Art got that old pit-of-the-stomach tickle. His eyes narrowed, that's our man for Grape Avenue.

He checked with the security personnel about how much longer they would be, and they told him they were winding up and would be out of the house in fifteen minutes.

Going to the bedroom, he took his overnight bag out of the closet and set it on the bed. He gathered a pair of his Dockers, a pair of socks, a solid red pull-over shirt, and a red baseball cap. Everything went into the bag and before he closed it, he grabbed another red cap and put it on his head then tucked his extra key to the house in the side zip pouch. His eyes roamed his room for any forgotten item. Satisfied, he closed the bag and snatched it up by the handle.

He carried the bag downstairs and into his office. He placed the call he'd promised to make earlier and listened as the answer came.

"I'm about to come over."

"Okay, I'm here.

Art locked his office door as he went out the front door carrying the bag with a set of clothing exactly like those he had on. Art backed his car out of the garage, got out and checked the front yard. His peripheral vision wandered the neighborhood for cars and any out of the nature facts he could store. Nothing. It was quiet and nice as always. The breeze picked up and rustled the trees in Judy and Irma's backyard. He turned the hose on and walked around his yard watering a bed of petunias by the living room window and some ferns tucked away under a grouping of elms to the right of the front yard. He made himself visible for as long as he thought natural. Walked back and turned the water off, rolled up the hose and stood there a moment for the entire world to see.

Art got into his car, backed out and drove down the street. Shit, I should have taken Daisy out one more time. That poor pup is getting the shaft. I can't help it right now. I have a job to do and more females to protect.

He pulled into the apartment complex where Murphy lived and carried the travel bag to Murphy's door.

His hand rose to knock just as the door gave a pop and opened. "Hey."

"Hey, back at you." Art slipped into the room and saw Willy sitting on the couch holding a cat. "I haven't seen you for a long time. How are you doing?"

She grinned big, her white hair up in the tight bun and decorated with a blue ribbon made her appear like a sweet little old lady. He remembered the pretty blue print dress she wore with the lacy collar that day they went to Amanda's office to hypnotize her for the Nelson case.

"I'm doing fine," she said as she raised her hand to be taken by Art.

He did and held her small, cold hand for a moment. "You've got a cat?"

She petted the cat and said, "This is Slippers, she was Sam Nelson's cat, but she's mine now."

Art nodded and slid his eyes to Murphy. He lifted the travel bag to make Murphy aware that he had something to show him.

"Let's put it on the table," Murphy said, moving toward the dining table that sat at one end of the room.

Art followed him, placed the bag on the table and opened it. "There's a complete set of my outer clothes here."

"I'm expected to wear your clothes?"

Art's expression slid into incredulous, his eyes narrowing, and his face hardening for just a second as he looked at Murphy before he registered the joking expression flooding across Murphy's face.

Art beamed too. "I need to change into your clothes and leave here with another hat. Anything will do if you can cover my red hair. Oh, and your car."

Murphy looked at the clothes a minute and then said, "I think I've got just the right thing." He removed himself from the room and came back a moment later carrying a fishing hat with a downward flange, it colors all browns and drab greens. He handed it to Art.

"This'll work," Art said. "Thanks."

"Now, what's the plan?"

Art walked over and sat down on the chair facing the couch. Murphy joined Wilma on the couch, taking Slipper's up in his arms. Wilma looked steadily at Art, waiting for him to speak.

Keeping his voice low and looking from one to the other he told them what was happening. Willy's eyes widened as she listened. Murphy kept his face plain as he rubbed Slippers from her head to the tail.

"I get it. I'm you. You want me to get shot at!"

Wilma's hand shot out and grabbed Murphy's arm. "Nonsense, I won't allow this. You cannot put yourself in harm's way."

Murphy looked down at her. "Willy, it's what I do for a living."

Art smiled, his brows raised and his eyes sparkled, "Better you get shot at than me."

Murphy looked from Wilma to Art. "Thanks a bunch, man," Murphy grimaced, "when?"

"He shot at me the first time when I was taking the trash out about five-fifteen. I guess one time is as good as another. Just before sundown. Let's do a dry run today."

Chapter Thirty-Five

4:36 P.M. October 7, 1995

A rt drove Murphy's vehicle and parked it two blocks away from his own house. He and Murphy were on the same page in this little drama as it was about to unfold. Now wearing Murphy's pants, shirt, and the camouflage hat his arm free of the sling he felt satisfied that he would not be recognized in his neighborhood. He moved away from Murphy's vehicle making every effort to appear as though his arm was normal and that he wasn't Art Franklin. He walked to the neglected side yard next to Judy and Irma's. Swiveling his neck to assure that no one was watching his approach, he came to a stop. He scanned around once more before placing his hand on the loose board.

He'd made a visit to this site late last night, thanks to Daisy who became his cover for the covert walks and made it easy for him to search out this particular fence line.

Art found the loosened board on the interior fencing when he first visited Judy and Irma's the other day. That made him suspicious of the outer fence. He felt certain that the son-of-a-bitch that targeted him must have been thorough. If he made the interior boards easy to move, he'd probably done the same to the outer fence line. When he'd found the loose board he knew he was onto the scumbag. Now with Murphy's help they'd get the S.O.B.

Moving the loose board to the right, he slid his body through the opening and pulled the board back in place. He stood in broad daylight in the empty field of trees and dried grasses next to some hay-like tumble weeds. Art pulled his hand through some of the knotted-up grasses and found them more hay-like in texture perfect for his needs. It had been there a long time and bound itself into the clumps that rested here and there. His footsteps made crunching sounds as he walked across the dried, cracked ground. He chose his spot just about ten feet from the loosened board that opened into Judy's and Irma's interior back yard. That board allowed entrance to the area where a sniper would be positioned to sight down his house line. Art checked his hidden container, the army surplus locker he'd dragged over last night. That little chore became the reason he couldn't get to sleep last night. It charged him up.

Art checked his time, 4:47 p.m. The trash company would come in the morning about nine. It had been his habit to put his trash out at the curb about 5:30 p.m. He didn't know when this shooter would make his next move, but he felt it had to be sooner rather than later.

Pushing the dried grasses off exposed the container, he pulled Murphy's shirt off and lifted the lid. He reached for the garment. Art looked all around. He was alone. He went to work pulling out the camouflage jumpsuit he'd bought with the Doehler footlocker. Soon he would appear like a hay pile. He slid his shoes off and dropped the pants. He stretched, lifting his shoulders to enjoy the feeling of the sun on his body. He looked down on the camouflage suit and was happy that the suit and the dried grasses of the area looked enough alike. Once I'm fully encased inside this thing, Art thought as he placed one foot inside the pant leg and slipped it to the end, I won't be recognizable. I can sit here until doomsday.

He slipped his arms into the sleeves and adjusted the shoulders. He had water and rations to last for hours. Art put Murphy's clothing into the Army box shut it, and covered it with the loose dried hay grasses. He pulled the headpiece over his head and sat down in a shaded area against the tree. This is the strangest stake out I've ever experienced. He chuckled to himself as he felt for his piece to be sure he could get to it if necessary.

Art sat as still as he could, trusting on his invisibility and his ability to be, at the moment, a grass hump. The problem soon became apparent; he had limited vision. Now and again he'd turned his head as he heard something but mostly he remained face forward and dead still.

A half hour went by and Art's car pulled up in his driveway. Murphy had arrived. He heard his garage door open, the engine rev as the car went into the garage and the familiar whine as the overhead door closed. Art listened, knowing that Murphy would now be impersonating him. Let the games begin. He sighed. "Now you son-of-a-bitch show up."

As instructed Murphy went into the house, he opened the back door and walked to a discarded cardboard box that had encased one of the new doors. Art left a cutter nearby and Murphy grabbed it up and began cutting the cardboard into pieces that would fit in the trash container.

He sliced long and hard and folded some of the cardboard over stepping on it to flatten before shoving it in the trash barrel. Art asked him to work slowly and to roll out the trash can to the curb as though it was his own.

After that to go into the house, turn on the TV, and a few lights until Art came.

After several minutes, Art couldn't hear anything coming from his property. Things got quiet, and he wanted to move and take a look. He knew better. He held his ground. Some birds chattered to each other, and that seemed pleasant as he sat on the ground, his legs crossed at the ankles. He blew with his mouth to move some of the fake grasses so that he could see clearer around him.

Nothing happened. Time passed, and he noticed a rock right under his right-cheek bottom. He didn't dare move to fix the problem. No grass would move that way, and he'd reveal his hiding place. He grimaced and rolled to the left to relieve the pressure point. He hadn't sat a stake out for six years, and he'd forgotten how mind draining it quickly became. He thought of Melissa, what she might be doing at the moment. How he hoped she'd be home soon and all this matter would be out of the way. His thoughts shifted to Amanda and lingered there. Somewhere, deep in his heart, he ached for her— the soft skin of her arm, the scent of her hair, and the gentle feminine quality of her voice.

The rattle of the plastic wheels cut though Art's reverie as Murphy rolled the cans to the curb.

The SOBs a no show. He took in a deep breath and as he did he barely heard crackling of dried twigs. Someone was coming.

Art stilled himself. Oh how he craved to turn his head and look. Be a pile of grass he reminded himself.

Its sounds like two people. They're coming my way. He shifted his eyes searching as best he could. He gripped his hands tight, and willed whoever it was to come into view. They moved like a cat. His hand glided to his gun resting on the surface, his finger slipping down the length of the barrel ready to wrap around the trigger.

211

Two forms moved in front of him by the fence. The grasses drifted over his eyes and cut off his vision. He puffed and let his breath move the grasses again and again until he felt certain that he knew those body shapes. His jaw dropped as one of them spoke. He wanted to stand up and tell Tango Investigations, Inc to take a hike. He couldn't, Yvonne had told him to stay clear of this property.

Knowing who they were caused him to leave his gun and slowly raise his arm until his fingers could move some of the grasses over his eyes apart and allow him a much better view of their movements.

"Okay, we've got to get on the other side of this fence," Lessie said.

He watched as she looked the fence area over.

"Give me a minute, and I'll figure it out. This dang fence isn't that high. I can climb it."

His eyes followed as she reached up and touched the top of the fence.

Yvonne used her cane to move over the uneven ground, "What?"

Lessie turned to her, "Put your hands together and give me a lift up. I'll go over the fence."

"I want to check this fence out," Yvonne said shaking her head while doing her best to stand her cane against the barrier. Each time she let it go it listed to the left and fell over. "You do the shadiest things, and you put my license in jeopardy."

Lessie's loose hand found her hip, "Oh, will you stop. You're beginning to sound like a broken record. You know I have to do this kind of stuff if we are going to be successful." Lessie looked directly at Yvonne, "You're too persnickety. Drop the cane. It won't go anywhere, help me!"

Art grinned as he thought he was watching a tennis match, working his eyes from one to the other.

"What if someone sees you?"

A hoarse whisper, "Us...don't you mean us? You're here, too!"

Yvonne said, "Are we going to discuss this all afternoon?"

Lessie gave her an exasperated stance and said, "Not if you listen to me and get my ass up there—," she pointed sternly, "—where I can get over this damn fence."

"I'm still the boss and I am going to take a moment to inspect this fence. After that I will tell you what we are going to do to proceed."

"Well damn!"

"Lessie you are the most —."

"Sassy?"

"Pain-in-the-ass."

"Yeah, but you love me."

Art saw Yvonne shake her head and turn toward the fence. She's going to find the loose board; she's only one board away. She found the board and moved it and Lessie went thought into the backyard of Irma and Judy's. Yvonne stuck her head through the opening and that's about all Art could make out.

It wasn't long that they came back to this side of the fence. They were looking at some pictures Lessie had taken of the area and they left.

"God! Art thought. He so wanted them out of here. Clearly, this stakeout is a stake off. He was close to letting his whereabouts be known to these two. Art gritted his teeth together until his jaws ached, finally releasing them to ease the discomfort.

Art managed to blow some grass away and turn his head. They were gone. At least they didn't know he was there. Art stood, looked around while pulling the headpiece off. He pulled his arm out of the right sleeve and slid the left sleeve off. The top dropped downward, and Art could remove one leg and then the other and was free of that uncomfortable outfit. He put Murphy's clothes back on and put the camouflage suit inside the footlocker, and slipped into his shoes. Everything looked right as he covered the container with grasses. Then he walked back to the fence opening and escaped the confines of the abandoned side yard.

He went back to Murphy's car and drove it to his house, parked it out front and walked to the front door and rang the bell waiting for Murphy to let him in his home.

As the door opened, Art started talking. "It was a bust."

Chapter Thirty-Six

5:28 P.M. October 7, 1995

Art strolled into his house, looked at Murphy and shook his head. "I wouldn't have believed it if I hadn't seen it with my own eyes." He closed his eyes with an expression that said he'd seen it all. "Tango showed up."

Murphy smirked, dropped his head, "Both of them? Yvonne too?"

"Come on," They moved into the kitchen. "I could use some coffee." Art filled the container with cold water then shoveled grounds into the filter and pushed the red button on the coffee maker and turned to Murphy, "It'll take a few minutes." He reached for some mugs, got the sugar, and placed the dish on the table, "You like cream?"

"No."

"Good, 'cause, you'd get milk." Art opened the drawer, took out a couple of teaspoons, and laid them by the mugs. "I'm sitting over there sweating myself like a sauna in that hay pile of a suit and along comes Yvonne and Lessie. They haven't a clue that the fence is rigged for entry. So Lessie decides to go over the fence."

Murphy's eyes widened. "Yvonne...went over the fence?

"No," Art shook his head. "Her back injury wouldn't let her. She found the opening and Lessie went through into the yard, they got some pictures and left shortly after that." Art looked at the pot. Not enough coffee had dripped down yet, so he turned back to Murphy. "What's that old saying, a watched pot never boils? Or something like that. I could sure use that coffee." He put out some cookies from a box in the cupboard. "Guess this was a dry run."

"So... what happened? You didn't tell them you were on the job?"

Art's eyes lit up, "Hell no. My shooter was a no show today."

"What are we going to do, wait for next trash day? That's a week away."

Art raised his good hand and placed it over his mouth as though to keep from speaking. He moved it away and looked up. "I don't know. I can't figure this guy out."

"You think it's a man?"

"I don't know." The coffee pot gurgled. He turned, picked up the fresh pot and poured both mugs full. "I don't know why I'm alive. He could have taken me out with the first shot."

Murphy stirred in two spoons of sugar and looked up at Art. "This guy is toying with you, wants to make you pay."

Art nodded agreement, pouted his lips and thoughtfully said, "But for what? Wouldn't he want me to know why this is happening?" Art got a questioning expression. After a moment he glanced down at his arm and raised his limp arm by the elbow, "I'd better put the arm sling back on, my arm's beginning to ache."

Murphy handed it to Art. "I don't know how you get anything done with that thing."

"I don't."

"Thanks." Art brightened, "Come on. Let's go out in the backyard. I need to get Daisy out for a walk on the wild side." He nodded toward his mug, "Get that, will you?" He leaned down, opened the cage door, and out romped the fuzzy white ball called Daisy. She played friskily with Art's hand as he corralled her and headed for the backyard. He and Murphy chose chairs suitable for viewing the river and letting Daisy roam.

"Maybe this person isn't coming back. Maybe he wanted to scare you and leave it at that," Murphy said.

"Maybe," Art sounded absentminded, as he sipped. "Then why'd he come the second time?"

"So what do you want me to do? Still impersonate you?"

"No," Art looked his way. "We can change back when we go inside." Art's eyes narrowed—. "Wait a minute."

Murphy turned to Art. "What?"

"It was getting dark that evening of the first shots. Maybe it's too early for trash day?"

"What time was it when you were shot at the next time?"

"Yeah, I see your point. But follow me. It happened one week ago. The first shots occurred at dusk as I took the trash out. The shooter had to know I'd be there to put the cans out and he waited for me—. We're too early." Art started removing the sling. He gulped the coffee. "Hot. God, that's hot." He handed the sling to Murphy and stood. "Catch that pup will you?" Murphy headed for Daisy and she raced off across the yard straight for the river and the boat ramp.

Murphy dashed down the sloping lawn his feet hammering over the boards of the private boat slip. As

Daisy readied to launch herself, Murphy scooped her up. "Got her."

Art headed for the house, and Murphy hurried to catch up tucking Daisy into her crate. As he straightened up he said, "I need more cardboard."

As Art pulled the green sling off he slung it Murphy's direction. "There's a bunch of it in the garage. I put up three doors, and you only cut one of them up earlier."

Murphy caught the sling and flexed his hand. A not so happy look covered his face, "Oh, thanks for that information."

Art could see Murphy was tired of cutting cardboard, but what else could they do? Art caught the time. "It's getting close to six. I've got to get back over there if I'm not late already."

"You carrying?"

"Yeah. You ready?"

Murphy nodded.

The two looked at each other for a long moment then Art left. "Later."

"Be safe and keep my ass out of trouble." Murphy said as the door closed.

Art hurried to Murphy's car to get back in place before the shooter showed up.

He hurried back to the area where the opening waited. He scanned all around to find anyone that might be viewing his actions. Everything remained quiet. He moved the board, slid through and hurried to the fence by Irma's and Judy's. He slid the board, and no one was there. Art took a deep breath feeling both relieved that he managed to get back here and at the same time sad that there wasn't someone already there ready to draw a bead on him. Art moved to the metal box, shoved the grass off. Unlocked the box and removed the outfit. He pulled it on over Murphy's clothes, concerned that he didn't have enough time to undress and get into the disguise.

Art recovered the box with dried grass, and situated himself on the shady side to play grass mound. He had that, "been-there, done-that" feeling as soon as things got quiet.

Murphy had dragged the trash container back and must be working on another cardboard box now. Art sat as still as a snail.

About fifteen minutes passed before Art heard the wooden fence behind him scrape and then the hollow sound of the board slipping back into place.

It has to be the shooter!

He gulped and tried to keep his heart from racing. Someone's foot pressed cracking dried leaves underweight. Another step and a twig snapped. The person stopped.

This guy knows his stuff. His ached to see who it was and he managed to get a clear view to his left where the camo suit seemed skimpier of dried grass. He kept his eyes turned that way, waiting.

Snap! Another step.

Please don't let it be Tango and Associates again.

The sound of advancement kept Art's muscles tense. His fingers tightened. He pressed his lips tightly together feeling his mustache stick his chin. Just a few more feet he urged. The person stopped. Art's hand gripped his gun. Art heard the sound of the person handling the ordinance.

Frustration tightened his neck muscles as his hand squeezed his gun. He stiffened wondering if the site hairs of that gun were pointing on this mound of grass. He didn't wait long to find out.

A larger full-bodied man stepped past Art, heading to the loose board in the fence. Arts eyes searched for anything familiar about this person. Somewhere on the outer fringes of his memory a glimmer pulsated, but wouldn't settle a clear thought. The man took a screwdriver from his pocket and made the opening bigger for his body to slide through. His work shirt scraped the wood as he pushed through. His leg the last to disappear into the backyard seemed like any leg to Art.

A large hand reached for the rifle, as the rifle slid through the opening in the fence, Art knew he had his guy. His hand wrapped around his weapon and he slid it free. Art's eyes bore into the fence ahead of him focused on the man on the other side who grunted as he dropped into position.

Art hoped Murphy still impersonated him and worked out in the open. He needed this guy to draw a bead on him and at the ready to fire.

Doing his best not to make any sound, Art raised up until he had his full height; his appearance like Bigfoot as he approached the fence opening. He pulled the board aside and could see the man prone on the ground, his cheek rested against the stock of the rifle. Art saw the barrel directed across the street. The man focused on dialing in the sight as Murphy dragged the second container to the curb.

Art heard the telltale sound, click-click, as the man's head moved closer to the eyepiece.

Then the intake of air.

Now or never, Art decided and his full authoritative command voice snapped out, "Freeze, you son-of-a-bitch!"

The man's head swung toward Art's voice, clearly surprised. At that moment he jerked back to his sight and squeezed off one round.

"I said, freeze! You fire one more round, and you're dead. Got that?"

The man took his hands away from the rifle and raised them into the air.

"Murphy, you okay?"

"Yeah."

"Get over here."

Murphy came running. He scaled the first fence, ran down the fence line, and slid through the opening in the second fence. A bit out of breath he arrived at Art's side. Art held his gun centered on the man. Murphy holstered his gun and pulled a pair of cuffs from his back pocket and slapped one around the thick wrist, "You have the right to remain silent...."

Murphy picked up the rifle as he recited his rights. "Do you understand these rights?" He handed the rifle to Art. "A nice piece. Mosin Nagant M 44."

Art stood the firearm against the fence without his gun wavering from the shooter.

"Get him up and let's get him out here."

"Come on get up."

The man could not get up with his hands cuffed behind his back. Murphy helped him get to his feet and ducked his head with his hand as he shoved the man back through the two-board opening.

As soon as they got him to the empty field side of the fence, they asked him who he was and why he'd been shooting at Art.

A gravelly voice demanded, "I want my lawyer."

"You have anything sharp in your pockets?" Murphy asked.

The man refused to answer as Art positioned himself a few feet away his gun trained on the man.

Murphy searched his pants and pulled out his wallet. "Michael McNamare."

The man hung his head.

That glimmer of memory he had earlier slid into sharp focus for Art. "You're Raymond McNamare's father?" Art asked, a perplexed expression crossing his face.

"I'm his Grandfather."

"Why are you shooting at me?" Art saw an expression in the man's face that said I'm sorry, and a belligerence that said, I'm a tough guy. Art thought, you shot at me ass-hole. What in hell is that all about? But he didn't ask, he figured he would have some time with this guy and could find all that he needed to find then. For now he watched McNamare from the barrel of his gun which remained pointed right at his heart.

Mac McNamare cast a hateful glare at the barrel of that gun and then at Art. Red shaded over his rounded cheeks, fire spit from his deerskin tinted eyes as they leveled on Art. He huffed as though out of breath and managed, "Don't you know?"

Art shook his head.

"All I hear day and night is that you killed our grandson. My wife won't let me be. She goes on and on and on about it day and night."

Art's mouth gaped a long moment, then his eyes narrowed and his nostrils flared as he took in a deep breath. "So killing me would make her feel better?"

McNamare grunted out, "I thought it would get her off my back."

"Get him out of here," Art said.

Murphy and Art moved him off the property to the sidewalk where Murphy called for a squad car to give the man a ride downtown.

In a matter of minutes, a car arrived and the officers took McNamare into custody, tucking him into the car to take him to the station. Murphy and Art told them they'd be down soon to give their reports. Then they exchanged a congratulatory look at each other. They shook hands, and headed for Art's house to exchange clothes and car keys. "Murphy, your car is around the corner parked near the old mill on School Street .

After Murphy left, Art put a call-in to Evelyn to let her know everything was okay and safe for Melissa to come home. He listened to the phone ring and got angrier by the moment. Finally the answering machine kicked in and asked if he'd like to leave a message. Yes, he thought, but it would not be appropriate to say what he was thinking on her machine. "Evelyn, call me."

Chapter Thirty-Seven

6:51 P.M. October 7, 1995

Walt came as soon as Art called, his humped over body shuffled up the walk, "Hey, you got the guy! I saw the rifle before I came here. That's really nice a sweet piece. Did you take a look at the sight. You could knock the wings off a gnat with that thing."

"So the question remains, why am I alive?"

"Yeah! Exactly."

Art leveled on Walt's eyes, "He didn't want me dead."

Walt nodded. "Do we know why?"

"Hey, that's not nice."

"Do we?"

"He said his wife rode him about my killing her grandson."

"Oh," Art said. "I've got something for you. I just paid a guy for hanging security doors on my house. His name is Stumper." He watched Walt's face.

Walt nodded, "Yeah, I talked to him."

"He's got a rifle across his back window of his pickup and a box of shells that would blow a hole wide enough for an elephant to walk through. That interest you?"

"I cleared him. He had an alibi for the time."

Art reached into the refrigerator and pulled out a package of sliced ham. His fingers teased the wrapper open, and he rolled up a piece, a nod to Walt to help himself as he stuffed his mouth full. "Maybe you should check that alibi out again," he muffled through the chewing. His expression screamed. You need to do it again.

"This is Roger Stumper?" Walt asked as he pulled a piece of ham free from the package and rolled it tightly up, nibbling a bit off the end of the roll.

"Yeah, that's the name," Art said taking another piece. "I'm out of bread, or we could make sandwiches. Oh—," Art pulled the refrigerator door open and brought out a large jar of sweet pickles and some sliced cheese. He tossed the items on the counter, grabbed the cupboard door and added a box of crackers to the meal.

"This is good just like this," Walt said. "I'm pretty sure his alibi was solid, but I can check again." He pulled his frayed notepad from his pocket, smacking his lips a couple of times as he turned the pages. "Here it is. James Wexford backed him up."

Art's eyebrows shot up, "Wexford?" He nodded and put another four cups of coffee on to drip. "I've got a feeling about him. He's your guy. Adora lost her life to him. Now you have to prove it. I'll give the doc a jingle and see what he tells me."

"Oh thanks, give me the easy jobs."

Art moved for the phone and called Doc Wexford. "What date and time do we need to clear for Stumper? Coroner fixed the time of death at 3:15 p.m. on the 31st of August?"

Walt finished the last of his ham roll, pulled a sweet pickle out of the jar and ate it in four bites. He wiped his fingers on a hand towel hanging on the end of the counter. "Yeah," he nodded as he spoke.

Art listened as the phone rang and rang. "What you need to do is get a picture of that pickup truck and show it to the woman that found the body. Maybe she saw more than she knows she saw."

Walt flipped some more pages backward, "That would be Ms. Mead, a widow, lives near Turner Rd. I've got her phone number right here. Got any idea where that pickup truck might be right now?"

"Hello, Doc. Any chance I can swing by your place for a moment; I've got Walt with me. Got a couple of questions for you."

Art nodded at Walt letting him know they were welcome to come over now. Walt put his pad back in his pocket and got off the stool. He looked toward Art who placed the earpiece back in the cradle. He moved over to the sink and rinsed his hands off, gathered everything up and put them away. "Okay, let's go."

As they parked at Wexford's Art said, tilting his head for direction, "There's your pickup truck right there."

Walt slid out of Art's car and pulled his Sony Cybershot from his pocket and snapped several shots of the pickup, getting the license plate, the front and sides of the truck. Walt focused on the rifle and snapped a couple. He slipped the camera into his pocket and walked beside Art to the steps of the grand house. "This is one of Lodi's historic houses," Walt said as he placed his foot on the first of five steps to the porch.

Their footsteps thunked across the wooden porch. Art pressed the doorbell and through the door they could hear a melody announced their presence.

Wexford came and unhooked the wooden screen door to allow them to walk into the mess of construction. After they got into the room and looked around the doc said they might be more comfortable sitting on the front porch. So they went back outside and over to the chairs.

Art explained Walt's interest in the whereabouts of Roger Stumper on August 31'st from 2 p.m. to 3:15 p.m.

"Was he working for you that day?" Walt asked his notepad at the ready.

The Doc nodded his head, "Yes, I hired him in July, about the 15th."

Walt asked, "He was working here on that day and during that time?"

The Doc nodded, his eyes wide, and looked straight at Walt. "He got here about 7 a.m. and worked all day. He's been a good worker."

"Were you with him all day?" Art asked.

The doc's eyes shifted from Walt to Art, "No, I had running around to do."

Art leaned forward, "How long were you gone?"

The doc seemed perplexed, shook his head and finally answered, "I don't know."

Art pushed on, "So, Mr. Stumper could have left anytime in the morning or afternoon and returned, and you would not know it for sure."

The doc's eyes widened, his shoulders raised, "I guess so."

Walt and Art left Wexford's and headed off to take pictures of two other used pickups. Art cleared his throat, "We need to get into his pickup truck and get one of those shells."

"I don't see any way of doing that right now and we sure as heck don't have anything to compare the rifling with."

"You're right. Still, I know he's our scumbag."

They drove over to the city lot where the employee's vehicles waited for their owners. Walt took some front and side views then he and Art headed to the department to print the pictures from a computer. As soon as they had the copies, they headed for Ms. Mead's for an unannounced visit.

The front of the white cottage sat back from the street and on a slight hill allowing the front lawn to drape down to the sidewalk. Bright red geraniums bloomed across the front of the house greeting them. They walked up to the security door and pressed the doorbell, setting off Westminster Abbey chimes.

M.L. WEATHERINGTON

A pleasant, white-haired woman said, "Yes, can I help you?"

Art and Walt introduced themselves, and she ushered them into her living room. They asked if they could show her some pictures and she nodded and asked them to sit down. Both Art and Walt chose wingback chairs. She sat on the sofa and Walt spread the pictures on the coffee table for her to view.

The woman's face morphed into a stone-serious expression.

"Have you ever seen any of these pickup trucks?" Walt asked.

Her fingers slid over her mouth as she stared at the pictures. She lifted each photo one at a time and set them on her coffee table all in a row. Slowly she shook her head and answered, "Yes. But I can't remember where. Why are you asking me?"

Walt leaned closer to her to get a better look at the pictures. "Which pickup?"

Her finger shook as she pointed to Stumpers pickup, "—I remember where." Her eyes misted, "I hope I never have that experience again." She looked at the pictures again. Her breath caught, "That's where I saw that truck. It was sitting at the curb when I came down the street and stopped my car. This truck," her finger tapped the middle photo, "was idling just sitting there. The man must have seen what I saw." An expression of shock crossed her face as she looked from Walt to Art. "He drove away as I got out of my car and walked to her. I remember I thought it strange." She stared off into space. "It was a gray-haired man. His hair was pulled back and..." She moved her graceful hand to her throat, her fingers brushing her skin, "he had a red scarf tied around his forehead. He looked at me and then drove off. I thought it funny at the time, but then forgot about it when I realized she was dead."

Art sat back; that was all they needed for the moment. They would run a picture of Mr. Stumper by her

and if she could ID that person as the man driving the
pickup truck Adora's cold case could go red hot.

Chapter Thirty-Eight

8:05 P.M. October 7, 1995

"How long do you think you are going to be before you come back to work?" Walt asked.

Art stepped out of Walt's car and glanced down at the left arm. "Don't know. I have exercises to do and physical therapy that I go to once a week now. To tell you the truth, I don't see any change."

"What do they tell you?"

"It will take time. Sounds a lot like they don't know to me." Art shrugged his shoulders.

"Time will tell. What are you going to do now?"

"I am going to call Evelyn again. I want to get Melissa back home. She needs to get back into school."

"I am glad it ended as it did."

"Yep. Talk at you later." Art smacked the side of Walt's unit sharply and stood up stepping back from the car. Walt moved the car away from the curb and Art watched a moment before he started turning toward his house.

"Art."

A sweet, demure female voice caught his attention; he turned as Irma came across the street toward him.

"Did you clear everything up? I mean concerning my house?" She looked at him with wide eyes. A touch of fear hinted in the sparkle.

He grinned at her and took her hand as she offered it when she stopped by his side.

"Everything is over. I caught the guy, and he's in jail now," Art assured her with his steady eyes.

"I am so glad to hear that. I worried from the time you came over asking to go into our back yard. I knew you wouldn't do that without good reason. What did the guy want?"

Art pursed his lips together wondering what he should tell her. He opened them and dampened his lips with his tongue. "Just a fellow with a grudge against me. He tried to scare me. It's over now. He won't come back."

Irma nodded her curly brown head, smiled and accepted Art's explanation. She placed her hand on his bad arm and patted. "Thank you for your service and for being my neighbor. I sleep better with you nearby. Is it okay if I get the handyman to fix the fence now?"

Art assured her that it would be just fine. She started for her home and Art watched her. He took in a deep breath and walked into his house and to the phone. He looked up Evelyn's number and dialed. He'd okayed a ten-day vacation, but now it wasn't necessary. He wanted Melissa back home.

"Hello?"

"Evelyn. It's Art. I called you before and left a message."

"Hi, how are you? I haven't checked my messages yet today."

"I see. I am fine, how's Melissa?"

"Oh, Art. She is wonderful."

Worry lifted its ugly head and set up shop in Art's heart. He put it aside as foolishness and plowed on. "Everything is okay here, and she can come home now."

M.L. WEATHERINGTON

Art listened as Evelyn handled the phone and breathed, taking her time.

"Art... listen. Melissa fits in here, and you've done a wonderful job to this point, but I think, as her mother, it's time for her to stay with me. A young woman needs a woman, a mother, during these years."

His hackles rose, "Wait a minute, Evelyn. Melissa has friends here, and a life here and she needs to be back in school."

"And she almost lost her life with you, because of what you do. You know that's the reason I walked away from you, I didn't want to hear one day that you were dead because of someone you didn't even know killed you in the line of your duty."

Art's cheeks bloomed red, and his eyes smoldered as he drew breath, "Evelyn, you didn't walk out on me, you got pregnant, and you didn't want a child hanging on you. I left you to raise Melissa. It had nothing to do with my chosen field of employment. Everything is fine here now, and I want Melissa home to go back to school this Monday."

"Well, I don't know if that's going to happen." Evelyn sounded like she planned to hang up. "I can put her in school here."

Art gripped the phone, his knuckles whitening under pressure and if he continued to squeeze as he did at the moment he just might have the earpiece in two halves instead of one piece. "This is not negotiable, Evelyn. I want you to bring Melissa back. When can I expect you?"

"She's old enough to make that choice herself. Let's ask her where, or, which parent she prefers."

"No!" Art wanted to wring her neck. "Melissa's a child, she's sixteen, and we should not put adult matters on her shoulders. We need to be on the same page, and you need to follow my orders and bring her home. Now!"

"Well..." she paused, "I don't think I want to do that Art. You've had her for the first sixteen years, and I will take it from here on out."

"Evelyn!" The line sang a disconnected song in Art's ear. He held it out, looking at it for the longest time, unable to believe Evelyn would do this.

He put the phone back in its cradle and jerked the drawer open, pulling out the phone book. Art spun the pages open hunting for the right heading. Finally, he pointed to the number and punched it in as though he had a score to settle with the square buttons. He made reservations for himself and two people on return flight at the airport. His flight left in 55 minutes.

"Murphy?" Art said when Murphy answered his phone. I need a ride to the Sacramento International Airport stat. He didn't listen to Murphy's answer; he slammed down the receiver and rushed upstairs. Art snapped open the closet and snatched up his ever ready travel bag. The one filled with a change of clothes and personal items like a toothbrush and toothpaste. Then he locked up the house. He moved his bag out to the curb and felt immediate relief when Murphy's car came to a sliding stop. Wilma sat in the front seat, and Art threw his bag in the back seat, and his body followed. He hunted for the seat belt and said, "Haul ass."

They headed for Turner Road. Once they crossed Lower Sacramento Road they were on Turner Road that was seven miles long to the Interstate Five freeway. The road proved empty at this hour. Tall trees draped their branches over the thoroughfare. Some walnut trees grew lining farmland to the right. Older farmhouses nestled along the road, a testament to a quieter lifestyle long past.

A grand new home sported tiled roofs and interesting elevations. Art didn't see any of it as they sped over that two laned road and finally eased into traffic on the I 5 heading north for Sacramento. "Don't know if I can get you there in time Art. This traffic's heavy."

"Then un-heavy it, get out there, and let's go." Art looked up as the seatbelt cut across his chest holding him back against the seat. His hand grabbed and jerked to loosen the webbing. He managed to get his fingers under and that seemed all that he could free himself.

The car swerved to the left as Murphy found an opening. Then jerked again as he made it into the fast lane. "We can go seventy here Art."

"You can go faster than that Murf. Just show your badge."

"Art that will take time. I'll do seventy-five. They won't bother us at that speed. Everyone else is going eighty. I'll stay with the flow of traffic as long as they are speeding I will too."

Ahead six eighteen wheelers were taking up the lanes, trying to pass the slower truckers. Art worried that they would get stuck in all that mess, but Murphy managed to get around them and hold their speed.

"Where are you going?" Wilma's voice almost carried away with the road sounds, caught Art's attention.

"I am going to get my daughter Melissa."

"Oh, where is she?" Willy's frail voice continued over the tire hum.

"She's in Florida." Art watched out the car window as they whizzed past new and used vehicles. He wondered what the driver's life stories were. Could they be any different than his? Would they be normal eventless existences? If so, how could he manage such a lifestyle? He looked at his watch as he spotted the sign for Florin Road. Would they make it? He willed the car to go faster and fought himself wanting to tell Murphy to pick it up. When did the next flight leave, five hours? He'd be sitting at the damned airport five hours? Art brought his bottom lip over his top, smoothing the mustache hairs in one long movement. Trees filled the edges of the freeway on the east side, some on the west. Businesses sprouted up here and there and mixed with open ground seeded in grasses turning golden. Here and there he noticed a horse, its head down grazing. He thought of Midnight. His teeth grit together. He hadn't spoken with Charlie, and I haven't paid the stall rent. He shook his head that he let so many things dangle lately. His life spun into one big mess, like he hoarded trouble. Maybe Evelyn's right. Maybe I'm not such a good parent. He dropped his gaze into the interior of the car and toward the floorboards. Just then they raced over a bridge, and the sounds of travel sounded hollow. Art noticed Murphy's car seemed clean and neat, no dirt anywhere. Just he and his bag filled the area. How do others do it, keep their lives from mucking up?

Finally, he brought his head up, refusing to sink into a dark pit of no return. The glass buildings of Sacramento gleamed as they swept around a curve and under an overpass. Soon, he thought, they would be out of old Sacramento and heading up the open road to the airport. His watch moved closer to the departure time. He'd have to run from the car. He'd have to fight that damn arm the whole way and manage his bag and get his ticket.

The car raced up the airport's entry road and sailed along to the front parking lot area and slowed as he came to the doors for the different airlines. "Which one?" Murphy's tenor voice sounded loud over the car and airport sounds.

"Delta."

The car stopped, and Art's body flew forward unsecured by the seatbelt. He grabbed his carry-on and slid it across the seat. "Bye and thanks."

Murphy leaned across Willy, "Let me know when you need a ride home."

"I'll call."

Art waved at them and rushed through the sliding door. He hurried to the counter and got his ticket. Art found the right staging area and door to load. "I'm on the flight to Orlando to leave now. How do I get on?"

"You better hurry, they'll be closing the door soon," the attendant said when looking at Art's ticket. Art ran toward the roped off area she pointed to and down the aisle. Trotting through a tunnel toward the humming sound of the plane's engines, he slipped through the doorway and felt the suction as the door sealed shut. He had his bag by his side; his arm ached with an almost sickening repeat throb. The dark-haired attendant grabbed his bag and told him to follow her. He moved sideways down the aisle to a seat on the aisle about midway of the plane. She opened the overhead and stuffed his bag up and in, closing the door. The stewardess moved out of the seating area, which allowed him to take his seat. He buckled up. After a few minutes the plane ran down the runway and lifted into the air. I'm coming, Melissa. Art unclenched his fists.

He pulled his gray jacket cuff back and looked at his watch. I won't be there for 5 hours and 17 minutes. That's 4:17 a.m. their time. Then I have to get from Orlando to Melissa. I wonder how long that will take. My return flight is for noon tomorrow, so I have to get her and head right back to the airport.

He sat back resting his head on the head rest and realized the person next to him, a middle-aged woman stared at him. At first her stare gave him the willies. Then he chuckled to himself. He might appear crazed to her.

"Hi, I am Arlene. You look frazzled; I am a good listener. Do you play bridge?"

Chapter Thirty-Nine

4:59 A.M. October 8, 1995

The plane landed, and colorful flags, snapped sharp by the wind caught his attention as he stepped off the plane's ramp. He walked to the car rental queue. Art followed the attendant who came to a stop and indicated the car Art would be taking. "Are you expecting a storm?"

"There's a tropical storm coming in tomorrow night."

Art looked around the lot and into the sky feeling the power of the storm building and he was glad he'd come for Melissa.

They stopped by a midsized Toyota, dark blue in color with a gray interior. Art walked around the car with the attendant, and they noted the existing imperfections together.

"Do you have a map? I need to get from Orlando to Kissimmee."

"Yeah," the young man said with a voice pattern slower than honey would flow on a frosty New England morning. "I'll set you up."

Art watched him filling out all the papers necessary for his car rental agreement. The day had been long now and he didn't need to prolong his ordeal.

"Wait here. I'll get you some brochures and a map of the area." He sauntered back inside the building. He is the only one working this late, Art thought. Art yawned again, looking up into the night sky and seeing that clouds hid most of the stars.

The man returned and said, "Here, these will help you. You just get on Florida's turnpike. It's about seven cents a mile, maybe a little less. You go south to Kissimmee. Take Magnolia Ave right out there toward SR 15 heading south. You turn left onto SR15 and in about sixty-six feet the name changes to W. South St. got that?" He looked at Art.

Art's brain was on overload. "Yeah, thanks." He felt he could follow a map much easier than he could follow this man's hand signals. "Then you take the ramp left and follow the signs for I-four west. At exit 249 take the ramp for Osceola Parkway toward Disney World. Ever been there?"

Art shook his head.

"No." The man's mouth hung open, trying to get his mind around how it could be that Art has not been to Disney World. "Well, there's a toll road. It will get you to Kissimmee in twenty or thirty minutes depending on traffic."

"Thank you," Art said and took the keys the young man held out with his copy of the paperwork.

That killed another hour he thought as he checked out the placement of all the driving equipment he'd be using. He switched on the headlights and started the car off the lot. Art drove over the Florida roadways in the still of the night along with several others. He left the toll road and ran over a surface road with low hanging electrical lines swaying in the breeze. The stoplight he waited at swung back and forth over his car. Finally, it turned green and he proceeded southward into Kissimmee.

He pulled over and dug Evelyn's address out of his jacket pocket. He could call but thought better of it almost as soon as he thought about calling. Art would show up and ring the doorbell. He'd thank Evelyn and take Melissa with or without her things.

He could darn well buy her new things. She needed new things as she had grown this past year.

Art stopped the car. The house number matched the one on his note. He turned the car off and removed the keys. A dog started barking as soon as he stepped to the ground.

Art walked over the front walk to the entryway and pressed the door buzzer. Finally, in a far-off room, he heard a door open, then pounding sounds like someone coming downstairs. He turned more to the door as he heard feet coming to a stop on the other side of the front door.

A tall, willowy, twenties-something brown haired girl opened the door.

"Evelyn, is she here?"

"Evie? hell no." The woman's head shook, her hair sailing back and forth.

"I don't understand, isn't this Evelyn's address? Does she live here?"

"Well, I guess she sure does, but she's moving the airplane."

"Where? Where is she?"

"Hell man, I don't know. She doesn't tell us where she's is, or where she's going."

Art let his shoulders slump. He felt tired, drained and his eyes burned. "How do you reach her?"

"Phone."

"What number do you call?"

"If Evelyn wanted you to call she would give you her number."

"I do have her number. I talked to her this morning. Now I want to talk to her in person. Where might I find her?"

The young woman sized up Art and said, "Well if you have her number why are you asking me?" The door slammed shut.

Standing in the night on what should have been Evelyn's porch confounded him. He stepped back, turned around and pulled his cell phone and entered Evelyn's number.

After a long moment, he got an answer, "Yeah,"

"Evelyn, its Art where are you?"

"What do you mean where am I. In bed sleeping."

"What's your exact location?" He held the phone to his ear as he stepped down from the porch walking down the sidewalk to the car.

"I'm at the airport, why?"

"What airport?"

"Kissimmee, why?"

"Just wanted to know where you were." He adjusted the phone in his hand and looked around the area. He imagined that the girl inside might be calling the police and he might have some visitors soon.

"I'll talk to you another time."

"Okay." She hung up, and so did he.

Thank God, I have this map of Florida. He moved the car to an all-night gas station and used the overhead light to find the Kissimmee Community Airport. Art drove there and walked up to the clerk. Spotting the clerks nametag he said, "Nick, hi. I am Arthur Franklin. I need to see Evelyn Conley. I understand she is here." Nick picked up his phone and made a call. She answered, and Nick told her Art waited for her in the office. She must have hung up because Nick put the phone down and smiled at Art.

"Is she coming?"

He nodded and went back to his crossword puzzle and mug of coffee.

Art cooled his heels for what seemed like a long time. Evelyn appeared disturbed as she sailed through the side door in her red robe.

"What are you doing here?" she asked.

Art narrowed his eyes on her. "I've flown across the country, driven to where I thought you lived only to find you here at the community airport." He let his voice rise with each word making the remark sound more like an indictment.

"Yeah."

Sounded to him like a sneer meaning "So."

"Where is Melissa?"

She smoothed her short locks back from both sides of her face, "I see where this is going. She's staying here with me from now on. So, if you want to wish her well in the morning, you can. Or, you can get on your high horse right now and ride out of here and leave her alone."

"Evelyn, Melissa is going home with me. You can't take a child out of state. She goes home with me.

"You don't have a leg to stand on, Bucko. You sent her with me. I have your blessing and God, how many people know it. Why? 'cause you thought you were being shot at. Oh, I think the courts are going to look at me as the best parent for her."

Art looked around the room. Nick, though his head seemed directed at the crossword puzzle on his desk, trained his ears on them. Art had to be careful. Perception is everything. "Okay, Evelyn, I can wait until morning. Where can I find a motel for the night and when can we meet?"

"Motels are all over the place just look for a sign that says they have an opening. Oh, watch out for the bed bugs, though, they can carry you away." She sailed back out of the office area, leaving him standing with Nick who watched Art through hooded eyes.

He walked out into the night and drove off the airport property for a motel. Just around the corner he spotted a sign waving in the strong breeze. It announced the motel had openings. He rented a room for the rest of the night. Art parked in front of his room, locked the car and lugged his carryon toward the door. The key card slipped through the key pass and the lock light turned green. The suction on the door molding let go and popped open. He was in and it elicited a weak smile as his foot sailed over the threshold. Art picked up his carryon and dropped it on the floor. He had one question bothering him now. What had happened between Melissa and him and had he lost his little girl?

Chapter Forty

3:13 A.M. October 9, 1995

As he entered the room he tossed his car keys on the table by the door and then headed for the bathroom. He felt much relieved then pressed down on the handle to flush the toilet. The room seemed quieter than he had expected. But then everyone was sleeping. Looking for a towel Art focused on the geometric design of the white on white, shower curtain. A shower would be good now. The curtain moved as he pulled it aside. The tub and shower looked clean and inviting. Art shook his head. He didn't want to wake up. I want to sleep.

The towels were decorations on the towel rack. Oh well, he thought and grabbed one of the hand towels and dried his dripping hands.

Without thinking, he moved to the window and drew back the drapes. The street on his side of the block had no parking signs with lights shining on them.

He shook his head and let the drape fall back into place. Art blinked his sleep filled eyes and brought his energy drained body to the bed. The cover felt heavy in his hand as he turned the pillows free of their entrapment. He had four small pillows. He only wanted two, so he sailed the extra two onto the adjoining bed.

M.L. WEATHERINGTON

Art pulled his shoes off. With his motel neighbors in mind, he set them on the floor. He tugged at his already loosened tie and pulled it off, allowing it to find its place on the bed. Finally, he twisted his waist and pulled his legs up to stretch them over the bright flowery cover.

His lungs filled with a deep breath and Art's head sank into the pillow. He slept.

Two hours later Art's eyes snapped open as the wake-up call came on the phone. His mouth felt like Death Valley in August. He dropped his eyes down to his arm. It ached. I didn't bring my pain pills. They are at home in my bathroom cabinet shelf. The pain would be his partner from now on out. He sat on the side of the bed and let his body lean forward. If anyone could see him now, he'd appear dejected. He held that pose for several minutes, finally standing and moving to the shower. When he came back out, he rubbed his chin. Stubble had started. Lucky for him his chin would be blond red and not so noticeable today. Tomorrow would be another story. He could buy a pack of razors if he had to, but right now it did not even merit a second thought.

Breakfast, at five a.m. in this town, circled in his mind. He left the motel room and locked the door. A heavy gust buffeted him. It felt warm. He looked up as he heard the wind in the trees. Amazed at the wind force bending their tops over he wondered Why didn't they just snap off? A newspaper stand held the headline 'Tropical Storm Suzanne Headed This Way'. He gripped his bag, looked down and saw his tie hanging around his neck ready to tighten. The wind smacked his face as he turned into the flow. He just needed a cup of coffee before he tightened the tie for the day.

Art opened the door to the motel office and approached the attendant. A sleepy look met Art's dead tired attempt at pleasantness.

"You leaving?"

Art nodded and placed the key on the counter. The attendant pulled some paper from the copier, tore the lower part off and handed Art his copy.

"Any word on the storm? Are the planes still flying?"

The attendant yawned and scratched his head. "Won't hit us until during the night. Planes will be flying today, maybe not tomorrow. We'll have to see." His eyes held tears as he stopped talking and looked at Art.

"It's sure windy now. Anyplace to get some breakfast around here?"

The clerk nodded and pointed to the right. "Go to the corner and you'll find Sherry's Cafe. She's open twenty-four hours."

"Thanks."

Art pulled the Toyota into a slot right by the door and went inside. Some locals were leaning over mugs of steaming coffee as Art chose a table. A woman, about five feet tall with blonde hair, slapped a menu down in front of him. She liked green eye shadow and had her makeup in place. Her dress, a crisp gingham check in soft green with a white apron gave her a fresh appearance. He nodded to her when she asked if he'd like coffee.

"The real stuff or decaf?"

"The leaded," he said, and the sound of his voice indicated to keep 'em coming.'

She poured, and he opened the menu and ordered scrambled eggs, sourdough toast, one pork chop, and a bowl of fruit. The place smelled good, and Art realized he'd missed dinner yesterday. He'd flown in during his normal dinnertime, and his thoughts were anywhere else but dinner.

He blinked his eyes and tried to look around the room at the other people just to practice his skills. But he found himself dog-tired and unable to think a clear thought. Besides, his arm did more than hang there. Today, it throbbed like a toothache.

Melissa. She filled his thoughts now. Where was she? That thought woke him up. Could it be that Evelyn, because of the impending storm, had flown her out of here?

Breakfast slid before him on a hot plate. His fork kept the pork chop in place as he slashed through the juicy meat and his mind took him where he didn't want to go. Fear crept in and the idea that Evelyn could have flown out last night or this morning just to get Melissa away plagued his peace. He had to get over to that airport and see for himself.

Back out on the street Art made a beeline for the rental and headed for the airport. He pulled up and went inside and met Nick, the same attendant from last night.

"Morning Nick. I need to see Evelyn, could you call her please?"

The man smiled at him and called Evelyn, asking her to come to the office.

She did, wearing the same red robe. She now fought to hold it closed against the strong breeze. The dark hair that circled Evelyn's head tossed wildly as she pulled the door open. A gust of wind whipped inside as she entered. There was a look of consternation on her face as she said, "What is wrong with you?"

Even though everything about her at this moment told him she was hopping mad Art felt relieved to see her. She hadn't flown their daughter out of here. His bag dropped to the floor. "Where's Melissa?"

"In bed! Sleeping." Evelyn cut him short while her robe settled at her slippered feet. Her eyes were stern as she crossed her arms.

Art steadied his eyes on her. "Get her. It's time for us to leave."

Evelyn's head tilted before she spoke, "Art, Melissa likes this life and she is learning about airplanes and is going to start her lessons to become a pilot next month. She is happy and content. She's not scared to death every

246

minute with me. Leave her be for her own good and yours. She's going on with her life."

"I want to see her, and I want to see her now."

Evelyn's head tilted the opposite direction, and her facial expression seemed stony. "Well that's just too bad, isn't it? She's my daughter now. Art, I can give her a safe, peaceful life. That's more than you have ever done." Evelyn shrugged her shoulders.

"I can call the police if I need to."

Her chin and chest rose, "Oh, you won't do that,"

A look crossed Art's face, steeliness as he set his feet apart and faced her square on. With a low deep threatening voice, he said, "I won't?"

"No," she looked at him as though she had him and she knew it.

He saw the grin spread across her face as her eyes narrowed.

"You'd be too embarrassed to admit you couldn't handle your own problem. Don't forget that I know you inside and out."

Their eyes locked together. Art was oblivious of the attendant or that Melissa had pulled the office door open.

"Dad!" echoed through space. She ran to him and slammed her body into his making his arm ache yet again.

They pulled apart, and he looked down at her. "Hi honey," he said as his good arm went around her and he took a couple of steps backward to steady both of them.

Evelyn raised her arms and reached for Melissa's shoulders standing behind her. Melissa turned her head and grinned at her mother.

"It's good to see you," Melissa turned back to Art, looking up into his smiling face, her head back so she could see him. He noticed her hair cut off and bobbed around her face. It looked good. But so different. He missed the long swishing red mass that had been a part of her all through her life.

"Your hair."

"Do you like it?" her hand left his arm and felt her hair, pushing it upward a bit and letting it hang. "Mom knows so much about," she took in a breath, "well, girl stuff."

Art's knees melted. Maybe Melissa did need her mother. Maybe she was better off with Evelyn. The breakfast weighed down on his stomach. He smiled a sick stretch of lips as he fought for what to say.

"Are we going home now?"

Art grabbed at the question, "That's why I came, everything is fine at home, and you need to get back into school."

"I so want to see Daisy and Midnight. God, I've so much to tell Sandy."

Daisy, shit I forgot the puppy. We have to get that flight! "Yes, baby. Get your things."

Melissa turned, pecked her mom on the cheek and raced away.

Evelyn held her arms out at her sides following Melissa's movement. "Melissa, what....?"

They stood silent, listening to Melissa's footfall as she raced away.

A gust of wind howled as the door closed behind Melissa and Evelyn said, "It looks like you won this one."

Art gazed at her feeling relieved.

"Just remember she might change her mind." Evelyn looked hopeful.

Art turned to her and with a kind expression said, "I'll let you know if she does."

"I bet you will."

Melissa and Art thanked Evelyn for everything. They invited her for a visit again soon and bid their goodbyes.

Satisfied that Melissa wanted to come home to Lodi and him let Art relax inside. His arm didn't seem to ache as much. That put a smile on his face as he drove them back to the airport car rental lot to return the car.

Once he'd returned the car he walked them into the airport.

"Dad?"

Art turned to her.

"I'm going in to freshen up."

He took her bag from her and nodded. After she left him he saw the time and knew that Walt must be up and at the office. A bank of phones was on the opposite wall, so he strolled over, placing the bags at his feet. He gave his old partner a call and waited for him to pick up. "Hey."

Walt caught him up on Stumper and Ms. Mead. She did ID his picture as the man she saw when she discovered the body. The rifle and box of shells fit the profile, and they were doing analyses for further proof. Walt had him in custody for the murder of Adora Stumper.

Art smiled a knowing smile that grew into a broad grin. This case would go down in his Franklin Log's as solved by him. He still had the stuff. All that made him happy, yet sadness lingered, and he couldn't quite explain that. Something was missing.

He had Melissa. They were going home. He could mark another case solved in his logbook. He explained to Walt that he had to make a call and told Walt he'd see him soon. When he hung up, he called Murphy and moved from one foot to the other waiting for the answer. He thought the phone was going to message just as Murphy's voice said, "Murf here."

"Murphy, get over to my house and get Daisy out for a walk in the back yard. There's some dog food in a can in the refrigerator and make sure the pup has some water. I forgot and just left."

"Where are you?"

Art looked around settling on the word 'women's' stenciled boldly on the bathroom door Melissa had entered.

"I am outside a ladies bathroom in Florida."

M.L. WEATHERINGTON

"You're what?"

"You heard me, hurry up on the pup okay? Melissa and I are coming in today and will be landing about 4:30 this afternoon. So I am hoping you can pick us up. Oh, the code to shut off the alarm is 04560.

"Sure."

Art had his head back on the airplane headrest as the craft flew through peaceful air. The impending storm in Florida was far behind them and was all but forgotten and the steady hum of the airborne plane pure music to his ears. His eyes closed when Melissa said, "Dad."

He answered a contented, "Hmm."

"Mom chased Amanda off. I told her you two were going to get married and we'd be a family. Are you listening to me? She told me she ran her off."

Art's eyes shot open, and a grin changed his expression. He felt lighter and that lost feeling that had hung around as though something was missing ended.

When they were home, Art called Doc Wexford, "I have a favor to ask. Would you allow me to have a picnic for two, Saturday, on your grounds by the rose garden? The one I saw from the front porch a few weeks ago?"

The Doc said yes.

Art asked for one more favor. "Would you please invite Amanda for four thirty p.m.? Tell her it's a picnic so she's expecting to eat."

He'd been working on a plan since that moment on the plane, when his head was back against the pillow rest, and Melissa spoke about Amanda. She was all he could think of. Happiness filled his heart. He knew at that point they were going home. Going where his life was, where their life was. It made him happy to know Melissa's looking forward to our marriage. She wants to be a part of a family too.

Art busied himself around the house when they got home. He made the note in his log book that another crime had been put to bed. Melissa seemed settled and happy to be back with school and friends.

Finally, Saturday arrived.

The appointed time came, and he'd dressed just as he'd been on their first date at the winery. Complete with butterflies in his stomach and damp palms. Only this time he came with a big grin and a bouquet of yellow roses wrapped in white tissue paper and tied with a green bow, her favorite color.

Art waited behind the giant redwood out of sight as the doc walked Amanda to the picnic with two chairs and a small thoughtfully decorated round table, Art gulped. She wore a dark green skirt and blouse. Her hair glistened in the afternoon light. She was exquisite, and he was in love.

The doc left her standing alone, just as Art had asked him to do. He watched her with her back to him looking over the table and the bottle of wine. It was the same vintage they'd enjoyed that evening at the winery. Her fingertips brushed the peach colored tablecloth. Amanda moved over to the rose bushes growing nearby and bent to cuddle a red rose. She placed her nose at the center of the blossom and smelled its fragrance and as she did she heard something. A twist of her head and she saw Art was coming toward her.

Her eyes went wide, and Art's heart took flight. His eyes sparkled as he held his bouquet of roses out to her and she accepted them. Tears glistened in her eyes as she gazed first at the blossoms and then up into his eyes. He held his hand out, and she took it in hers, and as she did he pulled her close to him. Smelled her fragrance and as she leaned into him he experienced her tremble in his arms.

He slipped his hand firm against her back and felt her melt into his body. With gentleness he brought his mouth close to her ear. "Amanda. You are my life, my breath, my world. I don't want to live another minute without you."

The end

The Gentle Giant Returns

Chapter One

2 P.M. October 14, Saturday 1995

Summer seemed lazy this Saturday, stretching its warm fingers into October's afternoon. A gentle breeze carried the floral fragrances from the garden to the little table. The day couldn't have been better arranged. Art lifted the almost empty bottle, as Doctor Wexford strolled across the distance from the house to where Amanda and Art sat. "I hate to break up this little party but..."

They both turned to him with contented grins plastered on their faces, the wine in their glasses almost gone.

"Any chance I can empty that bottle for you?"

Art looked at Amanda and with his eyes gave her a questioning look.

She nodded and Art lifted the bottle, "It's almost gone Jim, you might get a swallow." Art drained the bottle as the doc opened the wooden folding chair he carried along with his wine goblet.

253

He took the wineglass with the ruby liquid rolling around the bottom and upended it in one smooth move, "Aw. This is good," he brought the goblet down as he sat, "Let me see the label."

Art turned the bottle, and the doc nodded. "Made right here in Lodi."

Art stretched his legs out and looked at Doc Wexford. He knew this man wouldn't jump in where he probably wasn't needed for just any reason. He appraised the doc and waited. Then thought he's here about Stumper. "I talked to Walt, and they've got Stumper solid on murder charges. He's going before the Grand Jury."

"Why'd he kill her?"

"Well," Art looked at Amanda and could see she was all ears. "It seems that the ex, Adora, was artful at bleeding him dry. He felt he had nothing more to give and she was after even that."

"So he just got rid of his problem." The doc lifted his glass again to drink but realized that it was empty and he set it on the table. He looked at Amanda and smiled. "I am glad you two found your way back to each other."

"So are we," they chimed in at the same time, and then the three laughed.

Art relaxed in his chair as he took in the old house with its exterior a delight to study. The turned wooden embellishments had seen better days and the exterior needed paint bad. "You miss Stumper?"

"Do I. He was a worker." The doc shook his head. "I can do the work, but its help with the lifting on some of the jobs. I will find someone else. Hope he as good as Stumper." The doc looked at Art a long moment, and they listened to the breeze shove the heavy redwood limbs high above them. "What about the person that had you in their sights. Is that over?"

Art shot his eyes to the docs, and they locked. There was a deeper meaning behind this question, and Art knew. After a long moment he understood, he thought. "You're worried about Amanda. Is she safe with me?"

Jim nodded. "She's my friend, and I don't want to see anything happen to her. You could be a dangerous guy to connect up with. I don't know you all that well. No offense intended."

"None taken." Art looked at Amanda and could see she was very interested in his answer, and he wanted to say just the right things to make both of them realize that he was safe from that attack and that he would not involve her in anything dangerous. "I think the man who shot at me didn't want to kill me. He was making a statement with his wife who wanted me dead for taking the life of her grandson. I know it sounds awful. McNamare will be, and remain history."

"Is he going to jail?"

"Well, he didn't kill anyone."

"So he's going free?" Amanda sat forward her eyes wide with concern.

Art shook his head to make her feel there was nothing to worry about. "He'll be in the court system, he may get some time, he might have to go through therapy."

"Is that all?"

Art didn't want to tell them that he had a meet down town with Mac McNamare after the incident where he was captured. The eye to eye he had with the man left him secured in the knowledge that it was over. He just wanted his wife to see he was doing something. It didn't seem logical to Art that the wife would come-a-callin'. So as far as Art was concerned he was no longer a target and it was a done deal.

"Time will tell." He wanted to get them off this subject since he didn't know what the legal outcome would be. He'd looked in the man's eyes that day that he caught him, and he knew it was over, and he was safe from him coming after him in the future. How do you explain that to these two? "Well, you didn't just come out here to see how Amanda and I were doing, or to have a glass of wine. So what's up?"

"You can't wait, can you? You've got your nose to the, what is it with you, a scent of crime or something else that gets your juices going?"

Art waited.

He laughed, "Guess I'll let you figure it out on your own."

Art watched as the doc rubbed his palms together. "Remember, a few days ago before you left for Florida, I called and asked you to come over that I had found something and wanted to show it to you?"

"Yes."

The doc stood and pointed toward the house, "It's in the house, can you come now?"

"Both of us?"

"Sure."

They walked away from the little peach colored table, the ends of the cloth swaying in the slight breeze.

The doc reached the porch steps and flared his hand to show the way, "Maybe this is nothing, but I thought you might have some thoughts on what's down there and I should run it past you before I tear it all out in my demolition."

Their feet made clopping sounds as they walked across the wooden porch and the doc opened the squeaking front door. "Watch your step. There are building supplies everywhere."

Art took Amanda's hand, and she followed him as he walked behind the doc. The doc led them through the living area and the dining area dodging boxes and tools and one humongous ladder. Finally, the doc opened a door, and they approached stairs going down a long narrow passage. It smelled musty and made Art want fresh air, but they kept going down until they were on the floor.

"It's dirt?"

"Yes."

"A lovely house like this and the basement is dirt floor?"

"It surprised me when I first came down here. It's over here."

They followed him to the back wall, and they looked at some chains attached to the wall. They had cuffs at the end, and it gave Art chills when he saw them.

"Someone chained someone?"

"That's what it looks like to me too," the doc moved to their left, "but then I found this."

He and Amanda followed Jim to the end of the wall. Jim opened another door and before Art laid another set of stairs. These were cut out of the dirt. The side walls pressed in on him as Art scraped along the wall down the twenty steps to an area that would not allow him to stand full height. They were well underground at this point, the temperature a good twenty degrees cooler than outside, the smell heavy and earthy. Jim held a flashlight illuminating the area directing the spot of light across the wall then downward where it came to a stop. "What do you make of that?

Enjoy these novels from **Pynhavyn Press**

Funeral Singer: A Song for Marielle - Book One

by Lillian I Wolfe (Paranormal Suspense)

Singing at weddings, parties, holiday events, and street fairs with her band are all just another gig for musician Gillian Foster. Following a head injury, she begins to have unusual dreams. When she is asked to sing at a funeral, she discovers that her music connects her to the deceased. But this new talent also leads her to more trouble than she could ever have imagined as one of her "clients" demands her assistance in locating the person who killed her. Can she help her without endangering herself?

Funeral Singer: A Song for Marielle is paranormal suspense in the first book of a series of spirit mysteries.

Funeral Singer: A Song for Menafee – Book Two

by Lillian I Wolfe (Paranormal Suspense)

While Gillian Foster's unexpected gift appears to make her a "spirit escort" helping lost souls to cross into the light of whatever lies beyond the grave, she is finding that most go easily, some don't even wait, but here are those...

Helping one soul to move on brings Gillian into contact with another lingering ghost, who needs more than just a guide to the next life and she is his only hope. Does she have the skill to do it?

O'Ceagan's Legacy: Book 1 (O'Ceagan Saga)

by Lillian I Wolfe (Sci-Fi Fantasy)

Trained by her grandfather to command, Grania O'Ceagan expects to one day inherit the family's space freighter, but first she must prove herself worthy to be captain.

On a return trip from Earth to their home world, they take on two unplanned passengers and run into life-threatening events that could destroy everything. Grania must muster her crew and apply all she's learned to save her ship and crew from imminent destruction. Can she prove herself the leader she's trained to be?

For Eleven Million Reasons

by M.L. Weatherington - Police Mystery
If you think that winning the lottery is a dream come true, then you need to read the possible dark side of publicized sudden wealth. In *For Eleven Million Reasons*, mystery author M. L. Weatherington takes you on a suspenseful ride of murder and intrigue as Lt. Arthur Franklin pursues a killer. Don't miss this thrill ride of a first novel.

Bitter Vintage

by Riona Kelly - Suspense Romance
When the heir to the Claremont Vineyards in Northern California is killed in an accident, his sister Martinique returns home for the funeral, but she finds her father reclusive and odd, her estranged half-sister in residence, and a mysterious person skulking around the property. As she learns more about her brother's death, she is convinced there is more to the story and is determined to learn the truth.

Bitter Vintage brings the suspense of treachery, greed, and ambition along with romance and betrayal as the story unfolds against the California vineyards of the Napa-Sonoma region and the migrant workers' struggle for fair wages in 1964.

Alpha's Song (Les Loups-Garous)

by Angelina Fasano- YA Urban Fantasy
In quiet little Kennington, Massachusetts, dark secrets abound and some are buried deeper than others. Mysterious club owner Daniel Hawthorne keeps them close to his heart.

Following the devastating death of her mother, Christa Ellsworth never expected to return to the town where she grew up, but five years later, she finds herself dragged back to the scene of her family's tragedy. Christa's plan to finish high school unnoticed comes to a halt following a chance encounter with the devastatingly handsome club owner she can't get out of her head and she begins to uncover the extraordinary truth about the town she grew up in and an unusual birthright that is now hers.

Author Page

The wind was blowing that May day as I looked out over the mountains and wondered what I was going to do with the rest of my life. At sixty-nine, I had lost two husbands. The first, I was forty-four, and he was forty-seven, from an aneurysm, a sudden demise. The second loss was from massive blood poisoning, a long drawn out death. Clearly, I had enough experience with bereavement and so needed something else to do with my remaining years.

Enter my saving grace, the Chinese Fortune Cookie. As I pulled the paper free and popped the cookie piece in my mouth I read: There are dreamers and there are achievers. The difference between the two is action! I knew in that instance that the saying was right and what I should do with my remaining time. Write my stories. At eighty I dared to begin a new career, that of an author. I published my first novel, FOR ELEVEN MILLION REASONS and began writing the second in the Franklin Logs series, SIDESWIPED, the one you are holding in your hands.

Enjoy, I took pleasure in the writing.
M.L. Weatherington

Contacts: Blog: MLWeatheringtonauthor.com
E-mail: Weatheringtonmary@gmail.com